Revenge

BY JEROME G. SILBERT

Chapter One

Janine settled in the middle seat on the airplane. She fastened her seatbelt and looked across to her husband, Billy Dee Jackson, who sat next to the window. Baggage carts moved away from the plane as well as a gasoline truck with the word "Total" emblazoned on its side. She took her husband's hand.

"Well, it's back to Chicago, Billy Dee. What a trip we had."

Billy Dee nodded as he too observed the scene outside the plane. "Yep, back to the same old same-old. I'm look'n forward to it."

"What, you didn't like Paris?"

He sighed. "No, no…" They had spent five days in Paris as guest of Inspector Alain Ricard of the Paris police. Ricard had rewarded him for his assistance in solving an old murder case---the death of one Eduard Dumond.

Billy Dee closed his eyes for a moment. He thought back to those days when, as a retired Chicago cop he and his friend, Detective Jack Sheppard, became involved in the strange case of a bombing at the Palace garage in Chicago. What started out as a local crime became international. It led to a web of criminal activity that involved weapons and a terrorist group known as the SLA, Serbian Liberation Army. Little did he know at the time how this Dumond and his partner-in-crime, a woman who went by the name Susan, would lead him to Paris. But they had.

He turned from the window. "Paris was mighty fine, but

I like to eat dinner at a normal hour, say, six or seven o'clock. Starting at ten or eleven just don't seem right."

"You old, Billy Dee. Can't stand no change."

"Not true. I am old, but I can change on a dime, but…" He shook his head. "Glad you enjoyed," and returned to staring out the window.

He knew his wife wasn't satisfied with his attitude. To her, this was a trip of a lifetime. Every minute brought excitement and something new. Her suitcases stuffed with clothes, shoes, and knickknacks to remind her of her stay. She told him dinner at that late hour was how the Parisians did it.

"You didn't mind the food, once you got it," she sniffed.

Her husband continued to gaze out the window.

"Nor did you push away all the wine and after-dinner drinks, even after I warned you."

Still nothing.

"And what about all the cigars I let you smoke."

"Now, Janine."

"Uh huh, you spent a fortune on those Cubans, and, then have me bury them in my suitcase."

"Okay, Paris was great. Really."

"That's right, Billy Dee, Paris was wonderful."

The plane slowly backed away from the terminal.

"I wonder if them pilots have a rearview mirror?" Billy Dee asked.

"What? Are you lose'n your mind? Rearview mirror?"

"Well, explain to me how they do it?"

His wife gave him a stare that was a warning to be quiet. She leaned back in her seat.

"Don't wake me, Billy Dee, unless the plane goes down or for dinner."

He didn't reply. Instead, he retrieved a copy of *USA Today* from his knapsack and hunted for the sports section.

They landed on time at O'Hare International Airport

in Chicago. Billy Dee tried to stand before the cabin door opened.

"What's your rush?" Janine asked. "There's no one waiting on the other side of that door."

He semi-smiled and sat down. Seeing people move made him impatient for his turn.

"Come on, Janine, vacation is over. We'll need a truck to get all your bags home." He half-stood and waited for his wife to grab her packages and make her way toward the aisle. A traffic cop would have been useful to allow them into the mainstream of passengers.

The plane was nearly empty by the time he reached into the overhead bin to retrieve their two carry-on suitcases. He rolled his with Janine following. The crew said goodbye and thanked them for flying… He didn't hear the rest of it.

They made their way to Baggage Claim. The click-clack of his suitcase's wheels had a happy tone. He took a deep breath. "This is air. Good old Chicago air."

"Your allergies will soon act up. Good old Chicago air," his wife nearly spit out the phrase.

They took the escalator down to Baggage. A crowd had already formed at carousel 7.

Janine stopped. "Ain't that Detective Jack Sheppard over there," she pointed.

Billy Dee was a few steps ahead before realizing his wife had stopped. He turned and, then looked to where she pointed. "Hell, yes that's Shep. What the hell is he doing here?"

He called his friend's name. Through the din of the crowd, he called again and got Shep's attention. Shep walked toward them. "How was the trip?" Shep asked after giving Janine a kiss on the cheek.

"Beautiful," she answered, "but your partner here would be just as happy staying in the hotel watching sports, any sport."

"Naw, Billy Dee? Hard to believe." Shep smiled.

"Why are you here?" Billy Dee asked, not wasting any more time.

"Can't a friend do a favor?"

"I hope you brought a truck."

"You're grumpy already and jet lag hasn't even set in."

"Okay, sorry. It is mighty nice of you to do this."

"Damn right." Shep reached into his pocket. "I even brought you these."

"Cigars? Macanudos? I can't believe it. What's come over you?"

"Noth'n." He gently pushed Billy Dee a short distance away from his wife. "I got something to tell you."

"I'm listening."

"It's about your house."

"What about it?"

"Well, it's…eh…gone."

"Gone?" He heard what Shep said but didn't follow. "Where did it go?"

Shep's face paled. "There was an explosion of some sort."

Chapter Two

Brownsburg, Indiana
The Day Before

Charlie Topin, Tope to friends, rested his feet on the small wooden table in front of him. He held a glass of bourbon in one hand and a cigar in the other. His eyes focused on the clock that hung on the wall near the door of his small office. "Jest about that time," he said more to himself than to Pappy McDonald, his business partner.

The sign on the office door read *Topin and McDonald, Realtors.* A map hung near the wall clock with the town of Brownsburg circled and an arrow pointed to the near city of Indianapolis.

Pappy's gaze went to the clock. "I hope you know what you're do'n."

Tope took a puff of his cigar and blew out round rings of smoke. "Cigars are like dogs. They're your friend even though they have a potential to bite. It's all how you handle them."

"I think the liquor has gone to your head."

"Nope. Not at all. I'm as sober as a congressman."

"You should lay off that stuff for now. Your head needs to be clear to think."

He swung his feet off the table and rested the stogie on

its edge. "The trouble with you, Pappy, is you don't relax. You ain't one for drinking. A smoke is a sometime thing, and the hag you call your woman is usually with someone else."

"Now just a darn minute. Don't bring Priscilla into this. I get what I want from her when I want it. We just don't need it to be titled."

Tope, glanced from the bourbon to his partner. "I don't think I understand what you just said or…maybe I do. If that's the case, it's worth a drink." He put his glass down and went to the back of the office and found another. "Here you go, Pappy. Didn't know you were such a carouser. As my momma always warned, 'It's the quiet ones you need to watch for." He poured his friend two fingers full. "Go ahead, you have to drink."

"Tope, you know…"

"Honor, boy. To your pecker and Priscilla."

They clinked their glasses. Pappy coughed after downing his sip. "How do you stand this stuff? Jesus."

Tope shook his head. "You don't know good if it slapped you upside the head." He downed his drink and put the glass down. "Should be hearing by now."

Pappy glanced at the clock again. "Yep," he bit his lip. "We shouldn't have gotten involved. No sir."

Tope leaned forward and grabbed his friend's arm. "That safe will be filled with Franklins. And you'll be smilin' all the way to Memphis. Don't give me your shit. You're as much a part of this as me." He let go of Pappy's arm and sat back. "Drink-up, the world will be different after."

***

Chicago - The Day Before

A man in a black leather jacket drove an old white van

up 47th Street. It had a sign on the side that said *Vishkov Heating and Plumbing Contractors.* A woman, also dressed in black, sat in the passenger seat. She held her phone near her knee and studied the map.

"Jenko," she said, "it says to turn left on Drexel."

"Left? You sure?"

"Yah, left. The numbers go bigger going south."

"*Psikh* (crazy)," he said.

She looked up. "Huh? I don't understand Russian."

"Never mind, study the map."

She didn't like being dismissed. Was it because she was a woman? Or did he look at her as the poor Serbian cousin who always needed big-brother Russian help. She let it pass. They had a job to do. "Hokay, we're almost there. The address is fifty-two forty-seven."

"You sure? There's nothing but apartment buildings. They said a house."

"Pull over." She searched her pockets for the piece of paper with the address. *Oh my God, what I do with it?* Her heart raced.

Jenko drummed his fingers on the steering wheel. "Dijana, we can't stay here all day."

She brushed her long dark hair from her face. "*Uceuti* (shut-up), I'm looking." She emptied every pocket and found nothing. It was not like her to panic, but she broke into a cold sweat. They were to blow up a house belonging to a pig who had foiled many of their plans. Jenko was right. *What to do? Think.* She bent down and looked on the floor.

"Well?"

She straightened and was breathing heavy. Damn, why did she agree to do this job with such a conceited bastard? His blue eyes were ice. She tapped her jacket pocket again. "No, I don't have it." She met his glare. "Check yours, maybe you took it."

He laughed.

"Go on." she commanded.

"*Tupaya korova* (stupid cow)," he muttered as he stuck his hand in his jacket pocket. "Nothing," then pulled out a piece of paper. A second or two passed before he spoke. "Oh, you did give me the paper before we left. I remember now."

She could have rebuked him, but instead said, "Never mind. We have a mission and that's the important thing. What is the address?"

He read it off, "Five, four, four, seven."

"We go."

Chapter Three

Billy Dee felt weak-kneed after Shep delivered the news his house was destroyed. He grabbed onto his friend's shoulder.

"Lord, I don't…"

"What's going on with you two?" Janine asked walking over. She stared at her husband. "Are you all right, Billy Dee?"

Where he got the strength, he didn't know, but he took his wife by her arm and led her away from the crowd at the baggage carousel. He found an unoccupied chair in a corner and told her to sit. She protested but must have looked at his face.

"Billy Dee, you scaring me. What did Shep do?"

"Shep? Nothing." He took a deep breath. "Our…eh… our… Lordy, there ain't no good way to put it… Our house is gone."

"What you say?"

He held her hand and forced himself not to tear up. "I said, Janine, somebody blew our house up." He tightened his grip.

Her eyes didn't leave his face. Was it a second, a minute, but she just sat, her lips twisted, but no words were said— only gasps. She caught her breath.

"Get me some water, Billy Dee. I need…" She fanned herself with her free hand.

"Sure, anything." He turned. His eyes misty, he could hardly see where he walked. Someone grabbed his shoulder.

"Billy Dee, where are you going?" Shep asked.

"Water, my wife needs something to drink."

"I'll get it. You stay with her."

Billy Dee wiped his eyes. "Okay, sure. I'll do that." He stepped back toward his wife and barely had the energy to point. "Shep ... We'll wait, until..." He used the wall as support and prayed it would hold him up.

He spent decades as a Chicago cop, met nasty people in nasty places. He accepted the danger to himself, but never thought... not this... his house... Blown up?

He wiped his face with his hand and glanced at his wife. Hell, she could have been killed. He could have been killed. Beads of sweat continued to drip despite his efforts to mop them. This was not what he had bargained for. A hell of a price to pay for what was a gift from Inspector Ricard of the Paris police. Janine always told him, "Ain't noth'n free in this world." He must have smiled because his wife glared at him.

"You mean you found somethin' funny?" she asked.

He kept her words to himself. "No, Janine, I'm not laugh'n. Just think'n." Before she could ask anything else, Shep returned with two bottles of water.

"Sorry it took a while. If you want anything stronger, we can get a drink."

Billy Dee helped his wife unscrew the cap. "Take a few sips. You'll feel better." He took his own advice, but the liquid had no effect. His throat was still dry. They looked at each other while clutching the bottles.

"Why don't we get out of the airport," Shep suggested. "I've got all your suitcases and the car is out front."

The words must have awakened something in Janine. She looked up and sighed. "Yeah, sitting here won't do anybody any good. Where are we going?"

"I've arranged for a hotel at Fiftieth on the Lake. You can stay there until things get sorted."

Billy Dee helped his wife out of the chair. Shep motioned a skycap to follow with the luggage.

The four of them made their way out the terminal and to the car. Shep unlocked the doors and the trunk. Billy Dee opened the passenger side for his wife, then went to the back of the car. He poked his head under the lid. "Good thing you got a lot of space."

Shep grunted. "It's an old Ford. When they knew how to make them."

"Yeah, I can see." He straightened and moved closer to his friend. "When did it happen?"

Shep looked at his watch. "A few hours before you landed."

***

Chicago - The Day Before

Jenko parked in front of 5447 S. Drexel. He checked his watch: 5 p.m. Cars whizzed down the street as well as people, particularly kids. "I don't like it."

Dijana was bent over fiddling with the equipment in the backpack on the floor by her feet. She looked-up. "What is the matter?"

"Too many automobiles and people. This is not good time. We have at least a day. Let's wait."

She looked out the window. "It's dark, Jenko. People mind their business. We do today or tomorrow, it never perfect. There's always chance of bad luck."

"Yah, I like to minimize difficulties. Less is better, I say. No hurry. We get job done, Dijanaishka."

His eyes burned through her. Oh, the Russians. They charm with their Dijanaishkas or Alexandriashkas and believe by using endearments they get their way. She smiled. If he's not willing, what can she do? It will be another night spent with him. Another night of his hands and breath wanting to bed her and add to his collection. Another night…with those blazing eyes of his.

She brushed her hair from her mouth. "Hokay, tomorrow." *Did he smile?* Kopile *(bastard), he thinks he won again. I can make him suffer. Russian arrogance.*

She bent forward and lifted the pack from the floor and dropped it in the back. "Jenko, tomorrow. No more excuses, feelings, whatever. The pig must pay."

He tapped his forehead in a salute. "Of course. Now we know where. We'll start earlier, maybe park in alley. Tomorrow will be piece cake."

He grabbed her hand in a fast motion. His grip strong. She tensed and tried to move away. "Jenko, go, before people look."

"Dijana, you believe me. Yes?"

She nodded and he released her hand.

"*Khorosho* (good), we relax tonight and tomorrow…" He eyed her as he exited the parking space. "I'll call and tell them."

Chapter Four

Brownsburg
The Day Before

The phone rang in Tope's office. He and Pappy stared at the clock, , then the console.

"Answer it," Tope said.

"Me? No sir, I ain't—"

Tope's glare convinced him he would be better off if he obeyed. "Damn." He picked it up. "Hello?" He didn't get the other words, "Topin and McDonald Realtors," out. His clammy hand clutched the receiver, and he needed a handkerchief for his face. "Hello," he said again.

"The potato soup needs to boil," a male with an accented voice said. "Should be tomorrow before guests arrive." Click.

Pappy held onto the receiver. "What? Hello?"

Tope grabbed the phone out of his hand. He listened but heard nothing. "What the hell?" He dropped the instrument into its cradle. "Well…?"

Pappy had to take a few breaths. "…said something about soup."

"Soup?"

He shook his head. "Potato, I think. It ain't ready. Should be by tomorrow."

Tope sat back and refilled his glass. "Tomorrow, eh?"

He glanced at the clock, , then the safe. "The Bible says, 'Glory comes to those who wait,' or some sort of nonsense. Probably should go to church more often." He took a sip. "Priscilla, she a church woman, ain't she?"

Pappy looked up. "Huh?"

"I said… Never mind. Go home, Pappy. You look like you've seen a ghost." He got up and stood next to him. He put his hand on Pappy's shoulder. "It's all good. Better than good. Those people in Chicago probably figured something wasn't right to do the job today. That's good. They're professionals. The soup ready tomorrow means our pockets will be filled with Franklin crackers. Go home, Pappy. I'll take care of everything."

Tope could see on his friend's face a mixture of relief and concern. He patted Pappy again.

"You sure?" Pappy asked.

"Oh yeah. No problem."

"Okay, then, Tope. I guess I'll go."

"Thatta boy. Go see Priscilla. She'll have what you need to relax."

Pappy got up and took his coat and hat off the hanger. "See you in the morning."

Tope gave him a wave and waited for the door to close. He counted to thirty, then went to his desk and undid the lock. He grabbed a cell phone. He needed to make a call.

***

Pappy walked to his car parked in the lot behind the building. He'd grown up in this town. He was the first in his family to graduate high school. He could have gone to college on a basketball scholarship, but…it wasn't for him. High school girls swooned over him. That was his kingdom. Figured why leave a good thing.

He was born Harold McDonald but got the nickname Pappy from the bourbon the kids drank, then. He could hold his liquor and play a top-notch game—drunk. That's how good he was. In those high school days, he could do no wrong.

He unlocked his ten-year-old Nissan and started the car. He stared out the window. The clouds hung low and heavy. Snow was coming. It would be a bear driving tomorrow.

He drove down Crawfordsville Road. He could do it with his eyes closed. A few intersections up, turn right and there's the Walmart. What happened to him? The girls became women, and he stayed a relic of their past. Priscilla had been captain of the cheerleaders. They'd had a hell-of-a-time in high school. At least the fire hadn't totally burned out, then again, she was no longer that curvy cheerleader. Perhaps filling-out was one of the requirements to work at the department store.

Now he was almost 40 and still knock'n about town. He tried different jobs. Started his real-estate office same time he bought the car. Both had such promise. But promise don't mean success. The recession had kicked him in the teeth. Bills and overdue notices littered his desk, then Charlie Topin showed up, about two years ago. He knocked on the door, took a look around, and stuck-out his hand.

"I'm Charlie Topin. Most people call me Tope. I'd like to be your partner."

Pappy almost fell off his chair. "You…what?"

Charlie leaned on the desk with both his elbows. "Pappy, right? That's what folks call you?"

He nodded, surprised this stranger knew his name.

"I've been check'n you out."

Pappy could only stare.

"Things," He pointed to the mound of paper on the desk and made a tsk-tsk sound. "I'm going to make all that bad stuff go away."

"You are, are you? How? Why?"

Tope straightened. "That's what partners do. They help each other."

"I don't remember ask'n."

Tope paused and played with the brim of his hat. "Of course, if you'd rather drown and let everything go to hell, that's your choice."

Things did change but at the same time didn't. Tope was true to his word. The bills vanished, but hardly a client came through the door. Six closings a year didn't stretch far. But the light and heat bills were paid as well as the rent. Tope always gave him cash. Not an amount to set the world on fire, but, hell, more than he was worth.

***

Traffic became heavy. People were rushing home before the storm. He should drive by Priscilla's. Opening a can of something in his apartment didn't fire the appetite. Besides, he didn't want to be alone. All this cloak-and-dagger stuff got on his nerves. He never asked Tope where the money came from? Ain't for him to know. The bills got taken care of, and that was good enough. But this.

He made a left and checked his watch. Priscilla got off work about half-hour ago. She would be home by now. He parked in front of her small house. He shoulda called. He shoulda done a lot of things.

Chapter Five

Chicago

The drive to the hotel at 50th on the Lake was quiet. Everyone had their own thoughts. Shep tried to get a conversation going by asking about Paris, but Janine's answers and descriptions lacked enthusiasm. Billy Dee broke the unsettling air.

"Listen, Shep, before we get to the hotel let's go by the house."

"Not much to see in the dark."

"Maybe, but…"

"It's all roped off. It's a crime scene."

Billy Dee wiped his face with his gloved hand. "I haven't been away that long not to know that. I… we, want to see what's left."

Shep sighed. "Okay, if that's what you want." He exited the Dan Ryan Expressway at 55th and headed east. As they neared Drexel, Billy Dee took a deep breath. This was the house they bought after he'd been two years on the force. Their first big purchase. The realtor said it was a starter home, "needed some work, but built solid." She was right on both counts. If he ever added up the money for all the improvements, he probably should have moved. But he…they liked the neighborhood, the people, and most important, they could never get rid of decades of stuff. He chuckled as that would not be a problem any longer.

"What's so funny?" Janine asked.

Billy Dee licked his lips. "Well, I guess we can move now since everything is gone."

"That ain't funny. That's a tragedy."

He knew better than to explain further. He braced himself for the moment they arrived at the scene.

Yellow tape surrounded the border of the property. Police barricades were set at each end of the block. Shep slowed and flashed his star and was waved through. Two evidence trucks were parked near the house.

"Anyone hurt?" Billy Dee asked as Shep stopped the car in front.

"It was a clean job. Bomb and Arson arrived after a 9-1-1 call. The neighbors were evacuated as a precaution, but thankfully no one was injured."

"Thank the Lord for that," Billy Dee said.

"Amen," Janine joined in.

Billy Dee got out and helped his wife. Shep joined them. The three of them ducked under the tape and moved toward the house where there was more tape surrounding the destruction.

Billy Dee peered down in the hole. "Ain't much left. Jesus. How many bombs were used?"

Shep cleared his throat. "You're jump'n the gun. As you can see the ET boys are sifting through this mess. I'm pretty sure it was a bomb but that's not clear—at least not yet."

"What else could it have been?" Janine asked.

"Well, in these kinds of cases we have to rule things out. Could it have been arson, a gas leak, an electric short? That's why the boys are looking."

Janine drew her coat tighter around her. "It ain't no fire because there would be a pattern, and we had no problem with the gas or electric. I unplugged most everything before we left."

Shep nodded. "I'll make a note of that. Anything else you want to see?"

Billy Dee looked at his wife. "I want to come back tomorrow. Maybe there's something to save."

Shep patted his friend's shoulder. "Sure, no problem. Make sure, though, you call your insurance company first thing in the morning."

The Evening of the Bombing

"More vodka, Dijanaishka?" Jenko asked as he poured half a glass for himself.

She was feeling light-headed, but this was a celebration. There were too few occasions of happiness. She nodded. "*Sipati* (pour)."

He obliged. "What should we toast? Wait." He held up his hand. "To you, Dijanaishka. You are mistress of explosives." His eyes glistened from the vodka.

They were in a small apartment somewhere between Chicago and Indiana. They didn't know the owner. They were directed there after doing the job. The message on Dijana's phone was terse. "Wait further instructions." Orders from who knows who, but that was the life of a revolutionary. She downed her vodka. She probably won't be seeing Jenko again. If that was his real name, then again, what about hers.

"Jenko, come closer," she said, "I want to see what's behind those eyes."

He stood, glanced at her, and wobbled into the bedroom. "In here." He gestured her to follow.

"You took the bottle." She couldn't make out what else

he said. "What?" She slipped off her chair and stumbled after him. "Why you put no light? It's dark." She heard his laughter. Her eyes adjusted. In the corner of the bedroom, Jenko was on the bed, his shirt off. He patted a spot next to him.

"Come, we drink to this night. We drink," he held up the bottle-"to the pigs who stand in our way. Revenge." He didn't wait to clink their glasses but drank. "Now you toast," he said, and poured what was left into her glass.

She held the drink and was about to begin when he grabbed her arm and pulled her close. Their faces inches apart.

"Making love, Dijanishka. Is only truth in life."

"A quote from Tolstoy, Jenko? Or more Russian bullshit."

He let go of her arm and slapped his chest above his heart. "You hurt me. I talk of what's real."

"Fucking?"

"Yes. It's passion, the explosion of humanness."

"A philosopher too."

"It is not vodka talking. It is truth. What is more powerful?"

She considered that. At least tried to, but the alcohol and his physical closeness sent her thoughts swimming in all directions.

She had come close the night before of giving way. She parried his advances. "Must be alert and energized for tomorrow," she said. He waved that argument aside. His eyes so blue it shamed the sky. But she held fast. "Tomorrow," she said, "when it's over we celebrate." She kissed him on his cheek. He tried to grab hold of her, but she stepped out of reach. "Tomorrow," and blew him another kiss. Those eyes of his never left her as she made her bed on a couch. Sleep did not come easily. She thought of him, the caresses, the touching, of feeling him inside. She turned on her side and all that vanished, replaced by the mission that lay ahead. Opening the side door of the pig's house. She visualized placing the bombs in strategic places and setting the timers. All done without being seen. All done without getting caught.

She smiled and silently congratulated herself. It all worked. She and Jenko watched on TV. The pig received the message. Don't mess with us. We're bigger, stronger, and work in the shadows. She took Jenko's hand and placed it on her breast. "*Ssh*, Jenko. No more talk. Celebrate."

Chapter Six

Brownsburg
The Day Before

Tope searched his desk for his glasses. He used them when no one looked. Pappy left and the office was his, as it was most nights. He held his cell phone in his hand. He punched in the numbers and momentarily waited to hit the phone icon. He listened to make sure Pappy was gone. He sometimes reappeared, though. A sheepish grin plastered on his face to say he forgot something. What that was about, he could only guess. Hearing nothing, Tope pushed the icon again.

It was very early morning in Belgrade. Anton Majeskou would not be happy to have his sleep disturbed. Tope sighed while listening to the connection being made. After a few seconds, he heard breathing.

"*Zdravo* (hello)," Tope began. He didn't bother to say his name. The call identified who he was. His Serbian was rapid. "Mission postponed to tomorrow. Will contact after. Candy pick-up in the usual way."

"*Dobro* (good). Candy sent after confirmation of success."

Tope heard a grunt, then the call disconnected. He held onto the cell a minute or two longer, then locked it away in his desk. This called for another finger or two of bourbon.

If tomorrow went right, the real estate office of Topin and McDonald would mysteriously close…disappear as if it never was. Two years in this town was enough. Dealing with the locals and Pappy… He shook his head and took a drink. At least the liquor was good. He looked around the office. He was running against time. Even Pappy, as simple as he was, had to start to wonder. All Pappy knew about Chicago was an underhanded real-estate deal was taking place. A property owner who refused to sell. Even that might be too much for him.

Pappy didn't ask questions, but his nervousness betrayed the consent he gave. Tope wondered if the money was enough to pacify him. He eyed his drink and laughed. A silly thought. Pappy wasn't like other men Tope met. No, Pappy didn't want much. His world had beaten him down. He was a memory to most, a one-time basketball phenom who never made it. Give him a few nights with Priscilla, and a couple of bucks in his pocket, and Pappy was a happy man. Simple. He, on the other hand… He took another sip, stood, and walked around the office.

Who was he? Charlie Topin, a good old boy to some. A person who came into this town and rescued the firm and Pappy from further disaster. The people of Brownsburg whispered that Charlie was a fool, but, then as time went on, laid their doubts aside. It didn't matter…things seemed all right. Charlie minded his business and Pappy—was Pappy. Life went on. The cover was as good as any he'd had.

From this small town, he monitored goings on in Indianapolis as well as Chicago. His boss in Belgrade seemed happy with his work, then, a week or so ago, a woman contacted him. Not on his regular phone, but the other. The one locked in the drawer. She spoke with an accent, but her English was excellent. Her number was untraceable, at least by his means. Soon after, Belgrade called, and now...

His gaze went around the room, then he peeked under the window blinds and saw large snowflakes caught in the beam of the streetlights. History.

***

Pappy knocked quietly on Priscilla's door. Snow was beginning to fall. He looked at the sky and cursed himself for leaving his hat in the car. *Jesus, what can take a woman so long?* He knocked again. This time louder. When there was no answer, he looked around and noticed the door was slightly ajar. He stepped off the porch and went toward the back. He saw her car parked in front of her garage. He returned to the front. *What the hell?* He stepped inside.

"Priscilla?" Instead of a response, he heard a faint noise coming from the rear. "What you doing back there?" He stepped inside the home and moved toward the kitchen and bedroom area. "Priscilla, it's me, Pappy, just stopped by, you know." It wasn't a large house. In a few strides, he was in the kitchen. The light was on. He saw her purse on the kitchen table, and another light in the pantry area. "Priscilla?" He spun around when he heard the door of the bedroom open.

"Pappy?"

"What in tarnation?" His mouth was open as he stared at her dressed in a house coat that barely concealed anything.

"What are you doing here?" she asked.

"I…I…thought…we'd catch a bite," he said slowly, retracing his steps away from the kitchen. "Is this a bad time?"

She put a hand on her hip. He didn't wait to hear what she had to say. He moved with the speed that once graced him on the basketball court. He wasn't sure if she stood by the door and watched. Did she laugh…feel pity…feel anything? Whatever Priscilla's emotions, they wouldn't last long. Had he gotten there sooner it could have been him in that bedroom. He tore down the street in his car indifferent to the falling snow. That was the point. His indignation and shame were soon tempered by the reality of the road. He slowed. Despite Priscilla, he wasn't ready to wind-up in a heap. Not just yet anyway. Hell, Tope assured him by tomorrow his pocket would be full of cash. He wouldn't need Priscilla. Any gal would gladly be his once she saw the size of his wallet.

Chapter Seven

Chicago

Shep helped Billy Dee unload the luggage from the car. It took two trips to bring all the bags into the hotel room. Billy Dee surveyed the suitcases piled on top of each other. "Jesus, there were only two of us. We need another room just for this stuff."

"Quit your fuss'n," Janine said, "you should be say'n hallelujah, since we lost everything else. We got clothes and what we need until this mess can be settled."

Shep cleared his throat. "She's right."

Billy Dee turned to his friend. "Thanks for your two cents."

"No problem. I was just leaving. See you in the morning."

They gave each other a hug and pats on the back. "Thank you," both Billy Dee and Janine said.

Shep closed the door on his way out.

"Well, what do we do now?" Janine asked.

Her husband looked from her to the room. "It's late and we've been up more hours than I can count. We're home, thank God, in one piece. I'm going to sleep."

"What? How can you do that? Our house is gone. We have no place to go. Sleep! Aren't you…"

"Janine, there ain't noth'n we can do right now. I'm as pissed as you. It's go'n to be a long hard day tomorrow."

His wife sank onto the bed and covered her face, then

looked up. "Promise me, Billy Dee you're go'n to catch whoever did this. Promise me."

He went over and put his arm around her. "Yes, indeed. I'm go'n to catch the mother… who did this to us."

***

Billy Dee couldn't make-out exactly where he was. The area looked familiar, but, then he was seated at a café in the middle of a street. He examined closer and it was his street, Drexel. *Now how the hell could that be?* Seated next to him wasn't his wife, but Marc Gasol, the center for the Los Angeles Lakers. *What the heck?* Erin Andrews was across the table as well as another woman who fawned over Gasol. *What's going on?* The waitress, who had, down-to-the-shoulders blond hair spoke, French. He was sure of it. To his amazement everyone replied in that language except him. He was *tsk-tsk*ed by his companions. He told them he was having dinner later with his wife. They ordered for him anyway. The waitress, who called herself Danielle, brought wine to the table. Despite his reluctance to eat, he drank. The conversation around him was hazy, but he focused on the waitress. *Damn, she looks familiar. Where? How would I know anyone in… wherever I am?* The wine was good, and he heard himself smacking his lips. The woman next to Gasol leaned over toward him.

"What you say'n?" Janine asked while rubbing her husband's shoulder. "You mutter'n away and never heard your phone go off. Someone is call'n. Answer it."

"What? Phone?" Billy Dee opened his eyes and realized he was in bed with his wife in some hotel room in Chicago. "Okay, I'll answer…" He fumbled the phone and finally maneuvered to hit the green button. "Hello?"

"Bonjour, Monsieur Jackson, I hope it is not too early in Chicago."

"Early?" Billy Dee tried to make-out the time on the clock near the bed. "I guess not. What time is it?"

"It's two p.m. in Paris, must be around seven where you are."

"Seven in the morning?"

"Why yes. *Excusez-moi* if I woke you. This is Inspector Ricard."

"Inspector… oh, nice to hear from you and thank you for a wonderful trip."

"Our pleasure. What I called about was we picked up chatter about well, some sort of threat to…we, or I, think about you."

"What was that?"

"It's not specific, Monsieur Jackson. It was talk of doing something in Chicago…a house… or building… Not sure. I just thought, I should, as you say, give you heads-up."

"Uh-huh."

Janine perched herself as close to Billy Dee as she could. "What's he saying?" she asked in a voice disguised as a whisper.

Billy Dee moved the covers and stepped out of bed. He held his hand out to stop his wife's further questions. "Do you have anything else? Like who and…"

"I wish I did. Over the Internet under names and groups that pop up and, then gone. *Attendez*, I did write something."

Billy Dee heard static and rustling of paper.

"*Allo? J'ai compris*. I got it. The caption was La Maison du Cochon."

"What's that?"

Ricard cleared his throat, "The house of the pig."

The Morning After

Dijana stretched in bed. She felt tingly and energized despite the slight throb in her head from all the vodka she and Jenko drank. He was as good as she thought he'd be. His blue eyes added to the pleasure. All in all, yesterday from beginning to its glorious end was a triumph. That made her smile and with her eyes still closed conjured up all the gratifying touches and passion of the evening. As the images played, she felt her heart accelerate and a yearning for more swept over her. She reached out, but only felt the mattress. "Jenko?" She turned and stared at an empty bed. "Jenko?" She sat up and wrapped the covers around her. "Are you in the bathroom? Are you sick?" She listened intently for sounds, any sound. She checked the time. The clock on the nightstand read 7. Hopefully, that was 7 in the morning. She placed a foot on the floor as she got out of bed. Her desire changed to wariness. She heard a key thrust into the apartment door. *What to do?* Her clothes were strewn throughout the bedroom. There was no place to hide. Her gun was in her purse, but where the hell was that? Kitchen? Living room? She dropped the covers and ran down the hallway. She heard the click of the lock. She reached the kitchen, and spotted the purse slung on the back of the far chair. She lunged for her bag while listening to the apartment door open and footsteps.

***

Paris

It was early morning when he received the text on his mobile. French prisons, unlike those in the US, allowed prisoners to have phones. Land lines were installed in every cell. He didn't understand the reason for such leniency. But Jack Monte always pushed the envelope. Bribes, whether in the US or France, would always be the coin of the realm. A favor here, euros there, and voila, he had a mobile phone.

He rubbed his hands together in joy rereading the message. Finally, he was able to strike back…from prison. He marveled at his audacity and his adroitness. He was the one that asshole Detective Billy Dee Jackson and his shithead partner Sheppard nailed for a gun running spree in Chicago on behalf of the Serbian Liberation Army. Incidental to that plan were a few dead bodies, destruction of a parking lot called the Palace, a woman, Susan, who got away, and her mentor?... lover?... Eduard Dumond.

Dumond, the supposed mastermind of that deal. The very Dumond who he was doing time for in a fucking French prison thanks to being handed over by Jackson and Sheppard. The French, then found enough fools on a jury to convict him of Dumond's murder. Despite his lawyer's plea that Monte never pulled the trigger. As the French say, *c'est la vie*.

***

The Café Deux Magots was a Paris tourist must. Susan, who went by the name Danielle, neared the end of her shift. She had persuaded the manager, Felix, to allow her to work the evening hours to midnight. It was a bargain that benefited both. She was attractive and knowledgeable in the ways of Parisian charm.

Susan sat down at an empty table to close out her evening receipts. She knew without looking, Felix, had his eye on her.

"Danielle," Felix called, "when you're done, some coffee?"

That was how the game was played. A wink, a subtle smile, a slight brush of her hand on his shoulder, left him the promise of what the future may hold. The same cat and mouse scenario performed through-out the world, but in France… in Paris, it was *une façon de vivre*, a way of life.

She finished her tally and was about to give the receipts

to Felix when she felt her phone vibrate. She whipped the mobile from the back pocket of her jeans and read the text. She wanted to smile, but instead held herself steady. It was happening. A small payback for what occurred in Chicago a few years back. It was a start.

***

Chicago

Dijana reached inside her purse, but not fast enough. Before any words, plea, or scream, escaped her mouth, a masked person of medium height and girth, aimed and fired. The first shot missed, but not the second. She felt the bullet hit her shoulder. The next one struck her chest. Her legs collapsed and she fell. The room spun. She fought to stay conscious as she sucked in air. She watched the assailant come toward her and drop to one knee. He placed the barrel of the gun on the side of her head, then paused to survey the scene. His free hand grabbed her breast, ignoring the blood that spewed from the wound. He grunted, making an *unh* sound.

She tried to speak. Maybe she could say please, maybe beg or promise to fuck him…anything to live. He removed his mask. The last thing she saw was his bluer-than-the-sky, eyes.

Chapter Eight

Brownsburg

Tope had taken the call in his office the next day. It was the one he had been waiting for. The speaker on the other end said one word, "Done," and hung up. Tope turned on the TV and sure enough, the picture filled with fire trucks and police cars. The building that was there, was no longer. *Hell of a job.* He rubbed his hands together. The candy would be coming as soon as he sent Majeskou the YouTube of the news report. He prepared his computer. He typed underneath the video and sent it. Several minutes later he received a message: "candy on its way will be there tomorrow at the end of the day."

Tope leaned back. At least that will get Pappy off his back. All day long, he kept nagging about the money. Now he'd have an answer for him. Whatever got into him? Pappy was like a school kid who wouldn't take no for an answer. His agitation got so bad; Tope sent him home. He thought of calling but decided to let him suffer a little bit more. The chump probably wasn't getting any from Priscilla. That could make a man, Tope admitted, do about anything.

The next day was similar. Pappy arrived early.

"Did the money come?" he asked.

"No, it didn't. The message said end of the day. Don't you worry, you'll get your share."

That quieted him for a few minutes.

"How much is my take?" Pappy sat up from his desk.

"I told you. Several thousand dollars."

"Like how many."

"Jesus, Pappy, you're driving me crazy. You'll get a third. Just like me. There are expenses to pay, too."

That satisfied him for a while. Near going home time, Pappy started again.

"Listen, Pappy, I'm as concerned as you, but I can't make it appear on my own. Go home, I'll phone when it arrives."

Pappy, his eyes wide, his mouth downturned, gave the impression of a dog who's been kicked one too many times. He shuffled out the door with his hat held in both hands. "You call me now as soon as it gets here."

"Sure will. Have a good evening."

Tope retreated to his office as soon as Pappy left. He fired up the computer and thought about the message to send. It was well past the end of the day. Nothing to lose in reminding Majeskou. After all, the job was completed… successfully. He settled on "waiting on delivery." The line blinked on the screen. He gave it a little more consideration, then thought he heard the entrance door of the building creak open, followed by footsteps on the stairs. Without thinking, he pressed the button and closed the computer. He got up from his desk and opened his office door.

"Pappy? Is that you?" He took a step closer to the vestibule. "You've been mop'n all day long. The money hasn't come. What did you forget?"

***

Chicago

At least it was sunny, Billy Dee observed, peeking behind

the drapes. After an unrestful night, he had phone in hand and was on the line with the insurance company. No easy task even if he was patient, which he wasn't. *It wears me out talk'n to machines. They act'n like your best friend when they ain't. Could save a whole lotta time connect'n with a real person.*

His growling must have woken Janine.

"Whatcha go'n on about?" she asked.

He held up his hand and pointed to the phone. "On hold with the insurance."

She must have waited a minute or two before giving advice. "Call Jimmy our agent. That's what he's there for."

The instruction hit him like a bolt. He held on. The awful music played, occasionally interrupted by a concerned female voice purring about the importance of the customer. After what seemed like hours, he hung-up. "Jimmy, huh?" He checked the time. "Probably a little early," as it was before 9. "I'll get some coffee from the lobby. You want anything?"

"Sleep."

"No problem." He grabbed the room key from the table and left.

The line for the hotel's breakfast was short. He took his coffee and a sweet roll and found a chair that had a leftover newspaper. Before he could take a sip, he glanced at the headline and identified the picture below. *My house. My goddamn house.* He took several deep breaths and braced himself for the article. Nobody saw or knew nothin'. He slapped the paper down and snatched his phone from his pocket. The call went through

"Detective Sheppard, Bomb and Arson."

"When you gett'n your bony white ass over here?"

"Good morning to you, Billy Dee. You sleep well?"

"Sleep? As a matter of fact, no."

"I didn't think so. I'll be by in an hour. Have some coffee or something."

"I already did." He paused. "Sorry I'm a pain, just read the newspaper."

"Now why would you do that? You know you can't believe what's there?"

"That's the problem. There's noth'n there."

"I'll call when I'm downstairs. My best to Janine."

Billy Dee went back to the breakfast line for additional rolls and another cup of coffee for his wife. It was just past 9, and he felt he'd already put in a day's work.

***

Brownsburg
The Day After

Pappy had an extra bounce in his step as he got ready for work. Although Tope hadn't called the evening before, he had a feeling his luck would change this morning. He'd walk in and on his desk would be a stack of Franklins. Tope did those kinds of things. He loved cash.

He hummed an old song, *Tonight's the Night,* as he shaved. Oh, he was going to have a good time later whether it was with Priscilla, that bitch, or someone else. *One more time, ol' Pappy go'n be king.* He dressed and left. On the way he felt so good he stopped at Dunkin and picked up two coffees and a box of half a dozen donuts.

He drove into the parking lot behind the office and saw Tope's car parked. The son-of-a-gun probably had gone to the bank already and gotten the cash. What a guy. The entrance door to the building was open and Pappy climbed the stairs balancing the coffees and goodies. At the landing where the office was, he called out to Tope to open the door. There was no answer. He put the food and drinks down.

"Tope? You in there?" he asked turning the doorknob. "It's Pappy. I brought coffee and stuff."

He pushed the door open and let himself in. The lights were on. He stepped around the front and saw Tope's office. "Didn't you hear me? Jesus, I brought some…" His gaze settled on the empty space. "What the…? Tope? Stop fool'n around. Where the hell are you?" He went to Tope's desk. There was a glass with a half finger of bourbon still in it. He looked around. "Something ain't right." He went back to the front and felt an object under his foot. He looked down and discovered a cigarette butt, then a darkened spot several feet away. He knelt and stared at the wetness. He knew what it was without touching. He knew but told himself it wasn't. *Couldn't be. Why? How?* He straightened and looked wildly. He returned to Tope's office and stared at the desk. The computer…gone.

Chapter Nine

Chicago

Billy Dee waited in the entrance of the hotel for his friend. He was out the door as soon as Shep's car turned onto the driveway. He grabbed the door handle just as the car came to a stop.

"You in a hurry or something?" Shep asked.

"Hurry? Just don't want to waste time."

Shep had a cigarette dangling from his mouth. "You think by rushing over there you'll find the answer to who did it sooner?"

"Cut that out, Shep. I'm nervous and pissed. Can't just stay here all day and do nothing. I know investigations take time. I was a cop. I get it."

Shep put the cigarette down. "Does Janine know you're out?"

Billy Dee put on his big "ah shucks" smile. "She asleep. I 'm not go'n to sit in the room and have time tick by until she ready. I'm sure she'll call whenever she gets up."

Billy Dee noticed that instead of heading west, they were travelling north. "How you gett'n to my house?"

Shep glanced at his friend and smiled. "You may have eaten but I haven't. It's not a French bistro. I trust your palate still eats American?"

"Don't give me that. I was only gone…what…two weeks. But I just…"

"Manny's, my man."

Billy Dee let the name of the restaurant sink in. "They still have the cabbage soup and dark rye?" He asked after a minute. The taste of that dish pushed all other thoughts aside. "There wasn't a thing like that in Paris. It makes my mouth water."

"We'll have a decent breakfast and I'll catch you up on what we have so far."

"You're the driver. Hmm… I'm feel'n better all ready."

***

Brownsburg

Pappy crumpled into a chair. He had to think. Something had happened in the office…but what? If Tope was killed, where's his body? Nothing in the office was out of place. Tope's car was still in the parking lot. Maybe he had it all wrong and Tope went for a walk or got coffee.

Hell, even after all the years and time they spent together what did he really know about him? Did he have a girl? A boy? Pappy swept a hand over his face. He was letting his imagination run.

Tope kept things close to the vest. Pappy never even been to his place. *Jesus, how strange?* His head was bombarded with thoughts that went in all directions. *Should I call the police?* He drummed his hand on the desk. *That could lead to too many questions…like what happened in Chicago.* He jumped out of his seat. *Hell, what* did *happen in Chicago?* Tope told him it was a real-estate deal. "…just putt'n a little pressure on the seller," he said. Pappy never asked about the particulars. The promise of more money than he ever had was good enough. He walked around his desk rubbing his hands. Too much time passed playing the junior partner. Never ask'n questions when things seemed too good to be true. Yeah, his momma warned him.

She would watch him as he got ready to go out in his high school days. "Don't you believe everything they tell you, Pappy," she'd say. "Folks will do and say anything if they think it's go'n to do them good."

He didn't understand, then, thought it was an old lady talk'n sad about her dreams. He stood over the bloody spot. No doubt that's what it was. He'd seen it too many times on the basketball court not to know.

He stepped into Tope's office again and searched the top of the desk. He brushed through papers without reading them. *What the hell am I looking for? A note? Tope's phone?* His heart raced and although the temperature in the office was cool, he felt sweat drip down his face. He scolded himself. *Take it easy. It's all a big misunderstanding.* After minutes of blindly searching, he sat back in Tope's big leather chair. He almost laughed out loud as he conjured up the simple idea that eluded him. All he had to do was call. It was obvious. Tope wasn't in the office, nor was his cell. Tope's car was where it was supposed to be. He took a deep breath. *That's what happens when pressure builds and there ain't no woman. No matter what, that's going to change tonight.* He grabbed his phone from his pocket and dialed Tope's number. The call went directly to voice mail.

***

Chicago

The self-service line at Manny's had few people as the breakfast crowd was gone and it was a bit early for lunch.

None of that mattered. Billy Dee loaded his tray with a large bowl of soup, a stack of rye, two potato pancakes, a half sandwich of corn beef piled several inches high, and chocolate cake. Shep was not timid in his choices, either. They unloaded their feasts at a table.

"All that Parisian cooking don't hold a candle to this. They can keep their sauces and butter-soaked meals," Billy Dee said. "This is honest food a man can enjoy and understand."

"Amen, brother," Shep said between mouthfuls of his roast beef sandwich. He looked at the dishes piled in front of Billy Dee. "Will that keep you to lunch?"

"It could. We'll see." He dug into his food. "God, this is good."

"While you're feeling no pain, I'll let you in on the investigation," Shep set the uneaten part of his sandwich on the plate. "The ET boys were still running tests for fingerprints. Bomb and Arson believed it wasn't arson or a gas leak. They're still searching for the device or devices. Whatever was used packed a real punch but was set in such a way that only your house and garage were destroyed. That indicates this was no amateur."

"Shep, we both know who it was. Damn it."

"Billy Dee…?"

"Okay, go on. Anyone see anything?"

"Glad you asked. The day before it happened there was a white van parked in front. It stayed several minutes, then left. No one got out."

Billy Dee used his fork to push his potato pancake around the plate. "Yeah, so what does that mean?"

"I don't know, but it's the only lead we have so far."

"Did the same van come back the next day?"

Shep picked up his sandwich. "You're good, Billy Dee. That's what we're going to find out. Eat up."

Chapter Ten

Hammond, Indiana

Jenko struggled to stay awake. It had been a long day, and he had much to do before calling it a night. He realized he had a job, but… He did savor his time with Dijana. She was as good as he anticipated. Behind that cold Serbian aloofness and attitude was a woman driven like a man. He lost count of the number of times they fucked that night. He rarely got to rest. Thoughts of her made him miss on the first shot but the second was true to its mark. He felt bad he had to do it, an uncommon feeling for him.

As for the man in the real estate office, that was fun. The look on his face…confusion, that seconds later melted into fear, then astonishment. The pompous ass reduced to whimpering when he figured out this was his end. Jenko touched his side for his gun. That weapon transformed him from just a guy no one cared about to God. The look in the victim's eye near the final moment filled Jenko with power and excitement almost like sex just before climaxing. He pulled the trigger, and the act was done. It took more time than he thought to clean-up. His victim bled like a slaughtered pig. The fucker was heavy too as he carried him in the body bag out the door and threw him into the van next to Dijana.

It was late enough that there were few if any people on

the street. Besides, he knew from the reports given to him, that murders were infrequent in that town. People wouldn't expect those kinds of things to happen. Surprise was always his big advantage.

The instructions were to take the bodies and dump them a few miles apart in the Sag-Canal between Chicago and Gary, Indiana. The area stank from all the industrial waste that surrounded the waterway. By the time the bodies were found, if they were, the amount of chemical waste would make identification difficult. At least Dijana was naked and easy to slide from the body bag. The other would take a little time.

***

Paris

Felix brought a bottle of Tesseron Cognac to her table. He pulled a chair around and plunked down two glasses.

"A little celebration, after a night like this." He poured the drinks.

The café had had a successful evening. Lines of people waited for tables. It could have gone on all night, but even Paris cafés had to close if for no other reason than it ran out of food.

Susan studied the reddish- gold liquid for a moment before she took a sip. The liquid touched her lips and chased away whatever chill was in the air. "*C'est bon*," she said and took another taste. She set the glass down and found him staring at her. "What?"

"You are mysterious. You're here, but not always. That mind of yours is always in motion."

"I'll take that as a compliment. At least you don't accuse me of being a blonde ditz."

"Far from it. I watched you yesterday. You looked at your

phone and whatever you read made your eyes sparkle, then puff....gone"

She brought the brandy glass to her mouth to hide her expression, then she drank. The cognac went down smoothly with just the right amount of heat.

"You're blushing," he said.

"No, no, it's the *l'eau de dieu*, but I didn't know you were so interested."

He put his hand on top of hers. "You are intriguing. I like intrigue."

"Be careful what you wish for." Her gaze focused on his face. "Simple is always easier."

He gulped down his drink. "But not necessarily better."

***

Chicago

Early morning was still hours away. Jenko pulled the van into the wooden-broken-down, two-car garage behind what appeared to be an abandoned frame house in Posen, a poor suburb south of Chicago. He was bone tired but had one more thing to do before sleep. He vacuumed the van and emptied it, leaving only a knapsack in the corner over the rear wheel hub. Noiselessly, he climbed out and went to the vehicle parked next to him. Underneath the front tire was a key. He bent down and retrieved it. He unlocked the driver's door, threw his gear into the front seat, then backed out. When he was at least a block and a half away, he pushed a button on his phone. He heard the explosion and sped away. Once on the expressway heading into Chicago, he used the switch on his dash to make a call. As soon as it went through, he spoke, "The birds are gone along with the nest." He heard someone clear their throat.

"Which male bird no longer flies?" It was difficult to ascertain whether the voice was female or male.

Jenko kept an eye on traffic as his memory raced back to the victim. After a second or two he said, "What you mean?"

"Would you say the bird was tall?"

"Tall?" He closed his eyes for an instant. "No. I didn't take ruler to measure."

"Did he look like a flamingo? Tall legs and neck."

Jenko laughed. "No, I remember…no… legs were short… more like stuffed duck."

There was static on the line.

"Allo?" he said. "Allo." Jenko quickly glanced at his dash to determine if he was still connected. "You there?"

"*Dah*." The words came slowly. "It was the wrong bird."

"What? Again, please."

"Idiot, you failed your instructions."

Jenko began to sweat. His hands grew cold. "I-I don't understand." He heard a grunt through the phone.

"Follow the plan. I'll contact you later."

The line went dead.

Chapter Eleven

Chicago

"I was shocked. I grabbed my Patti and hid under the bed. Patti was so scared, she barked constantly, and I couldn't keep her quiet. After, I don't know, a few minutes, I went toward the window and looked out. Your house was gone. I couldn't believe it. I was shaking so. I called Fred to come home," Ellie May Tyson dabbed her eyes with some tissue. "I'm so sorry for you and Janine. Terrible." She shook her head.

"Thank you, Ellie May. When you looked out on the street did you see a car, anything strange?" Billy Dee asked.

She blew her nose, , then said, "Besides your house blowing up? No. There was so much dust and debris… I…but the day before I said to Fred, what's that van doing in front of the Jacksons' house."

"Van?"

"Well, you know Fred. I interrupted his TV programs, and he probably didn't hear me. Fred gets that way. I don't know if his hearing is going bad or what."

Billy Dee stole a glance at Shep and suppressed his smile. Ellie May had lived across the street from him for years. She was the neighborhood watchdog and gossip.

Poor Fred, he was well versed in the art of selective hearing and seeing. As he would say, "When the bed is only used for sleeping it affects your ability to hear and see."

"What about this van, Ellie May?"

She paused and crinkled her face trying to remember. "Well, I was sitting right over there." She pointed to the chair facing the front window. "It's not like I stare into the street all the time. I'm not one of those busybodies. Well, you know, Billy Dee."

Billy Dee nodded in agreement. "What color was it?"

"Color? Hmm, I…white, yes it was a white van and had some kind of name on it."

"Go on."

"That's what it was. I didn't understand why a heating and cooling company would be in front of your house."

"Do you recall the name?"

Ellie May went to the window in the front. "Name? I'm trying to remember. I said to Fred, "You ever hear of this company?'" She turned to face Billy Dee and Shep. "Well, I was talk'n to the wall. He never listens to what I have to say."

"Ellie May…the name?"

"Oh yes, the name. It was foreign if anything. Vish something… that's it…Vishkov Heating and Plumbing."

"Vishkov? You sure?

"Ain't it a strange name? Fred tells me I never forget anything."

Billy Dee smiled. "I'm sure he's right. Thank you, Ellie May."

She gave him a hug as he and Shep took their leave.

"Give my best to Janine. If you need anything, you know where we're at."

"Will do."

***

Brownsburg

Pappy went through the day. He made excuses as to Tope's whereabouts to the few who asked. Every few hours, he'd go to the parking lot and check on Tope's car. Only to find It hadn't moved. The rest of the time he sat at his desk, staring at the front door and, then his desk phone. A few times he thought of calling the police. What would he say? *Maybe tomorrow if the son-of-a-bitch don't show*, then he thought to give Priscilla a call. *Line her up early, so that she can't make other plans.* He picked up the receiver, but after punching a few of the digits he hung up. *A man got his pride. She should be calling him after what she did.* One thing for sure, tonight, he was not going home. Nor would he be alone. He would park his ass at Joey's Bar and either get drunk, laid, or both.

He checked the hour on the big wall clock. *Getting near quitting time and no Tope. Son of a gun.* He got up and went to Tope's office. *Hell, maybe there's a spare car key or something.* He opened the top desk drawer, then the next. The bottom one was locked. He gave it a good look trying to figure out why that would be. *What is Tope hiding?* He was about to pull hard on the handle but stopped. *What if the bastard showed?* It wouldn't be right for him to go into Tope's drawer. He certainly wouldn't like it if Tope went into his. He sat back in Tope's chair. He did like the feel of it…all genuine leather and worn to the right suppleness. He should move it to his desk…if… He slapped the chair's arm and chided himself for being selfish. He leaned back a little, and something caught his eye on top of the desk. *Holy crap.* A car key lay on a small silver-like dish. He snatched it and clutched it in his big hand. He allowed himself to lean back and close his eyes. Yeah, he could see it. Driving to Joey's Bar in Tope's Land Rover. The women would be all over him. Why not, for one night, be the big man in town once again?

***

Chicago

"Did you get all that?" Billy Dee asked Shep as they walked across the street to the hole in the ground that used to be Billy Dee's home. "Ellie May is something else, but basically good people."

"Yeah, I got it," Shep said, slapping his notebook shut and putting it in his pocket.

"You ever hear of such a company?"

"No, but that doesn't mean it don't exist," Shep answered.

"True." Billy Dee gazed at the debris-laden space in front of him. "What's left…shreds of papers, maybe some photos, broken furniture, Jesus…this is for shit." He shook his head. "The bastards who did this sure knew what they were doing."

Shep looked up. "You used the plural? You think there's more than one?"

Billy Dee kept staring at the hole that was his home. "I don't know, but it wouldn't surprise me. One to drive the van, the others to plant the devices. It would make sense. Just a feel'n."

The site still had yellow tape around it. There were police technicians taking soil samples, others photographing. Billy Dee saw remnants of a wall where the back of the house used to be. Other bricks were strewn in helter-skelter fashion, as if a mad artist had been at work.

"You want to go down there?" Shep pointed.

Billy Dee hesitated. He wiped his face with his hand and sighed. "Might as well, this ain't go'n to get easier."

Shep introduced Billy Dee to some of the technicians, then went toward the rear. "What do we know?" he asked a man wearing a well-worn apron with an unlit cigar between his teeth stooping near the remains of the back wall. Shep watched as the man studied the residue on the brick.

"Well," he said, standing up, "I'll bet anything that some sort of fertilizer nitrate was utilized. The same stuff used in that Oklahoma bombing."

"Hold on, you think something that powerful?" Billy Dee asked.

The cigar man looked at Shep. "I know who you are, but who's he?"

"Sorry, this is Billy Dee Jackson. He's an ex-cop and the victim of this…" Shep circled his arm over the destruction.

"Someone wanted to get even with you." Cigar man nodded, then spat. "Dennis Thompson," he stuck his hand out toward Billy Dee. "Been doing this a long time and always learning something new. The bad guys keep innovating. Keeps us on our toes. Anyway, the boys call me Den." He spit out some loose tobacco leaf. "Your neighbors said they saw a white mushroom cloud, , then red-brown smoke. That indicates ammonium nitrate. We'll know a bit more when we get some of the dirt and bricks analyzed."

Billy Dee took a deep breath and turned to Shep. "The bastards who did this will pay; Lord have mercy."

Shep patted his friend on his back. "We'll get them. Don't you worry. We'll get them."

"Damn right." Billy Dee began to walk away.

"Where you going?" Shep asked.

"To the car. That van with that crazy-ass name on it. Let's find it."

Chapter Twelve

Paris

Jack Monte's mobile phone buzzed, and it woke him. He sat up from his cot. He made sure no one else was watching before retrieving the phone from a pocket sewn into the underside of the mattress. Satisfied there were no prying eyes, he grabbed his cell and read the latest text. It took him several minutes to break down the code. The message informed him that an agent may have botched a killing. He scratched his day-old beard. This wasn't information he wanted to be associated with. This was trouble. He got up and began to pace.

He had sought revenge on the cops who'd had him deported to France. He still had contacts with the SLA, Serbian Liberation Army.

The conversation with the liaison was brief.

A few days later, there was a message for him and a number to call.

"*Zdravo* (hello)," the voice answered.

Monte couldn't quite place the accent or the sex of the person. But it didn't stop him.

"Where am I calling?" Monte asked.

There was a pause and static, then, "Belgrade. Unless you have business, this conversation ends."

"Wait. I do. Do you know who I am?"

"Of course. Otherwise, I would never answer."

"Good." Monte went on to explain his plan.

It didn't take much to convince them to get on board. A plot was hatched, and it succeeded. Billy Dee Jackson's house was blown up. Monte thought he was done. Now, this latest message of a killing gone awry. He understood screwups always cost, and he desired no part of it. He got what he wanted, the rest, well, was on them. He took a deep breath and closed his eyes for a moment.

He was smart enough to know his plea of innocence wouldn't get him far. His earlier trial made that clear. He closed his hand over his phone. Even if he got rid of it, that wouldn't be enough. He sat down on his cot and returned the phone to its hiding place. He swept his hands over his face. He had to be careful. Everyone in prison was a potential enemy…fellow prisoners and of course the guards. It was him against all. Revenge was not as sweet as he once thought. He felt the walls of his cell close in.

***

Susan waited for Felix to finish his walk-through of the café before he locked the door.

"Another night done." He checked the time. "It's too early for bed."

They began to walk down the street. "You sound like a little boy past his bedtime."

His lips formed a half-circle as if he would cry. "I am a child. How else could I act as *le grande maître d'* and smile at the parade of *les cochons* all day long."

"Not all of them are pigs. Some turn out to be very pleasant."

He took her arm. "When they have you to look at, of course, but me…? I do not have your…eh…charms."

"Very funny."

He leaned in to kiss her.

"Felix."

He stopped. "What? A kiss. What's the big deal? I may be a little boy in there," he pointed, "but here…"

"You're all grown up and want to do adults things?"

"*Exactement.*"

She took a step away and studied him. "*Bon.* If that's the case…then see me at my place in an hour."

"*Vraiment* (really)?"

The hunt, she knew, was as exciting as the conquest. She left him with his mouth watering. He surely had visions of spending the night. She had other plans. Poor boy, she giggled. He was in for an unfulfilled *une nuit de désir*, (a night of desire). It was a most Parisian thing to do.

She lived in the Montmarte area off the rue Novins. The train ride to her apartment took fifteen minutes. From the station, it was a five-block walk to her place. Once inside, she turned off the alarm. She visually searched each of the five rooms and the kitchen. Satisfied all was in order, she poured herself a cognac, then sat on the couch with her feet tucked beneath. The night's labor receded along with the tensions it brought. She emptied her jean pockets of the tips she was paid as well as her phone. The pile of money rested on the table in front of her. She took a sip of her drink and sighed, then remembered Felix. She reached for her cell.

"*Mon cher,*" she texted, "I am so sorry to disappoint us, but a family matter has come up and I must attend to it. *A demain*, Danielle."

She reread the message, then pressed Send. She took another sip and congratulated herself. The note was short, gave just enough detail, and most importantly gave hope to his denied passion. He would be angry at first, then disappointed. But all possibilities live for *a demain* (tomorrow).

Now that Felix was out of the way, she placed her cell

alongside the cash and went to her bedroom. A small safe was stowed inside her closet. She twisted the tumbler according to the combination. There was a click, and the door opened. There, amongst papers, a bankroll of hundreds and, a notebook containing names and addresses was another phone. This one had apps that spoofed calls to make it appear they came from different locations, along with telephone numbers that matched. The virtual sim card had an adjustment for voices, male or female, and languages. It was a technological marvel. She would never be able to explain how it worked, but it did. She reviewed her messages, then went to her bed. The clock on the side table read 3:30 a.m. She calculated the time difference, then set her alarm to make the call at the appropriate time.

***

Brownsburg

It took Pappy a while to figure out where he was. He remembered he went to Joey's Bar in Tope's Land Rover. He distinctly recalled sitting on the bar stool buying drinks for whoever was nearby. The liquor flowed as his head could attest. There was a woman who had an eye on him before things went blurry. It wasn't Priscilla. No, this one was thin, with a country farm face. She kept smiling and laughing when he was sure she couldn't hear his jokes. He guessed she was in her late twenties, early thirties. He sidled up next to her. She didn't mind. Said she was staying at the Holiday Inn up the road. She was in town for a meeting or something. He didn't care what her reason was. His focus, between shots and beers, was on her tits that screamed to be freed from her skin-tight sweater. That was pretty much all he could think of. He remembered helping her into Tope's Land Rover. Heard her say how impressed she was. He didn't think of how she got from the Holiday Inn to Joey's. Hell, he was in too much heat and drink to stop and figure. She gave directions and he managed to get to her place. It wasn't Holiday Inn. It didn't matter. She was making him feel *sooo* good along the way.

He sat on the side of the bed trying to recall what happened after they got inside the apartment. He looked over his shoulder, but no one was there. He rubbed his face with his hands and beat himself up for not remembering her name. Frustrated, he yelled, "Anyone home?" No one answered. He stood-up slowly but felt a bit dizzy. He found his pants at the foot of the bed. His wallet was there, but the cash was gone. He checked his pockets for Tope's keys. They weren't there. He found the rest of his clothes scattered around the bedroom. He tried all the pockets. *Shit, I don't even know where I am.* He dressed in a hurry. The apartment had another room, a kitchen, and a small bathroom. The door to the place had a skinny chain but no lock. Anyone could come in. He started to sweat. His hands grew cold, and he felt nauseous. Not the time to get sick. He had to get out. He tripped going down the one flight of stairs but caught himself before he fell. Once outside, he huddled in the doorway. The prairie wind stung his face. There were several cars parked on the street, but none were Tope's Land Rover. *What the hell do I do now?*

Chapter Thirteen

Chicago

Billy Dee's phone went off as he climbed into Shep's car. "Let me guess, the Missus.?" Shep said, putting the key into the ignition.

Billy Dee ignored him and answered. "Good morning." He tried to sound cheery.

"Good morning?" Janine said, "that's all you got to say? It's afternoon, and I'm sitting in this hotel room with these four walls wondering where the hell you went. You brought me coffee, but that don't go all that far. The insurance man, Jimmy, called too, and you weren't here."

"Janine—" Billy Dee attempted to interrupt.

"Don't you hush me. I know you with Shep and probably ate good at one of them downtown places." She caught her breath. "Billy Dee, you tell Shep to bring you back here. I don't care what you're do'n or who you arrest'n."

Billy Dee sighed and moved the phone away from his ear for a moment. The damn thing was more of a nuisance than anything else. But of course, he had to have the newest and best model, though he barely knew how to make a call much less take a photo. "Okay, Janine, you made your point." He hoped his voice didn't carry. He could feel Shep lean toward him and heard him snicker. "We're about fifteen minutes away. I'll see you." He kept the phone to his ear for a few seconds after the call ended.

"I guess no more investigating for you," Shep said.

Billy Dee rested his cell on his lap. "I don't see it that way. Janine will be cool. I was away a bit too long. She'll see the light when I tell her we may have a lead. You'll see. Besides, it will give me time to rent a car. You can't be driving me all over the place, though I do appreciate it."

Shep put the car in gear. "Man, I admire you. Even after the dressing down, you just keep going. That woman has a hold on you."

"I guess she do. Hell, she's put up with me all these years… even more than you."

"She's got me there. You retired on me." He didn't say anything for a moment. "You know the wife and I bailed on our marriage. We couldn't stand each other after the years piled up. Whatever you two have that makes it work, God bless."

"Amen to that."

Shep dropped Billy Dee at the hotel. "I'll get back with you later this afternoon."

"Thanks, Shep. It's all good." Billy Dee flashed a smile that disappeared the moment his friend left. *Lord, you play'n with me now. My house burned down, my wife is pissed, and I don't have a pot to…"*

"Afternoon, sir." The doorman's remark interrupted his thoughts.

Billy Dee looked up. "Afternoon." He walked past him, took a few steps into the lobby, then turned. "Say, you know where I can rent a car?"

"A car? No sir, I don't, but maybe someone at the desk can help you."

"Okay, just a thought. I'll check it out a little later, thanks." He didn't have the time to wait in line for that information.

He knew Janine was fuming. *Best get on upstairs and put the fire out.*

The elevator sped to his floor. He got out and walked with a purpose to his room. He was about to knock when Janine opened the door. "You bring anything?" she asked.

"Bring? ...like what?"

"Someth'n to eat. Billy Dee, it's afternoon already and coffee ain't food."

He stood in the entryway trying to think of the right thing to say. "You right, I shoulda stopped and got you somethin'. Hey, why don't we order in."

"From the hotel?"

"If you..."

"That'll cost a fortune."

"Okay, there's places in Hyde Park that will deliver. What you hungry for?"

Janine sat down on the bed. "Well...I haven't had pizza in so long."

"Done. I'll order from our favorite place...Medici."

"I can't stay angry at you. Make it a large with extra sausage. What did you and Shep find?"

"Hold on, I'll place the order."

He actually figured out how to find the number on his phone. "See, I'm gett'n the hang of it," he said to Janine as he dialed.

He placed the order, then hung up. "They say forty-five minutes. Might as well sit and put on the TV." He took three steps and picked up the remote. He stared at the instrument. "Lord, they don't make it easy. How do you turn the damn thing on?"

Janine took the device from him. She pressed a few buttons and the picture spread across the screen. "What do you want to watch?"

"Sports."

"As if I didn't know." She went through the channels. She paused at the local news.

"Wait," Billy Dee said, as she was about to flip the station. "Let's hear what's go'n on." Billy Dee grabbed a chair from the corner of the room. On the screen, a reporter described a fire of a house and garage in Posen. Billy Dee got out of the chair and stepped closer to the TV as the reporter described the scene.

The authorities claimed the cause of the blaze was unknown. A fireman interviewed on camera believed the fire started in the garage. He went on to say they found remnants of a burned-out van, but the place appeared to have been vacant.

"Praise the Lord," Billy Dee said at the end of the report.

"What's got into you?" Janine asked.

"I think… I…" He looked at Janine. "I got to call Shep. I've got a feeling that fire has something to do with us."

"You crazy. It's in Posen."

"I know. Boy, do I know."

Chapter Fourteen

Chicago

The phone's ring woke Jenko. At first, its sound intruded on his dream. The persistence of it penetrated his consciousness until he no longer could ignore it.

"Allo?" His voice a hoarse whisper. He looked widely around the room trying to remember where he was. There were cracks in the wall, and a bed that had held too many occupants. The one shade was so thin that the lights of the street made it seem like daylight, then again, maybe it was daylight. He tried to read his watch. "What time is it?" he asked.

The voice on the other end was not sympathetic. "Why you in bed? The day is half over. You still have job to do."

Jenko breathed into the phone. He didn't like to be lectured or yelled at, particularly when he awoke. "What you talking? I did what was instructed. Where is the money?"

"Did you forget the bird? You did the wrong one. If you want your money, go back, and do what you are paid to do."

"*Poshel na khuy.*" Jenko let slip a *fuck you*. He quickly became apologetic. "Sorry, sorry. I just woke-up. *Prostite menya*, forgive me, I…" Jenko slid his hand through his hair. "Yes, you are right. I'll take care of it."

"When?"

"Soon, yes, very soon."

"Better. You have till end of week. Get rest and do the job."

"Of course. I won't disappoint."

"*Da*h. You'll receive more information regarding the bird so no more mistakes.

"*Da*h. I promise. Excuse, but I am low on…"

"Don't you worry, Jenko. You meet Vera in two hours on Halsted and Jackson. She is tall with straight black hair. She has envelope for you."

He said his thank-you to a dead connection.

***

Brownsburg

Pappy worked up the courage to step away from the door stoop and took a closer look at the street. There was no Land Rover in sight. He caught a glimpse of a street sign that helped him figure where he was…miles from his neck of the woods. He gripped the phone in his pocket. At least the bitch left him that. Besides feeling the cold and wind, he was mindful that there was no one else walking. He swallowed hard as he went toward what he hoped was a main street. His route led him past buildings that had plywood where windows used to be and black soot on the facade. He was definitely in the wrong part of town.

He'd try Tope. If he answered, that would solve most of his problems except for the missing car. True, Tope would be pissed. He'd be called every name in the book, but Tope would get over it, especially after he explained his reason for taking the Land Rover. Besides, insurance would cover it.

Pappy cursed the cold taking the phone from his pocket and punching Tope's number. It went directly to voice mail. He stopped and let the wind take its bite. He took a deep breath. "Shit." His money was gone along with his credit card. He didn't have the kind of friends that would jump in their car and do him a favor, especially drive to this part of town. As he saw it, he had no other choice but to call Priscilla. The irony wasn't lost on him that he should have started last evening with her in the first place.

"Pappy? I can hardly hear you. What?" Priscilla asked.

"I need… a… listen, can you… the damn wind…."

"What do you want? I'm at work." She looked around determining if anyone listened.

"I've been robbed."

"You've been… I don't understand. You're sobbing."

"No… ROBBED, like… took my money."

"Are you okay? Did you call the police? Oh my God." She put her hand over the receiver and whispered to a nearby coworker. "Pappy been robbed."

"Priscilla, I need you to come get me."

"Come get you? I'm at work. Where are you, anyway?"

"I think I'm in Danville."

"Illinois?"

"No…no, Indiana. It's about ten miles from you."

"Ten… I… can't you call a cab? I'm working a full day. You want me to up and leave?" She covered the phone again and told her friend what Pappy said.

"Priscilla, they took all my money and credit card. I'm ask'n for your help."

"Well…you're ask'n one hell of a favor."

"You're still my girl, Priscilla."

"No… I am? After you walked in on me? You've got rocks in your head, Pappy. I'm nobody's girl and plan to keep it that way."

"Okay, okay, I don't mean I own you or somethin'. You're good to do whatever. Jesus its freezing. Please…"

"Stop whining, you pussy." She held the phone from her

ear so her friend could hear. After a few seconds she agreed. "Okay, tell me where you are."

Pappy pulled as much of his coat lapels as would reach over his ears as he waited. After what seemed like a day, he saw Priscilla's car inching toward his street corner. She pulled over, and he jumped in. It took a few minutes for him to stop shivering and catch his voice. "Thanks," he finally said.

She made a U-ey. Her tires squealed. The force of the acceleration splayed him against the seat. "If I had known where you were, I'd never would have done this. You better bless God that I'm so good-natured."

He lifted his head. "Thank you again. I appreciate it."

"How the hell did you get out here, anyway?" She gave him a sharp glance.

Oh shit, what do I say? He rubbed his hands a bit longer than necessary. "Well… I…"

"Pappy!" Her stare went through him.

He bit his lip and looked away. "I…eh…", then glanced toward her. "I got a call from a potential client, at least I thought it was. She wanted me to check out some property. The rest you know."

Priscilla didn't say anything. Instead, she turned on the radio and caught the end of a tune. The disc jockey came on, cracked a rude joke, then launched into reading the news. "A Land Rover crashed into a building, killing the driver at the border of the town of Danville and Brownsburg. Police are investigating."

Pappy put his hands over his face, then realized that she glanced at him.

"What's the matter with you?"

He didn't reply.

"Didn't your partner, Tope, have a car like that? Say, why didn't he come and get you?"

Pappy turned and stared out his window. "He's gone."

Chapter Fifteen

Chicago

Billy Dee was unable to reach Shep. He left a message on his voice mail and sat down. Within a minute or two, he stood and walked around the room.

"Stop," Janine said, "all your walk'n is wear'n out the carpet. I'll flick on some sports. Sit down."

Her words caught him in mid-stride. "Did you say something?" He looked at her face and knew he annoyed her. "I'll take a seat." He went to his chair, stared at the TV for a moment, then popped up.

"If you're so antsy get yourself a car and go out there. Lord, it better than you pace'n and stare'n at that phone. I'll save you some pizza once it gets here."

He could feel his smile stretch across his face. "Right idea, Janine. I still got my badge. See, there was a van from some sort of heating and cooling company outside our house before it blew-up. It had a strange name painted on its side. I don't know if one is the other, but I have a strange feeling."

"I've lived with you long enough to know about your 'feelings.' Get out of here and check it out."

"I'm blessed," he said as he got his hat and coat. "I'll check-in with you when I know something."

"You better be back around dinner time. The pizza won't last for all the meals in the day."

***

Jenko held the phone as if it were a dead fish. Was it the speaker's tone that unsettled him? Was it…? Shit, he hadn't caught up with his sleep. He fumbled around for his watch, then realized the damn phone had the time. He better wake up in a hurry. Who knows whether this Vera was bringing money or… his end? He rubbed his eyes. *Der'mo* (shit). He sniffed his undershirt. Phew! Sat up. He carefully placed his feet on the floor and glanced around the room. *Is not Moscow Ritz.* He stepped carefully to the bathroom. The wallpaper hung from the wall like a prizefighter hit one too many times. The dim yellow glow of the one bulb didn't hide the black crust that colored the sink and toilet bowl. He looked at what passed for the shower and thought twice as to whether to use it. Another whiff of his T-shirt convinced him. The knobs for hot and cold turned with a screech. After waiting several minutes, he realized there would be no hot water. The shower would be quick. After a hurried rinse he didn't bother with towels, even if there were any. He dug into his knapsack and put on fresh underwear and yesterday's clothes. Whoever's apartment this was could keep it. It was barely fit for human occupation. He tried locking the door behind him, but the hole wouldn't align. *Sukin syn*, son of a bitch, he muttered. He walked down the flight of stairs to the lobby and placed the key in the mailbox. The poor slob who comes after him was not his problem. *Do svidaniya.*

The car was where he left it. He was thankful for that. He turned on the engine, and the car's dashboard sprang to life. The GPS told him he was at 31st and Talman. He pressed a button and recited an address. The screen changed and a female voice instructed the route to follow. He flicked on the radio. He smiled as he drove past streets and highways.

He wondered if anyone knew who he was and what he had done.

In Russia he was surely a nobody. Just another young man among millions who drank vodka and lay around doing not much of anything except occasionally bedding a woman. The movement made him "a somebody." He saw the world. All because he was good with a gun. He rarely considered the consequence or the morality of his act. Killing was his profession, and like a doctor or lawyer, each case had its rewards and aggravations. Certainly, Dijana was a plus. She was competent as an explosive expert and from what he could tell, committed to the movement. Why she had to die, he couldn't fathom. That wasn't his job. She was a great fuck, but that didn't interfere with his job. That was why he was a professional.

The voice of the GPS told him he was a half mile from Halsted and Jackson. As he got closer, he searched the side-walks for anyone meeting Vera's description. A parking spot opened near the corner, and he took it. He could wait in the car, but that was not his instruction. He reached under his seat for his gun and slipped it in his jacket pocket. He checked his surroundings again. People were all around and the traffic was heavy. There were different Greek restaurants lining both sides of Halsted. If this was a setup for his demise, this Vera would have to do it quickly and use a silencer. That's what he would do if given the same assignment.

He leaned on a sign pole near the corner and took a cigarette from his pocket. He cupped his hands to light it. The taste of the smoke made him hungry as he realized he hadn't had breakfast. People walked by their pace hurried due to the cold weather. For him, Chicago's winter was warm. In Russia this would almost be considered spring. He made a clucking sound with his tongue as he kept watch.

About a block away a woman stepped out from one of the Greek restaurants. She had a cup in one hand and the other was concealed in a coat pocket. She was tall, and even at a distance, he could tell her hair was dark. He studied her movement. She took purposeful strides. She looked neither left nor right but straight ahead as if she was immune from the wind and cold. He dropped his cigarette and walked toward her. He put his hand in his jacket and rested his finger on the trigger. They were a third of a block away from each other and closing. She never looked at him.

***

Posen

"Who did you say you were?" The desk officer's name tag identified him as L. Johnson.

"Billy Dee Jackson." He flashed his Chicago police badge.

The desk officer scratched his head. "Now, what's a Chicago cop doing way down here?"

"The news reported a garage fire. It may have something to do with a case in Chicago."

"How so?"

Billy Dee licked his lips and tried not to let his frustration show. "There was a van in the garage that may be tied to…"

"Yeah, I follow, but you just show'n up and all." He shook his head. "Just don't know about that."

Billy Dee flashed a grin. "I don't want to interfere with anything you guys are doing. Only want to talk to the investigating officer."

"Uh-huh. I know what-you talk'n about, but…eh…when it comes to arsons, Posen don't got nobody. We use the sheriff's department."

Billy Dee felt his face flush. "The sheriff's department?"

"That's right. Cook County Sheriff. Probably they're over there now."

"Really." He let that tidbit of information settle before saying, "Thanks."

"No problem, Officer…?"

"Jackson. I'll go over there and have a look." He started out the door, then stopped. "Can you give me directions?"

The desk officer's eyes widened. "Directions, yeah… it's a ways. Sorry, I can't leave the desk and drive you there myself." He, then busied himself with papers he probably viewed a dozen times.

Billy Dee was tempted to speak his mind, but marriage had taught him it wouldn't do any good. "Guess I'll find it myself," and walked out the door.

Chapter Sixteen

Paris

Susan appreciated technology. She didn't understand the how's and why's of it, but it made her work easier. The clock by her bed told her it was a little after noon. She stretched under her covers with the realization that her day had begun. She had set in motion the pieces on the imaginary chess board like Dumond had taught her.

Eduard Dumond had been many things…a thief, embezzler, lover, and a raconteur. He had a large appetite and lived life as a moveable feast. He was her teacher, friend, and at times, she had been his mistress. Thinking about him, she realized Dumond could never fill his soul, no matter how many triumphs. He loved the game more than the gains. It was the dare of the edge. Unfortunately for them both, he lost his last intrigue.

He had sent her to Chicago to buy weapons for the SLA. A woman had shot Dumond at a hotel as he waited to finish the deal. In Chicago, she too was almost killed, and fled back to Paris.

It wasn't easy to pick up the pieces of her life. Dumond had had enemies and disgruntled investors. But he had also left hidden files of customers and contacts. She had paid attention when she was with him and he, in his manner, not overtly but subtly, told her where to look.

"I love the classics," he once said. "I have at times in my life come across beautiful first editions of some of the greatest of French literature. Dumas, Hugo, Zola, even the Marquis de Sade."

Susan was quite aware when he said, "he came across," he really meant he appropriated them. The how was not important, but Dumond had them. The obvious places to search would be his safe or bank vault. Susan knew he had neither. He did, though, have multiple safe houses throughout Paris. One by one she had located them. Sometimes it sat plain as day on a bookshelf, in others mixed in with cookbooks, pans, or laundry. Inserted between the pages, she found Dumond's lists scribbled on note cards or lined paper. It took time, but she not only had Dumond's files, but also those lovely books that paid for many, many things.

She swung her legs over the edge of the bed and headed toward the shower when she heard the door buzzer. She grabbed a sheer bathrobe and put it over her naked body as she moved toward the door. The ring gave way to a knock.

"Danielle, open the fuck'n door."

She stopped. She knew that voice… Felix.

She put the chain on the door, then opened it slightly. "Felix, what are you doing here?"

"You lied to me, and I don't like that. I drove around all night trying to understand why you brushed me off after you led me on. You're a bitch, and if this was another time, I'd fire your ass, but…" He caught his breath.

She undid the chain and opened the door a bit wider. "You can't…given the unions and that I also make a lot of money for the Café." She could see his eyes work hard to penetrate the thin fabric that adorned her. The anger on his face melted away, replaced by a tingling of lust. As Dumond often told her, "Show a man the hint of tits and ass along with the possibility, and a woman gets what she wants."

"So, Felix, you think I made up the story about an emergency?"

She could see him search for a pleasing answer. An embarrassed grin crept over his face.

"Well…eh… it's just…you know… as soon as you got home… the message…"

"Did it ever occur to you that I didn't know before? I was looking forward to it too."

"You were? I mean, of course we both…"

She swung the door open. She enjoyed the look on his face as he took her in standing in a sheer robe that went just below her thigh. He was putty. "Do you want to come in?"

He took a step toward her. His arms ready to embrace but, then stopped. "I…" he sighed. "The time! I must be at the Café. How about we pick-up after work?"

"Felix, that's a million hours from now. It's a shame our timing is so poor. We'll have to see what the evening brings, *mon ami*." She smiled as she slowly closed the door. "*Au revoir*," she said just before it shut. She would have burst into laughter but was afraid he'd hear. She replaced the chain and made her way to the shower. There were more important things to think about than Felix. There were plans to arrange and details to tidy, and best of all, technology made it possible to hide it all.

***

Monte trudged from his cell to the dining mess. This was usually the time when he and his fellow inmates socialized, such as it was. Gone was his smile and his ability to joke. Every word an inmate spoke was analyzed. *The bastard laughed when he spoke. Was there a threat lurking behind the pleasantness?*

"What is the matter with you, Monte? You are not your

usual self. Where are the treats you bring to make us jealous? Out of money, *mon ami*?" asked Pierre the Corsica, or, as the others referred to him behind his back, *le petite Napoleon*.

Monte mumbled a response, but apparently it wasn't sufficient.

"*Mon ami*, no chocolates, or cigarettes? Look at him, maybe a woman tired him out during the night. Poor man."

The remark elicited laughter from the four others at the table.

Monte drew himself up. "At least I'd know what to do with one given the chance."

Pierre took the challenge. "Besides everything else you've regaled us with, you now propose you can teach Casanova a thing or two. We are eager students. Tell us your techniques. We have a lot of time to practice."

That drew a crescendo of laughter.

Monte jumped out of his chair glaring at the circle of men around him. "Go fuck yourselves." He took his mug of coffee and left. He knew he couldn't leave the room until the buzzer rang, allowing another shift to enter. He searched for an empty table and found one near a corner. He was angry at himself. He had let the news of the text received last night cloud his thinking. True, anyone could be part of the Serbian Liberation Army, prisoners or guards. The group had the means to bribe and worm their way in anywhere. But being paranoid leads to mistakes. He took a sip of what passed for coffee. The bitterness of the liquid made him gag. *Tastes like shit.* He would order better from the canteen. That thought improved his attitude. After all, the path leading to him from a killing gone awry somewhere in the States was a long stretch. How could he have anything to do with it, being cooped up in jail? He laughed. This prison was his defense.

***

Chicago

Jenko's finger rested on the trigger of his gun inside his coat pocket. He drew near the woman. Her movement was quick and practiced. It happened fast. He almost failed to grab the envelope with his free hand. He continued to walk a few seconds more before he turned. He searched the sidewalk populated by several people, but she had vanished. *This Vera very good.* He glanced at the packet. The only markings on it were his name. He put it in his pocket and went to his car. Once inside, he checked the front, then the back of it. Nothing else was visible. He tore it open. There were ten one-hundred-dollar bills. He took the money out and counted it again. A small scrap of paper fluttered to his lap. He retrieved it. On it was a phone number and nothing else. Coincidence? Mistake? He held onto the note as he stuffed the bills into his pocket.

Chapter Seventeen

Chicago

"Where are you, again?" Shep asked.

Billy Dee couldn't tell from his friend's tone whether he was enjoying the frustration he relayed or concerned. "Lord, you do try a man's patience. I said I was in Posen."

"What the hell you do'n way down there?"

"Have you been listen'n to anything I've said?"

There was a slight pause. "Yeah, heard every word. You want me to drop what I'm do'n and join you."

"I didn't say that, but now you're talk'n. Well?"

"I can't."

Billy Dee sighed and gripped the phone a little tighter. "You can't or won't?"

"Never you mind. If you weren't so giddy-up and waited some, I could have saved you all that trouble. Here's the name of the sheriff's investigator, Bennie Ochawa. He's expecting you."

"No shit? You the best, Shep. My man."

"Yeah? A minute ago, you thought I was an asshole."

"Now…"

"Didn't you?"

"Come on, Shep, be nice. All is forgiven. Thank you. You're a prince."

"Sure, I am, and you're welcome." Billy Dee looked at

the address Shep gave him. He took out his glasses to read what he had scribbled on the back of a card … 145th and Palmer. *Easy, just plug it into the map app.* It didn't work. If only Janine was with him to help. She'd figure it out in a minute. He thought of calling but how the hell could he talk to her and fiddle with the phone at the same time. He'd just have to deal with it. He wiped away drops of sweat as he continued to punch in the address. *To think, these devices were made to make things simpler. Not on your life.* He fumbled, swore, repeated, and finally succeeded in obtaining the route needed to get to the wanted location. *Yeah baby, I did it. Who said you can't teach an old dog new tricks.* He replaced his glasses and stepped on the gas.

Two fire trucks were on the scene. He flashed his badge and a sheriff's officer let him drive through the blocked-off site. He parked behind several other police cars and walked to where a group of officers stood.

"Afternoon. Can anyone tell me where I can find Investigator Bennie Ochawa?"

Billy Dee drew several looks and after a few seconds one of the officers pointed toward the charred wooden frame house in front of them.

"You'll find him in back."

"Thanks." Billy Dee stepped carefully over the puddles of water and debris and made his way to the rear. There were several more officers along with firemen in heavy gear busying themselves where the garage must have been.

"Investigator Ochawa?" Billy Dee called.

A tall Asian fellow looked up. "Yes?"

Billy Dee flashed his badge and introduced himself. "What happened?"

"Chicago Police? News travels fast." He said a few words to another officer, then went back to Billy Dee. "To my best guess, someone didn't like this place. Although why is another question since the house seemed to have been abandoned."

"And the garage?"

Ochawa took a step closer to the smoldering ruin. Billy Dee followed. "See that?" He pointed to a partial skeletal frame of a vehicle. "Makes no sense. Why a vehicle would be parked behind an empty house."

Billy Dee glanced over at the wreck. "Looks like what used to be a van."

"You think?"

"Well, I'm no expert but… Was fire the cause?

"There was a fire all right, but that's not what started it."

Billy Dee stepped closer.

"I'd stand back. There's still gasoline from whatever was parked there." Ochawa chewed on the end of his pen, then pointed toward the rear of the structure. "See that?"

Billy Dee tried to follow. "What am I looking at?"

"The left of the rear passenger tire on the driver's side. The rubber is gone, and the wheel rim melted. I'd say that's where the explosion occurred."

"Explosion? From a bomb?"

"For now, let's call it a device. Yep, someone decided some-time this morning would be a good time to make noise. Pieces of that vehicle and garage rained all over the place. The men are retrieving what they can." Ochawa stooped down and picked a 2x4 charred piece of metal from near his shoe. He called one of the officers to mark the spot and bag it.

"Can I see that?" Billy Dee asked.

Ochawa shrugged. "Suit yourself. By the way, your partner mentioned something like this recently happened in Chicago?"

Billy Dee studied the object. It was smooth and flat. He glanced at Ochawa for a moment. "Yeah, the other day, a house blew up. We also think there was a device used." He held the piece out away from him and turned it over. "Is that writing?" He showed it to Ochawa and the other officer. While they examined it, Billy Dee grabbed his glasses. "Let me see that again. Ain't that the letter 'V'?"

Ochawa looked over Billy Dee's shoulder. "Could be. Yes. Or a 'W' with part of it missing. The lab boys will check it out. Anything I should know if it is a 'V'?"

Billy Dee continued to study the piece. "Neighbors said there was a van in front of the house the day before. Painted on the side was a strange name V-i-s-h something Heating and Plumbing." Billy Dee handed the metal back. "It's the little things that lead to something big."

Ochawa nodded. "I'll keep that in mind. Right now, all we have is a maybe."

***

Brownsburg

Priscilla pulled her car over to the side and stopped. "What do you mean, Tope's gone? Where did he go?"

Pappy's hand shook. "I… I…don't know. Can't get ahold of him."

Priscilla's eyes widened. She got that way when excited.

"A man don't just disappear and leave everything."

"No, you right," Pappy said, "but…he was always a strange fellow. He came out of nowhere…remember?"

She tapped her fingers on the steering wheel. "How long has he—"

"A day or two," he answered before she finished. He could see she was thinking.

"So, you're saying Tope upped and left…and took nothing. Ha. You know what that means?"

"I don't like where you're go'n with that."

"Why, you already used his Land Rover and got it stolen. Oh, Pappy…" She moved toward him and planted a kiss on his cheek. "You're cute, so cute. Don't you think we should head over to the bank?"

"The bank? How come?"

She unzipped her coat and leaned into him. She took his hand and placed it over her breast. "Well, Pappy, I'm the girlfriend you always wanted me to be."

"You are? You mean you will be? No more play'n around?" He fumbled at her shirt buttons.

"Now, Pappy, there will be time for all that but first…" She brushed his hand away.

"Sor…ry. I get what you mean. This isn't the best place for fool'n around." He sat back for a moment but didn't take his eyes off her. He slapped his leg. "I got it. Before the bank we should stop at the office and…" He took a deep breath. "Celebrate the fact I'm runn'n the show."

"Really, that's how you want to party?"

He thought for a moment. "Yeah, sure do. We can do it on his desk. That's a statement."

"Hmm… on his…?"

Pappy felt electric. "Why not? I'm the boss now. Why can't I do…*my girl*." His stomach jumped. Saying those words was like making a three-point shot with seconds to go. "Don't you worry, we'll get to the bank soon enough."

She batted her eyes, then sighed. "If you think that's the best way. I mean, it's not like we hadn't done it before. But, since I'm now your girlfriend I'll go along with it." She put the car in gear and began to drive. They got about a block before she took her eye off the road and said, "But we better get to the bank right after."

Chapter Eighteen

Chicago

Jenko had choices to make now that he had money in his pocket. Breakfast, not at a fast food, but a sit-down where ladies and gentlemen ate. Or a hotel room where there were clean fresh towels in the shower and a comfortable bed. He felt he had earned a little time, even though his instructions were to clean the mess left in Brownsburg quickly. Besides, what if the scrap of paper with the phone number led to… His cough interrupted his visualization of the dark-haired Vera sharing the nice cozy bed. A killer had to be calm, and what better way to ease tension? He laughed. He drummed his hand on the wheel. Food or sex?

He put the car in drive and inched his way down Halsted. He hadn't gone a block or two before he saw the sign for the Crowne Plaza Hotel north of Madison on the east side of the street. It was big and shouted "'class." He made the decision and drove up the driveway and parked. He told the valet to wait and entered the hotel. There was a small line, but it moved quickly. American hotels were efficient; at least this one appeared to be. He asked for a room for two nights and the rate was easily affordable.

"A credit card, please," said the young man behind the reservation desk.

Jenko's mouth went dry. "I don't use such things. Cash."

The man smiled. "You can use cash, but we need a credit card, in case, well, you know…"

Jenko shook his head in disagreement. "I don't know. I pay in full. Here." He took four one-hundred-dollar bills from his pocket and pushed them toward the receptionist. "Good, yes?"

The young man's smile disappeared. "I…I… the rules…"

"I pay for room," Jenko said, "now give me key, please."

The receptionist gulped and took a step back from the counter. He looked one way, then the other, and finding no one else to discuss the matter, finally nodded, and handed Jenko the magnetic card pass. "Have a nice stay," he quivered.

"Sure," Jenko said, and went to retrieve his bag from the car.

His room was on the 20th floor. The drapes were drawn, but he could tell there was a balcony. He threw his duffel on the bed along with himself. This was a bed, sturdy, spacious, and comfy. The perfection would be to share it with another. Vera. He went through his pocket for the slip of paper. He sat up and dialed the number on his cell. Would she have a low or high voice? Would it be flirtatious? He heard various beeps and clicks on the line and thought it strange, but, then Vera was in a similar business as he. Precautions?

"Allo?"

***

Paris

At first, Monte heard a sound. Was he dreaming? It was still night, or so he thought. His dream slowly evaporated, replaced by a noise coming from underneath his mattress. It finally clicked. His phone. Someone was calling. Who?

No one knew his number, no one, but… Why? A call? He reached for his cell and in a hoarse whisper said, "Hello."

"Vera? Is this Vera?"

The voice he heard was accented. Russian, Eastern European? Was *Vera* a code word that he should know? Monte felt his heart race. "Who is this?" he asked.

"Jenko, we passed on street this morning."

Jenko? Street? Monte wiped his face with his hand. He knew no Jenko and he definitely wasn't on a street. "You have the wrong number," he said.

"Wait. Is this…? Maybe number is house Vera stays."

Monte felt a little relief as he realized this guy must have dialed wrong. "There's no Vera here. You called a prison in Paris…France." He hung-up. He held onto the phone for several seconds before returning it to its hiding place.

Monte lay on his bunk with his eyes closed, hoping to fall back to sleep. *Crazy*, he thought. *How? The fellow's name was what again? Jen… Jas… ah what difference does it make. It was a wrong number. That happens all the time. But the number he recited was not Paris, or France, it was USA.* Monte turned on his other side. *The cellular network must be fucked up. Vera? Who the hell is she?*

***

Chicago

Jenko quickly disconnected. Paris? *Did he say prison?* He stared at his phone and the number dialed. There was no "011+1", or "33." How in hell could that have happened? He stared at both the paper and his cell, , then tore the scrap. *Jesus. No more thinking, Vera, sex, …* His stomach growled. *Food, I need.*

He concealed his gun in his jacket's pocket and took the

elevator to the main floor. He followed the crowd around the reception desk and saw the sign for dinning hanging above its entrance. He walked over. A waiter brushed by and told him to sit anywhere. He chose a booth near a window. A busboy filled a glass with ice and water. Jenko quickly emptied it. He put the glass down and, in a growl, ordered coffee. It came along with another waiter.

"You can choose off the menu or take the buffet," he said.

"Buffet? Where?"

The waiter pointed to an area in the corner.

"Is any good?"

"It's free if you're a guest."

"Dah. Buffet."

The waiter left a plate.

Jenko took a sip of his coffee before filling his plate. *Not bad. At least it had taste. Not Russian coffee, but...* He held the cup to his mouth and for a second closed his eyes. When he opened them, a tall thirtyish woman with long red hair took a seat across from him.

She put her index finger to her lip. "Ssh. I followed you here. I'm informed you fucked up in Brownsburg. I'm to make sure no such thing happens again."

Jenko still clutched the cup. He stared at his visitor. "Vera?"

"Shut up. How many nights you pay for?"

"Two."

"Under what name?"

"Mine. Jenko."

"How stupid can you be?"

He put the cup down and slowly moved his hand.

"I wouldn't," she said. "Your balls will be gone before hand makes it to jacket."

He flashed a smile. "You are good. I thought so when we did exchange. You had dark hair this morning. Now red. It is becoming, Vera."

"I don't know what you talk. If you think I'm Vera, , then it's Vera. My name is not important. The job is and I will make sure…"

He put his hands over his ears. "Yah, yah, I understand." He looked straight on at her face. "Tell me, you want to eat first or fuck."

Her foot caught him in the testicles. As he coughed and doubled over, she said, "Eat, you probably can't do the other."

Chapter Nineteen

Brownsburg

Priscilla pulled into Pappy's office parking lot. "You sure this is what you want?"

"Are you kidding?" Pappy smiled from ear to ear. "You're my girl now."

"Sure, sure, but let's not take too long."

"Honey, when I'm through you'll be in heaven."

"Maybe after the bank," she said under her breath.

"What'cha say?"

"Heaven, you're right. Can't wait." She flashed a smile.

They got out of the car. She started for the office without waiting for Pappy.

"Hey, wait-up now. I got the key, remember."

She stopped. "You hav'n a problem walking? You should be ahead of me with those long legs of yours. But maybe there's a part slowing you down."

"Stop that, Priscilla." He slid his arm around her waist when he reached her. "This is go'n to be great."

All she could think about was whether Tope was really gone. She glanced at the parked cars but didn't see his. That was a good sign. She'd give Pappy what he wanted. In her mind that was only fair. She wasn't a complete bitch. But then she got to thinking how much would be in the account.

She could imagine all the things she'd buy while Pappy did his thing. *I guess that's heaven too.*

Pappy got the office key out of his pocket. Last night's pickup was a long-ago memory. It took getting robbed and Tope's car stolen to get what he really wanted: Priscilla.

He cast a sideways glance at her. She was a good-looking woman always had been. Her curves weren't as sharp as they once were, but, then again, he'd put a little pastry on too. What he remembered was she really got into it. That's what made doing her so enjoyable. He wondered how the heck had bad luck turned into something so good. Life does play tricks.

"Once I open the office door, I'll get you the key to the bathroom if you want to freshen-up," he said as they climbed the stairs.

She wrinkled her nose and half shut her eyes, then sighed. "No problem. First let me see Tope's desk. I don't want splinters on my ass."

"Huh? Oh, no, no it's all polished."

He opened the door and stepped inside. He checked the counter and secretary's desk near the entrance. Nothing had changed. He glanced around the room. The blood spot was barely noticeable.

"Whatcha doing?" she asked. "Where's the bathroom key?"

"Oh, oh yeah." He swiped it off the hook on the wall. "Here. I'll be in there," and pointed to Tope's office.

The office was the way he had left it last night. Tope's papers and things were still there. He cleared the desk, then sat in Tope's comfortable leather chair. To think Tope always rode him about his relationship with Priscilla. *Well, ain't this go'n to shock him? I'm go'n to do her on his fuck'n desk. How's that for take'n control. Who's the sap now?*

Her voice broke his concentration. "You go'n to turn yourself around?" she asked.

He swiveled in the chair. She had let her hair down and the only clothing worn was her blouse that just brushed her thighs. "Ain't you a sight," he said, "one goddamn pretty one."

She sashayed to his chair while unbuttoning. "You like?"

"Do I?" He reached out to grab her.

"No, no, stand," she ordered.

He didn't have to be asked again. She grabbed his belt and unhooked it, then unbuttoned his pants. They dropped to the floor. He had one leg out, when he heard a knock. Her hands pulled on his briefs. The knock came again. He looked up.

"What's wrong with you?" she asked.

"What? Didn't you hear someone at the door?"

She froze.

Now the sound was unmistakable.

"Anybody there?" A male voice asked. "This is the police."

Chapter Twenty

Posen

Billy Dee had that confused moment when he looked for his Chrysler 300, then realized that it was gone…lost when his house exploded. He had rented some foreign-made car. He looked down the street and after refocusing, found it. *Sure, wasn't like my baby.* Everything from the hood to the trunk was compacted and there were too many buttons and gizmos. The pick-up on it was nonexistent. *Better not get into a chase.* He opened the car and fell into the driver's seat. The door, unlike the Chrysler, made a tinny sound when he closed it. *Lord help me if I get into an accident.*

The street was still blocked with fire trucks and police personnel. He took a cigar from his pocket that Shep had given him the night before. It was as good a time as any to light it. After the first few puffs and approving the taste, he stared at the unfolding scene. A mobile lab truck squeezed through and stopped on what once was the lawn of the destroyed building. Ochawa came alongside the truck and pointed toward the garage and the remnants of the van. They seemed to be in a long conversation. Was it about the "V" or "W" that was found? He went to flick ash into the ashtray and in the process glanced at his rental contract lying on the passenger seat. At the top of the page was the VIN, the vehicle identification number. *The VIN. Of course.*

Damn, Ochawa must be looking for it. If it was found, that would be a huge step in discovering ownership. He should have asked. He left his cigar in the ash tray and got out.

"Hey, Detective Ochawa," he said, ambling toward him.

Ochawa stopped. Billy Dee couldn't tell if the detective had a look of "now what" or "don't bother me" either way, Billy Dee sensed his welcome time numbered. "I'm sure you're looking for it, but thought I'd ask. Any luck on the VIN?"

The detective flicked his eyes upward and mumbled a response.

"Whatchasay?" Billy Dee asked.

"I said we're looking for it. The explosion blew van parts all over." He spread his arms out. "I'll let you know if we find anything."

Billy Dee nodded. "Thanks. I won't stay in your hair. I'm sure you're on top of what needs to be done."

"Damn right." Ochawa walked off and left Billy Dee midway between his car and the destroyed garage. "Don't mind me," he said quietly to Ochawa's back, "I'll just wander a bit and see what I can find." He walked past other officers and got near the remains of the vehicle frame. From previous experience, he knew sometimes the VIN was stamped on the driver's side opening or the engine block. He put his glasses on and stooped near that side. There wasn't much left of it. Shep had once told him to look for a pattern from the explosion point. He stood and surveyed the scene. If the device was set off at the rear of the vehicle, the front part, if not melted by the heat, would be hurled forward. *Why not have a look-see?* The evidence boys were behind him on all fours searching for whatever they could find. Billy Dee walked in the other direction with his head down. He walked through the grass and dirt until he got to the curb. No luck, nothing. He straightened and calculated the distance he had come. *I guess Shep's rule of thumb was wrong or the heat from the blast melted everything.* He rubbed his chin, deciding whether to call it quits. He took a step into the street. Something caught his eye. Lying almost flat against the curb was a business card. There was a little dirt on it, but other than that in good shape. He bent and retrieved it. He took his glasses out again and read, *Topin and McDonald's Realtors, Brownsburg, Indiana.* He flipped the card on the other side and noticed a brownish-looking spot. He rubbed his finger on it. Dried blood? He rubbed the substance again but wasn't sure. He turned it over and reread the other side. *Brownsburg, hmm where the heck's that?* He guessed it wasn't close. He held the card and weighed whether to keep it. *Could be nothing or… What the hell?* He put the card in his pocket and walked back to his car. Brownsburg, where in Indiana was it?

***

Brownsburg

Pappy stumbled putting his leg back into his pants. "Oh shit," he repeated. After two attempts he succeeded and pulled his slacks up. "Get some clothes on," he told Priscilla. "Hurry."

He answered the door with his shirt half-in and half-out. "Yes, what can I do for you?" his voice strained as he allowed the officer to enter.

The officer built like a linebacker stepped in. "I'm looking for a Mr. Topin."

Pappy steadied himself by resting one hand on the entrance counter. "Charlie Topin? That's who you want?"

The officer looked at the piece of paper he held. "Yeah, Charles Topin."

"He's not here. I'm…I'm his partner, McDonald, folks call me Pappy."

"Do you know where I can find him?"

Pappy rubbed his chin. "No… no I…" Before he could complete his sentence Priscilla made her entrance from Tope's office. Her blouse was buttoned but that's all she wore.

"Officer, Mr. Topin told us he went on an extended vacation and left the running of the place to Mr. McDonald."

Pappy nodded. "That's right. I'm in charge."

The officer's gaze darted between Pappy and Priscilla, lingering on her. "Well, I…eh, do you know if his vehicle is missing?"

"Missing?" Pappy let out a breath. "You don't say. Tope drove a Land Rover if I recollect. What do you mean… missing?"

The officer refocused his full attention on Pappy. "When did Mr. Topin leave for his vacation?"

Pappy's fingers dug into the counter. "Why… eh…"

"Day before yesterday," Priscilla answered. "He called and said, 'he had to take care of some out-of-town stuff and didn't know when he'd be back'. That's the last we heard from him."

"I thought you said he went on vacation?"

Priscilla strained the first button on her blouse as she not so subtly thrusted her shoulders back. "Absolutely, I thought it was strange too. I mean, probably he took a working vacation. Mr. Topin wasn't very good in the explaining department."

The officer's stare went through her. Pappy figured he was focusing on what he was seeing too. She certainly had God-given tits. Looking at them made him for an instant forget the cop was still there, then he remembered. "Anyway, Officer Reynolds, what's this about?" Pappy said, looking away from Priscilla and reading his name tag.

It took a second or two before Reynolds responded. "We think his car was stolen. A Land Rover was found in Danville. The driver was a woman."

"No kidding. Danville? Indiana or Illinois?" Pappy asked.

"Indiana."

Pappy shuffled his feet. "Danville, what the heck?"

"Do you know if Mr. Topin had business over there? Or a girlfriend?"

Pappy let the questions sink-in. "No…no, I don't. Danville? My word, don't know what he'd be doing way over there. Our business is pretty much in town."

Reynolds reached into his pocket. "This is my card. If Mr. Topin calls or returns, please tell him to contact me."

"Sure will, Officer Reynolds. I'll tell him, first thing." Pappy took the card.

Reynolds turned toward the door.

"Oh, by the way, who was the woman?" Pappy asked.

Reynolds stopped and took a breath. "I can't give out the name yet. She's dead."

Chapter Twenty-One

Paris

Susan made sure she looked especially seductive when she came to work at the Café Deux Magots that late afternoon. It wasn't for the tips. She considered the extra money pocket change. It was for Felix. Her French Musier jeans fit her curves as if they were sculpted, and her silk beige blouse accented what he had wanted to see and touch. A man's brain will follow his eyes and led properly, the checks and balances he'd normally apply…vanish. Viva la conquest!

Felix led the wait staff meeting before the café opened. He was supposed to explain the specials for the evening. Perhaps it was lack of sleep, but she could tell his concentration was not on the new menu items. He tried to hide his frequent stops by clearing his throat or searching for words. He'd pause in the middle of a sentence and give her a quick glance. For a Frenchman, he failed Ogling 101. The staff surely got the impression he had the hots for her. She could see it in their eyes. She had heard the staff's clucking and warning about Felix's wandering eyes and hands. They thought she was the lamb being prepared for his feast. What they and Felix didn't know was the price he'd pay, then again, what was an hour or so of heaven worth? She looked away from his frequent glances and feigned embarrassment. She had acted in this theatre many times and knew the role.

The café had a busy night, and Susan's "pocket money" bulged out of her tight jeans.

"I see you've done particularly well tonight," Felix said. His gaze focused below Susan's waist.

"And you, *mon ami*, have also done fabulously. You will be manager of the year," She laughed and brushed some hair from her face.

"Danielle, why do you torture me? I can't think straight with you around. I'm sure I've not attended to things I should. I hope I won't be fired."

She patted his hand. "Poor boy. You've been thinking with the wrong head. But someday…" She shrugged.

"*Oui,* someday what?"

"*Mon cher*, so eager." She closed her eyes and leaned toward him.

"I can't kiss you here…now. There's still customers and others."

"*Mon Dieu*, you are right. I forget myself," she said in a playful but subtle, mocking tone. She looked at her watch. "We'll be closing in a few minutes. I'll turn in my receipts."

His eyes spoke, "say more," but she didn't. She knew Felix better than he knew himself. She went to a far table and laid out her factures. It wasn't long before he joined her.

"I don't want a replay of last night," he said.

She concentrated on the papers before her.

"Are you listening?"

She stopped counting. "I can either count or listen, but I can't do both…well. Which would you like?"

He hesitated and ran his hand through his hair. "Okay, finish what you are doing, but don't leave before we talk."

She gave him a mock salute and returned to her task. It didn't take long to complete. Before turning in her tally, she heard the bartender shooing some overserved customer out. Someone called "*fini*" and she saw Felix lock the front door.

She stayed at her table near the back as the staff members said their *"bon nuits."* They smiled that French inevitability of what they thought was about to happen when they glanced toward her. Tomorrow she'd be yesterday's meal. Felix would be hunting for new prey. They didn't know her.

Felix had his back to the entrance door. He took a breath and strode to where Susan sat.

"So?" he asked.

Susan met his stare. "Would you like me to disrobe? Take me on this table? I am not your appetizer or dessert. I'm thankful for the opportunity of working here, but I do it well. I've heard all the chatter about you. Here's the deal. Let's not play cat and mouse. You're attracted to me, and I'm attracted to you, but it's not a one-nightstand."

"Of course, I didn't think…"

"Felix, your reputation proceeds you. I know that look in men. That hunger for something they can't have but want very much. I've been there, too."

He pulled a chair from under the table and sat. "You are a puzzle, Danielle. First you come on to me, , then you tell me to go to hell. I'm having difficulty in following."

She covered his hand with hers. "I'm not that complicated. Time will hopefully bring us both what we want." She smiled.

"Now what?"

"Now we go home. You know the days I'm off work. Call. It'll be a date."

"A date?"

"Yes, that is what men and women do. Besides, I have a favor to ask."

Creases showed on his forehead. "Yes?"

"This is a bit bizarre, but you'd be a doll if you did it. A relative, distant, of course, a Canadian, got into trouble and is in prison in Paris. I need you to visit him and deliver a letter from his Canadian family. I guess they wrote personal things and would rather not have the authorities read it."

"I…eh…"

"That was why I couldn't see you last night."

She retrieved the item from her purse and laid it on the table.

He gazed at it as if it was an animal about to bite. "You want me to visit a prison and deliver this…this letter to…" He picked it up and read the name. "Jack Monte."

"*Oui*," she said, as if it was the most natural thing to do.

Chapter Twenty-Two

Chicago

Jenko doubled over from Vera's kick and gasped for breath. He heard her say something about food, but he had no appetite for it. Putting a bullet through her head replaced those cravings.

"Take water," she said, "you feel better."

He slowly sat-up. "*Ty suka* (you bitch)." He glared.

"Watch your mouth. It can happen again."

He quickly moved his hands to shield his crotch.

She leaned over the table. "Let's get straight. I'm not plaything. We have job to do. Either work together, or one of us be left behind. What is your pleasure?"

At the moment, he felt his choices were limited. "Hokay. No sex or talk of it. We finish job."

"*Dah*. Now eat, then go. With luck we'll be Brownsburg in four hours."

He shook his head. "Not me. We go tomorrow. I don't think I walk four steps because of you. I'm tired and hurt. Tomorrow."

She jumped out of her chair and in a step or two stood behind him with her mouth to his ear and her hands gripping the back of his neck. "*Svoloch* (bastard), you fucked the job. Our orders are to do it now. You sleep in the car."

He stared into his water glass. "Move your hands." He felt

more pressure. "If you are trying to kill me, then go ahead. We all die sometime. But soon people watch what you do." He twisted his neck as she released her hold. "Better. Now, sit or go. We leave in morning at six to avoid traffic."

***

Paris

"Monte, you have a visitor," the guard known as Le Rouge called out. "Get your ass out of your bunk."

Monte sat up still in the clutches of sleep. *Who the- hell- comes to see me?* He rubbed his eyes, then matted his hair with his hand. "Who is it?"

Le Rouge shrugged. "I don't know. I just came to get you. Maybe it's a girlfriend," he laughed.

Monte stared at the redheaded guard. "I don't know anyone." He sat unshaven, rumpled, and didn't move. He eyed the guard whose real name he had forgotten if he ever knew it. Real names were meaningless. It was how one was known that counted.

"*Connard* (shithead), I don't care whether you come or not. Decide." The cuffs dangled from his hands as he waited.

"*Va te faire foutre* (fuck you). For all I know you're getting your jollies waking me. I'm going back to sleep."

"Suit yourself, asshole." He took a few steps away from the cell.

Monte heard him walk away. "Wait. On second thought, why not? It may be a new lawyer who'll get me out of this stink'n hell."

Le Rouge walked toward him. "Keep dreaming. Do you want to go or not? I'm wasting my time with you."

"*Oui.*" He stood and waited for Le Rouge to handcuff him.

"Very well." Le Rouge signaled for the cell door to open.

He applied the restraints and led Monte to the visitor center. They entered a small room with plexiglass between them and a chair for the guest on the other side. "Sit. Your visitor will be here in a few minutes. I'll be outside the door to take you back."

***

Felix woke unsatisfied and frustrated. His first thought that morning was Danielle was playing games. His second, she had taken control of the relationship. This rarely happened to him. The female staff of the café was his personal playground and he hired accordingly. Danielle had filled all the requirements. Now, to win favor, he had to deliver a letter to a jailbird. Was he crazy? There were other fish in the sea. Why bother?

He took his shower and shaved, then went out for a coffee and croissant. A plan formed as he sat munching his breakfast. The letter had to be delivered. It didn't matter who did it. He downed his coffee. The morning was young enough to accomplish several things. He hit the button on his phone and called a past lover and former employee, Denise. She wasn't as sexy as Danielle, certainly not as complex. Show her a good time and…a smile came over his face. All he had to do was put up with her simplicity. He silently congratulated himself. It was a win all the way around.

***

Monte waited and wondered who this visitor could be. A new lawyer who the SLA hired as a reward for his loyalty. Possible. After all it was his idea to blow up Jackson's house. A little reminder that there was payback in messing with one of theirs. He licked his lips. Of course, they'd seen the light. This was his lucky day. This was the first good thing that has happened since that unfortunate message he received about a murder. Probably, wasn't meant for him, anyway. He heard a click and the door on the other side of the plexiglass opened. He moved closer to the partition. Seconds passed before the light on the other side went on.

"Who…who the hell are you?" he asked as he attempted to focus on the woman who plunked herself down in the visitor's chair. She had dark frizzy hair, wore a baggy sweatshirt, but the kiss of youth remained on her face. "Are you from the…" Thank God she didn't hear the last part as she started talking.

"I'm Denise. Felix sent me to deliver this letter, but…" Her hand touched the partition. "Hey, how can I do that?"

"Who are you? Monte asked again.

"Denise. I already told you. Anyway, here's the letter." She held the envelope to the glass.

He didn't recognize the handwriting but read it was addressed to him from someone in Canada. He swallowed. "I can see that it's for me. Who is Felix?"

"Oh, he was my boyfriend. Sorry, I should say after this morning, he is my boyfriend. He was quite good if you know what I mean." She giggled, batted her eyes, paused, then said, "Sorry, you probably don't. Anyway…" She shrugged. "I can leave it here on the ledge."

"No, no don't do that. Why don't you open the envelope and put the letter to the window so I can read it?"

"That's a great idea. I should have thought of that. Felix always told me I was a little slow in that department." She laughed as she tore open the seal. "But I make up for it in other ways. Not that it's your business." She took the single sheet out and held it to the glass.

Monte got as close as he physically could to the divider. He read the two words on it typed in small letters… "we know".

Chapter Twenty-Three

Chicago

"I know I've been gone awhile. No, I… Let me explain… Janine," Billy Dee moved the phone from his ear, then sighed.

"You know it's long after dinner time. You said you'd be home by now."

"We've gone over this. It took longer than I thought, and traffic is bad."

"Uh-hum. What am I supposed to eat?"

"Isn't there any leftover pizza?"

"No, there is not. If you remember, I had no breakfast, and lunch was hours ago."

"Well, order another one. I'll be home as soon as I can." He clicked off his cell. He felt a little bad hanging-up on his wife, but not that bad… Nothing he could do about it, anyway, stuck in a never-ending construction zone with cars bumper to bumper.

The situation did give him time to think about the blown-up vehicle and garage in Posen. He tapped his fingers on the wheel. He'd have to call Shep and fill him in. Further dealings with Ochawa had to come from him. No reason why Ochawa seemed pissed off. *Jesus, today everyone had an axe to grind.* He ran his hand over his face. *Sure, glad I no longer have to deal with bureaucracies and bosses. The wife is enough.* His eyes fell on his cigar resting in the ash tray. He relit it and took a puff. His phone rang at the same moment when he exhaled and tried to bask in its taste. He looked around for any State Police before answering. He hadn't figured out how to pair his device with the car. *Just my luck some cop will bust me.* He quickly glanced at the number. He didn't recognize it. It's probably a Nigerian Prince or some other crank

calling, but the ring was persistent. He gazed around again for the police, then picked up the phone.

"Yeah?"

"Allo? Mr. Jackson?"

What the…? How did…? "Who is this?"

"Not important. Your house blown up, yes?"

Billy Dee could feel himself breathing hard. *Thank God traffic wasn't moving.* "Who is this, please?" It was difficult to tell whether it was a man or woman speaking. There was a definite accent, but he couldn't make out from where.

"I have answers for you."

"You… what do you… Answers?"

"You police, yes?"

Billy Dee gazed out the front window, his one hand tightened around the steering wheel. "Who told you that?" He heard a chuckle from the other end.

"Mr. Jackson, you play like newborn baby. But like in old days, information always costs. You aware of old saying, vith money you rule world. It's true."

"Yeah? I wouldn't know."

"You know very well. Here proposal. Twenty thousand for information. I'll call back in two days at this time."

"Twenty thousand? Are you—" The call went dead.

***

"You look terrible," Janine said after opening the door of the hotel room. "What happened? Are you sick? I told you not to run around. Let Shep do it. He's real police. Now you sit in that chair. I'll get you something to drink."

Billy Dee sank into the seat and wiped perspiration from his face. "Shep should be here in a few minutes," he managed to say. "I called him from the car."

"Naw, baby, you need to rest and eat something. A man your age can't…"

"What about my age?" Billy Dee stood. "I may be older, but… Damn, Janine that has nothin' to do with it." He waved his hand in exasperation. "Wait till Shep gets here, I'll explain everything."

Janine sat on the corner of the bed and eyed her husband. "I can't wait to hear."

He ignored her comment. "He's bringing a bucket of fried chicken with all the fixings."

"Can't wait. We'll all feel better after eating."

He looked at her. "Maybe."

***

Paris

Susan held her phone and stared blankly at it. Too many thoughts went through her head. Too many moving pieces to keep straight. Closing her eyes for a second or two, she felt Dumond's presence. He gently patted her shoulder. A thin smile appeared on his lips as he nodded approval.

"Surprise is the best weapon," he'd say, "Keep your mark off balance, that's the key."

She opened her eyes and felt reassured. She knew Dumond was a character, a rogue, a lover, a teacher, but he was gone, dead. He made a mistake and it cost him. His wandering eye for women was the death of him. She took a breath and was about to put her cell away when her other phone rang. She knew who it was without looking.

"Felix, are you calling to claim your prize?"

"Ah, *non…oui…*maybe. The letter was delivered."

"*C'est bon*. How did the prisoner look? What was his name…ah yes, Mon…te."

"He looked… I'll be honest, I had someone else do it. She assured me he got the letter."

"She?" Her voice went up an octave.

"Just a friend, Danielle. Nothing to worry about, I mean there's no worries, because we… well…"

"Are just friends, too?"

"*Oui, exactement.*"

"In that case, *bon*, I'll see you at work tomorrow."

"Wait. How about dinner or something?"

"A date?"

"A… well… okay… *oui*, a date. Meet me at… Allards. I have the address on my phone. I'm searching… here it is, Forty-two Rue Saint-Andre des Arts. How about at eight?"

"Hmm. The bistro is *très cher…oui*?"

"For you, why not. Besides, I know the chef."

"Very well. I'll see you at eight. *Au revoir*." She pressed Disconnect and held the phone to her lips. All through dinner, the poor boy will be thinking of one thing. Such fun, but will he get what was not on the menu? She sighed. *C'est la vie*, but the price will truly be *très cher*.

Chapter Twenty-Four

Chicago

Farmers who swear they wake with the sun would be in for a surprise living in Chicago. Their timepiece wouldn't work for weeks. The sun's overcast and gray cousin took its place and was in no hurry to leave.

Jenko would have overslept had it not been for the alarm. He partially woke to a blackened room and with a mind to continue his sleep. But even through his bleariness, the clock read 5:15 a.m. There was little room to negotiate… another five minutes or so? But it wouldn't be sweet with a part of him eyeing the time. Best to get going. The bitch, he knew, wouldn't be late. Anything to avoid another kick in the balls, or worse. He turned on his side. Where does a she-devil spend her time? She had left the hotel as abruptly as she'd entered. Didn't hear from her the rest of the day. Pity, all that time gone to waste. He threw the covers off. He did feel rested, and after his shower and a cup of coffee, he was in good shape and able to handle most anything, including Vera. In the end, she too was human with all the frailties it implied. All he had to do was wait to find them.

He left his room and went down to the first floor. He decided not to check-out. Hell, he paid for 2 nights. The job would be over and done with in several hours. More than enough time to get his money's worth…maybe even

with Vera, whether she wanted to or not, and if not, well…
whatever the day brings. He stepped outside the main door
with his duffel bag so that it would appear he had packed.
She had 10 minutes.

Two minutes to six and no sign of her. He felt his superi-
ority restored as the time trickled down. She'd be late. She
was human after all. He concentrated on his watch and saw
the seconds disappear. It was 6:01 and she was nowhere
in sight. He was jubilant. Another few minutes ticked by
before his phone vibrated against his hip. He grabbed it
out of his pocket.

"*Dah*. You're late. Where are you?"

"Watching you. *Durak* (fool). I've been across the street
in your car."

He wildly looked around. "Where?", then he saw. She
was parked behind a white truck. *Damn her. How the hell
does she have my car?* He figured it out while walking toward
her. She must have another set of keys. *Shit.* He better find
her weakness sooner than later or he may never return to
the hotel for one more night.

***

Brownsburg

Priscilla turned on her heel the second the cop left and
walked in the direction of Tope's office. "You didn't mention
that partner of yours could be wanted for murder. You said
he left." She lowered her tone and tried to mimic Pappy.
"I don't know where he is." She returned to her own voice.
"My ass. You're shilling for him. I'm getting outta here."

"Hold on will you listen for a minute? Jesus." He moved
toward her. "I don't know where he is. Really, but it's not
because of the accident. He… Will you stop your fuss'n?"

"Where's my clothes? Goddamn it." She marched around the office searching.

"Priscilla? Your damn clothes are probably in the bathroom." He stood in the doorway. "The truth is Tope hasn't been here for a couple of days. His car was in the parking lot. I took it last night."

"You?"

"I didn't hit nobody. Remember, I told you it was stolen."

"What ain't you tell'n? I'm smell'n something bad."

He lowered his head and mumbled, "I picked up a woman."

"What did you say?"

He looked directly at her. "I fucked someone last night and she stole the car this morning. Happy?"

"You, you… and I was going to put out for you. Not on your life. Get out of my way."

Pappy left the office soon after Priscilla. His old car waited for him in the parking lot. The driver's door squeaked when opened. *This ain't no Land Rover to be sure.* He settled in the well-worn driver's seat and thought for a minute where to go. His apartment? To do what? Drive to Priscilla's and plead with her to take him back? He'd done enough begging. *If she hadn't been fuck'n around the other night that woman I picked up wouldn't have died and Tope... Jesus, this is all too much. Where the hell did he go and why?* He mulled that thought. In all the time he and Tope had been together, Tope never invited him to his house. He hit the steering wheel with the palm of his hand. That's what he was going to do. He remembered Tope lived in the Clermont Heights section off from Route 132. If he could only recall the exact address. He began to drive hoping he'd recognize the house by the pictures Tope had showed him. Unlike the area he lived, Tope's neighborhood had expansive lawns and stately homes. It had never occurred to him to wonder how his partner managed to live that well while he… It didn't matter. Now he had so many unasked questions.

The hours slipped by, and Pappy realized that daylight wouldn't last much longer. The streets in Clermont Heights twisted and turned; some formed cul-de-sacs, and others were one-way, which he had to back out. He pulled over and decided to Google Tope's address. He was quite proud of himself for that insight. It took several seconds before an address popped up. By the time he reached the right block it was twilight, and the streetlights turned on. They were dim. He figured bright lights would disturb the rich in whatever they were doing. He went slowly up the street searching for a house address. If anyone saw they'd think he was either a pizza delivery or up to no good. He decided to park and walk. He was certain he was near.

The home to the left and to the right of the one he stood before had outdoor lights that bathed the bricks in a soft hue. The one in between was dark. He approached the front door. There were pamphlets and other mailings on the ground as well as newspapers. He looked toward the street and the neighbors next door to see if anyone watched. The darkness, though, hid him. He was able to glean the street number from the bronze numerals nailed on the front doorframe. *This must be the place.* He rang the doorbell and waited. A minute passed and he rang again. He got close to the door. "Tope, are you there? It's Pappy." Nothing changed. He grabbed the doorknob without thinking and twisted. To his surprise it opened. He stepped into the entryway "Tope, are you home?" He felt the wall for a light switch and succeeded. A muted glow spread throughout the room. The place smelled stale. There was a recliner, a table in what was the living room, and nothing else. *Has the place been robbed?* He walked through to the dining area. It was empty but for a card table with a couple of folding chairs. The kitchen had a pot on the stove and no other furnishings. *What the hell?*

He took the stairs to the second floor and found the master bedroom. It was empty. He checked the drawers and the closet. Several suits and shirts were hung, and there were a few pairs of underwear balled up in a drawer. *God damn. Old Tope lived worse than me.* He almost felt sorry for him. He moved the clothes to the side and discovered a small metal safe resting on the floor at the back wall. *I'll be damned* and let out a low whistle. He stooped down and fiddled with the tumbler but had no luck. He stood. *Now what?* He leaned his weight on the side of the metal box and moved it several inches. *Jesus.* He squinted at it, then decided. *What the hell?* It's like weights he used for basketball practice. He crouched and picked it up. It was heavy but manageable.

On his way down the stairs, he stopped at the landing that was close to the front door and caught his breath. He rested the safe against the wall and realized there were no pictures anywhere. Nothing in the house had a personal touch. He managed to shut the light while holding onto the safe with one hand and, then the door.

It wasn't easy but he made it down the street to his car. Breathing heavily, he fumbled for his trunk key. The lid screeched as it rose. He dumped the container, then looked around before slamming it shut. *Thank God old cars have large trunks.* He trudged to the driver's side, opened the door, and sank into his seat. He sat there wishing to make sense of everything. Something was going on, but he couldn't figure it. He never had a head for think'n a few moves ahead. But his gut sensed trouble…a lot of it.

Chapter Twenty-Five

Chicago

Billy Dee checked his watch and wondered what was keeping Shep. "He should be here by now," he said. "Not even he could eat all that chicken he ordered."

Janine gave him the eye. "Why are you fretting so? I'm the one who hasn't eat'n." She switched the TV station. "Probably the line was long. We ain't the only ones having dinner."

Billy Dee looked at his wife. "Since when you defend'n Shep? A miracle."

"Never you mind, he's nice enough to think of getting food, not like…"

"Okay you made your point. What's that humm'n?"

Janine gave him the "you fool" stare and went to the desk and picked up his cell. She glanced at the face of the phone. "It's your homie, Shep."

Billy Dee grabbed the device and pressed Accept. "Hey, Shep, your ears must be burn'n, we're just talk'n about you."

"I bet. I'm downstairs. There's better food than a bucket of chicken."

"There is? Of course, after all, we just got back from Paris."

"I'm sure you can tell coq au vin from poulet de Brasse."

"Cocco what?" He paused. "Sure, I …."

"While you're pondering that, why don't you and Janine get in the car. We'll go for a good dinner."

Billy Dee stopped talking and looked at the phone for a second. Janine, who was close by, must have heard as she got her coat.

"You heard him," she said, "let's go."

***

Paris

Susan looked at the clock in her bedroom and knew she would be tardy. Felix would be at Allard fussing with the silverware, taking sips of water, , then wine. He would check his watch, look at the entrance, and wonder where the hell she was. She envisioned the scene.

A table for two with him sitting nervously and looking around. She was at least 20 minutes behind schedule. When a waiter would approach, he would up the ante and order a scotch. He'd look at his wrist, , then his phone and wonder, *Is she coming? Did the bitch stand me up?*

Delightful, it will make her appearance that much more appreciated. She didn't want him to suffer but, there's a line between anticipation and taking one for granted. She went for the former.

Dumond, amongst his talents, had an eye for fashion. He preferred her in black, said she looked her best in that color. She agreed. An "LBD" was always appropriate and made a statement of elegance with a little tease. The dress showed enough cleavage to delight the eyes and the length to excite them. She twirled before the mirror and was pleased by the reflection. She brushed her hair, then put on a simple necklace and bracelet. She hesitated before leaving about whether to take her other phone. Afterall, events were in motion. She could always excuse herself if necessary. *Bon.* She placed it in her purse in a secret compartment, then smiled at the prospect of it going off while she and Felix were indisposed. As Dumond would remind her, "Business is business, and pleasure is a business too."

***

"WE KNOW" played in Monte's head. *What the fuck does that mean? And who was that stupid girl who delivered the note?* She said her boyfriend was Felix. *A nom de guerre or real?* He sat on his bunk in his cell rubbing his face while rocking himself. *I'm losing my mind,* then he looked up. *Attendez une minute*, he had never been a man to be trifled with. He had the ability to see things most missed. That's how he survived. Has jail mottled his brain? He got up and began to pace. That ability didn't disappear because he's in a cage. "*Un, deux, trois,*" he counted the steps between his bunk to the other wall. He had done it many times. *Trente-six,* that's all there was. Thirty-six steps between one side of his cell and the other. He repeated, "Trente-six," then the phrase "we know," as he walked. Was this the SLA's way of saying thank you? Pin another murder on him since he was already doing time for Dumond's death? If it was, why in the United States? He babbled out loud.

"Knock it off, Professor," an inmate yelled from a cell across from him, "I'm trying to sleep."

Monte stopped pacing. He was called many names in prison. Professor was one of them, although not out of respect. Monte glared in his direction. "*Excuse-moi, mon ami,* I know you need your rest because you put in such a busy night."

"Whatcha mean by that, you shit?"

Monte knew this would draw the attention of the rest of the wing. It was entertainment for them and if he was honest, for him as well. It was like tennis but instead of a ball they smacked insults. Although, matching wits with a dumb fuck was not Broadway theatre in the making.

Monte rubbed his chin, then responded, "How do I know what you did at night? But whatever it was it had tired you out. You even admit it." He could feel his opponent's anger wash over their distance. Reality set in. This idiot could make Monte pay dearly or take his life in the exercise yard. He would make amends.

"*Mon ami*," Monte called, "Accept my apologies, I do not mean anything by it. I'll try to keep my thinking to myself."

"You better, you professor shit, and I did nothing last night for your information. *Rien,*

like I do every night."

"*Bon*." Monte returned to his bunk and lay down and stared at the ceiling. The hoots and clamor of the wing died down. *Why would the SLA want to get rid of me?* If it was knowledge of crimes, they could have done it a long time ago. He proved to them he could keep his mouth shut. If it's not the SLA, then… He sat up his hand dug into the side of the bunk as he swung his legs to the floor. *Someone else? Who knows I'm in a French prison besides the Chicago flics*, then it hit him. It had to be. How? He didn't know. Some way, he had to find the dumb girl who delivered the letter along with her boyfriend, Felix. And who better at finding people, then the Serbian Liberation Army. Later that evening he would contact Belgrade or wherever his long-ago phone call went.

✳✳✳

Chicago

Janine got into the back seat of Shep's car while Billy Dee sat up front. "I'll let you two boys talk, just don't take forever to get to a restaurant."

"We'll talk later," Shep said. "If fried chicken is still on your mind, I know a great place, Luella's."

"Never a bad time for fried chicken. Right, Billy Dee?"

"No, never a bad time…" Billy Dee agreed.

"It's a ways from here but traffic is light. It'll take ah, about forty-five minutes."

"I've waited this long," Janine said, "what's another few minutes?"

"You won't regret it."

Shep drove north on Lake Shore Drive. He passed downtown, the River North district filled with expensive hotels, condos, and skyscrapers.

"We go'n way on the northside?" Janine asked.

"Yep, Lincoln Square. There're more restaurants in a one-mile area than in most of the Southeast side."

"Damn, Shep, why is that?" Janine asked.

"Money."

The word triggered what Billy Dee had been holding in since he returned from Posen. "Shep, we do have talk'n to do, and we need to do it real soon," he said softly hoping Janine didn't hear.

"It's all right, Billy Dee, you and Shep can say whatever. I'm go'n to close my eyes until we get there. It's been a very long, hard day."

***

Dinner was, as Shep promised beyond good. "I haven't had chicken like that since my Momma made it for the Sunday meal after church when I was little," Billy Dee said. He wiped his lips with a napkin, "then to top it off with the beignets. Lord I must have gained ten pounds just look'n at the plate."

"Shep, you outdid yourself," Janine said. "That Nashville spice made me forget everything."

"Glad you enjoyed. The place is a gem," Shep said. He motioned the waiter for coffee. "If you don't mind, Janine, Billy Dee and I will take our…"

"What? And leave me out. No, sir. Whatever you two got to say, I want to hear. The food energized me. If it's about our house, , then it's about me too. It was our home."

Billy Dee touched his wife's arm. "But, Janine, remember what you said in the car?"

She stared straight at him.

Billy Dee tried a different tack. "You know better, Janine. This is police business. We can't be disscuss'n these kinds of things with, eh, what's the word… civilians."

"You a civilian, or did you forget you retired from the force."

"Okay." He raised both hands from his elbows. "I'll make an exception, this one time." He looked at Shep. "All right with you?"

Chapter Twenty-Six

Brownsburg

Vera drove Jenko's car like an elderly person out for a Sunday drive. Jenko peered at the speedometer. "You can go faster," he said in Russian. "Cars are going all around you."

"The State Police watch this road. I don't want to get stopped," she said.

"Vera, you kidding me? The way you drive, you advertise for them to do that."

"Keep quiet."

"*Suka*, (bitch)," he muttered and reached for the radio button.

"What are you doing?"

"It's called radio," he said turning the knob. "Music." He pointed to his ear.

"I don't want."

"You're not the only one in car."

"I need quiet to concentrate."

"Pull over and I'll drive."

She gave him an icy stare. "Not on your life. Study the file. No fuck-ups this time."

"Four hours to stare at a picture and a few notes? I'm not an amateur. I've done this before."

She grunted. "Mr. Professional, you did so well, that's why we're going back."

He could feel his anger. His hand slid into his right jacket pocket. One shot and dead, one shot, he just had to figure when. He steadied his voice and pretended calmness. "You right my Vera, it won't happen again."

"*Khoroshiy* (good), is best for both of us."

***

It was midmorning when Priscilla got dressed and drove to Pappy's office. It was not to make amends. She had gone over yesterday's events in her mind and concluded Pappy owed her big time. Not only for going to the end of the earth to pick him up in that godforsaken neighborhood, but he had betrayed her with a floozy or whoever the whore was, God rest her soul. To top it off, now the cops could be involving her in Tope's mess. How that would happen didn't matter. The plain fact was her name was probably in some report, and she didn't like it.

Her plan was to get her hands on a check and run to the bank. Yesterday cost her a half a day's salary because she took the afternoon, then add the "fucking" she agreed to do to get her hands on the money. She calculated a few thousand dollars would cover it. She hadn't decided on what the "few" would be… certainly more than one, less than five? She was worth every penny.

She drove down the street and parked a half block from the office and near the bank. She scouted the parking lot for Pappy's car She was in luck. It wasn't there. He must be with a customer looking at property. She laughed at the thought. Pappy didn't have a big clientele. Probably Tope's client. With luck the office door would be open. Few people locked them in this town.

She marched up the stairs and found the door slightly ajar. While that surprised her, she attributed it to Pappy's neglect. The man was irresponsible. It was another example of him going through life believing he had a free pass. She opened the door and stepped into the vestibule. She didn't say his name. Nothing appeared out-of-place. Although she thought she heard noise, maybe a ruffling of papers coming from Tope's office. She stood still and listened. The sound repeated. She called, "Pappy? Are you here?... Tope?"

It happened so fast. Two figures dressed in dark colors stepped out of Tope's office. One was a woman, the other a man. Each pointed a gun at her.

"Who are you?" the woman asked in an accented voice.

Priscilla froze unable to find her voice.

"Speak, who are you?" the woman asked again.

"Pris…cilla," she managed to say. "Who are—"

"Quiet. I ask questions."

Priscilla heard the woman speak to her companion in a foreign language. Their voices seemed to be animated and angry.

"I left it in car. Why take file?" The man said in English to the woman. "I stare at picture for hours. Why didn't you take it?" His gaze never left Priscilla.

"Idiot," she said. "One thing to do and… Hokay, Miss, where is man of company?"

"What?" Priscilla swallowed hard and fought to control her breathing. "You mean Tope?"

"Tope?"

The woman turned to the man and what sounded like words spoken in a mad guttural rush asked something. The man repeated "Tope," then shook his head. "Pappy," he said.

"Where is this Pappy?" she asked Priscilla.

"I…I don't…"

Out of nowhere, the man slapped her face. "What are you doing here? You work here?"

"No… no…" Priscilla touched her face. "I don't… Pappy isn't here."

The man glanced at the woman. A smile crossed his face. "We know that. Listen…" He put the gun down by his side.

"I…I don't know where he is. Really."

The man grabbed her shoulder and shoved her out of the vestibule toward the office part. "Are you girlfriend?"

Priscilla tripped but righted herself. "Girl…" She glanced at the woman who kept her weapon pointed at her. The man was besides her. "We're… ah …friends. Yes, we're just friends."

The man slapped her again. "I don't believe you."

Priscilla felt her eyes water and tears inched their way down her face. "What do you want from me?"

"Where is Pappy?" they both asked.

***

Chicago

Shep sat back with his hand around his coffee mug. "Let's hear it, Billy Dee. What did you find in Posen?"

"A few things. Ochawa is an okay dude, but I think I wore out my welcome. They're looking for the VIN numbers on the vehicle that was blown up. Doubtful they'll find it. Whoever detonated that garage did a hell of a job. There was possibly lettering from the vehicle that the lab boys are looking at. They found what may be a V. You never know, but…"

"That it was the truck used in the bombing of our home," Janine jumped in.

"It's a stretch, but not impossible." Billy Dee took a sip of his coffee.

"Ochawa called me," Shep said and raised his eyebrow.

"You're right about his attitude toward you." He paused, "but they will send their findings as to the device used. It could be similar to ours."

"Now we're getting somewhere," Billy Dee said. He took a card from his pocket. "I found this near the site. It has a little dirt on it. Mean anything to you?" He passed it to Shep.

Shep examined the card and flipped it over. "No. Brownsburg, Indiana means nothing to me." He stared at the dirty spot. "Whatcha thinking?"

"It seemed out-of-place. 'Topin and McDonald for all your real estate needs'," he read. "Why would anyone in Posen, Illinois be think'n of Brownsburg, which I looked up, is outside Indianapolis?"

Billy Dee felt his wife's hand touch his arm. She smiled at him. "You sure are a detective, Billy Dee. It's in your blood."

It wasn't often his wife complimented him, and he wanted to savor the moment. "One more thing," he began, "on the way home I got this phone call." He showed the number on his phone to Shep. "The person said he or maybe it was a she, hard to tell, had information about our house and wanted twenty Gs by the day after tomorrow."

Janine's hand left Billy Dee's arm. "They wanted what?" she asked.

"Not so loud," both Billy Dee and Shep said in unison.

"Excuse me. Isn't that some kind of blackmail or extortion?" she said a little more quietly.

Both men nodded.

"You ain't go'n to pay that?" Janine asked. "My Lord, our house is destroyed and now they want money too. I can't believe it." She reached for a napkin and dabbed her eyes. "Ain't right, I tell you. Bastards."

Billy Dee put his arm around his wife. "Calm yourself. Noth'n like that is go'n to happen. We go'n to check it out. Right Shep?"

Shep looked up from studying the number. "Yeah, sure we are. I'm writing it down. Hopefully that bad boy can be traced. We'll stall a bit and get IT involved."

Janine turned to her husband. "Then what?"

"Luck, Janine, it go a long way," Billy Dee said.

Chapter Twenty-Seven

Paris

Susan entered Allard. The aromas that hit her were a gastronomic delight. The bistro was like a proud grandparent maintaining the old ways in a sea of new. There were white tablecloths on each table. The wood floor as well as the bar was polished to a high gloss. The seating was spaced so that waiters moved inconspicuously and with grace. The maître-d' in a black waistcoat led her to Felix's table. She spotted the emptied glass of scotch as well as the one clutched in his hand. She was late and the effect was what she visualized. Felix got up clumsily and she was sure he wanted to tell her off, then his eyes roamed over her little black dress. The surly look quickly dissolved into a wide smile, as if tardiness never crossed his mind.

"Danielle, you look…" His mouth hung open, but his gaze never left her.

"Are you lost for words?" she said as the maître-d held the chair for her.

He made a stab at gallantry. "Your beauty overwhelms mere words."

Not bad, she thought, and kissed him on each cheek.

After being seated, Felix launched into the history of the place and extolled the virtues of the original owners who came from Burgundy in 1932 and introduced peasant recipes that were followed to this day. The liquor he consumed may have had something to do with the amount of talking he did. The bottles of wine, from chardonnay to Bordeaux, kept appearing through and after every course. The boss persona that Felix exhibited at work was nowhere to be seen. For a moment she wondered what had she done? Anything she asked or said seemed appreciated. He agreed or laughed at the appropriate place. His eyes rarely left her. In sum, he ate out of the palm of her hand, as the expression goes, but for how long? She felt Dumond's hot breath in her ear cautioning her not to be fooled. But the wine and his doting were like a rare perfume that intoxicated and swept the warning away.

"Danielle, we must indulge in dessert wines." He snapped his fingers and beckoned the sommelier. The wine master hurried over and in clipped tones suggested a 2010 Chateau d'Yquem. Felix's eyes lit up.

"Isn't that..." She didn't say the rest as Felix waved away her concern.

"It's our first date. A wine that is almost as beautiful and complex as you."

She could feel herself blush. Felix was over the top in dripping charm. She responded, "*bon*" and allowed herself to drift along the sway of the gentle evening.

She didn't remember leaving Allard or the cab ride. The contentment of a fine meal and her head light with wine made everything so Gay Paree. She recalled Felix held her under her arm as they ascended the staircase to a third-floor apartment. The hallway landings filled with their laughter and several long and passionate kisses. The click of a door lock and the flick of a light switch rushed past her memory of all the rest...

"Felix?"

***

Monte waited until after the last security check of the night. Each cell, then was plunged into a quasi-darkness and only the glow of dim section lights remained. He reached under his mattress. His fingers searched for the indentation of the hidden compartment. Slowly he worked the opening until he reached in and grabbed his mobile. He had ingeniously found a way to charge his phone through a thermoelectric device called Power Felt that used the difference of his body temperature and room temperature to create a charge. He powered the phone and saw the battery 75% full. He lightly kissed the screen and thanked God for his good fortune. He moved quietly to the darkest corner of his cell. With his back facing the front bars he quickly checked for messages. There weren't any. He, then went into the file marked 'Recent' and found the number. No one answered after his first try. There wasn't even voice mail. He redialed. He let it ring for what he thought were several minutes and again he was met with silence.

"*Foutre*," he said, and peered over his shoulder to see if he woke anyone. He counted slowly to 100, , then turned back, holding the phone in the palm of his hand and close to his chest to block the phone's small screen light. Was this the number? Did he dial correctly? He scrolled through the list of recent calls and decided the number and date matched. He'd try one once more. He listened to the connection tone as it buzzed six or seven times. His thumb hovered over the Disconnect button.

"Allo?"

Almost simultaneously as someone answered, Monte accidently hit End.

***

Chicago

"It's an 'app'," Shep said to Billy Dee.

"Good morning to you. What are you talking about?"

"The number you gave me last night. The IT guys checked it out."

Billy Dee cleared his throat. "Okay, what does that mean?"

This time Shep paused. "You know when those fellows start explaining it's hard to follow. The bottom line, I think, is the app bounces the call to another number. Since we don't know the phone carrier it will take a while to get the needed information."

"Uh-huh. So, what you're saying is that number I gave you is a fake. It doesn't exist."

"Sort of. That app switches the call to another. Plain speaking, the area code and number displayed is not necessarily where the call came from."

Billy Dee held his phone and stared at the digits in question. "You mean this call could have come from anywhere… Chicago… Paris?"

"That's what the IT boys were saying."

"Lord have mercy." Billy Dee ran his free hand through his hair. "And you found this out before I even had a cup of coffee. Don't you sleep? It's not even eight."

"Billy Dee, you're a retired man. Your day doesn't begin before ten. I'm still working."

"I'm going to let that slide. I've also done a little digging. Last night after we got home, thanks again for dinner, I Googled that real estate company. It's real, then, before you called, I was on the phone with the police department over there. Spoke with an Officer Reynolds."

"Yeah, so."

"Strange thing. This Topin fellow seems to be missing.

The police found his crashed vehicle with a dead woman behind the wheel."

Shep let out a low whistle. "Hmm."

Billy Dee glanced at his sleeping wife, then said quietly, "Interested in a road trip?"

"Where? … You aren't suggesting Brownsburg?"

"Indiana is nice this time of year. I even bet there's some good eating."

"In Indiana?"

"There's people there…they eat."

"I'll call you in an hour."

Chapter Twenty-Eight

Brownsburg

Jenko grabbed his captive's shoulder and pushed her into one of the offices.

"Sit," he said and pointed to a chair.

She did as order. If she was this Pappy's girlfriend, he didn't do bad for himself. He moved a few steps away and studied his shaking prisoner. The blush was coming off the rose but there was still enough vitality and youth to make the experience worthwhile. Vera interrupted.

"We need to get rid of her," she said in Russian.

"Not yet. She still has information to give."

Vera's gaze went from the girl to him. "Information or something else?"

"Milaya devushka sweet girl, you forget again, I am a professional, but I like what you suggest." If Vera's eyes could have shot him, they would have.

"You are a *svoloch*, you bastard. You think I'm going to stand around while you rape her?"

"But shooting her is all right?"

"That's an unfortunate part of the job."

Jenko scratched his face with the barrel of his gun. "Vera, what if this Pappy was an exquisite example of a man and there was an attraction. Would you not want to sample…?"

"Shut-up you horrible, stupid creature."

The tone between Priscilla's two assailants made her more fearful. It was hard to tell which one was more of a threat. The woman was curt and angry. Priscilla tried to follow. Was the woman pissed at her or him? She got the sense though; she was part of whatever was upsetting them. It was like watching a tennis match but there was no love. The man grabbed her shoulder again, then slid his hand down her front to her tit.

"See, Vera, she does not mind," he said in English.

Priscilla froze. Her gaze was on his hand. "Please," she whimpered and struggled to hold back tears.

He took his hand away. "Tell us where we can find this Pappy."

Her lips trembled. "I…I…please, I'd tell…you if I…knew."

The woman spoke rapidly in their guttural language. Whatever she said, the man didn't like.

"I don't think so," he said in English and looked back at Priscilla.

He grinned. His piercing blue eyes were on fire.

"This is not a big town." He shook his gun at her. "She knows. We'll find a way to make her remember."

***

Paris

"Felix?" Susan said again, this time louder. She sat up and pulled the linen around her. He didn't answer. Instead, she heard rustling from another room. "Who's there?" She glanced around. She could clearly make out objects as sunlight streamed in from a window. A nightstand was besides the bed. There were closet doors opposite her and a dresser along with a mirror in front of a wall. Her dress as well as

her purse were nowhere in sight. She pushed the sheet away,
, then crept out of bed. She was not shy about her nakedness.
Besides, a covering would only get in the way of her arms
and legs if she had to use them.

She hugged the wall until she reached the doorway, then
edged out into the dark hall. She regulated her breathing and
waited several seconds, straining to hear any sound. When
she did, she moved with agility and speed, passed a bathroom to an area where she glimpsed a dim light. A shadow
made her stop a foot or two from a room's entryway. Her
back was to the wall as she turned to listen and watch the
silhouette's movement.

"Allo, allo, who is this? *Merde*." He walked into the hallway
holding a phone to his ear.

"Felix?"

He stopped; his hand holding the phone dropped to his
side. "Holy… what…? You just scared the hell out of me."
He gasped.

"What are you doing with my phone?"

His gaze fell upon her body and his tone mellowed. "It
kept ringing, and I didn't want to disturb you." He stepped
a little closer. She eyed the bulge in his shorts, then she let
her gaze move up his body to his shirtless chest. He certainly
was in physical shape.

"You shouldn't have done that."

He ran his hand through his hair. "Okay, *excusez-moi*.
I tried to be nice." He was within inches and about to
touch her.

"*Non*, no more. Give me the phone."

"What's the big deal? Whoever it was hung up. Another
lover?"

She furrowed her brow. "Not your business. We are not
married or lovers."

"What was this evening?"

"A first date. Give me the phone."

"That's all?" He tried to kiss her, but she grabbed his face between her thumb and forefinger.

"Don't ruin a good thing." She held out her other hand.

"Okay, okay, you go from desire to bitch in a hurry. Here."

She grabbed the cell from him. "I should go. Where are my things?"

Brownsburg

Pappy was too tired to bring the safe to the office. Unfortunately, unlike Tope's home where there was a driveway and a two-car garage, Pappy had neither. His neighbors must have been partying as there wasn't a parking space near his house. Instead, he found one two blocks away. He decided to leave the safe in his trunk. The neighbors' laughter and loud music pierced the night air as Pappy trudged to his front door. He wasn't in the mood to join any celebrations. Too much had happened, and he needed to think. He opened the front door of his small house and stepped over a heap of clothes he was going to take to the cleaners but hadn't gotten around to. He flicked on a light. He moved a pile of papers from a chair in the living room and plopped himself down. The events of the day flashed through his mind like a series of coming attractions and before he could call a time-out, he was asleep. A noise startled him awake. At first, he didn't know where he was, then his neck reminded him he had been snoozing in a chair. Without a further thought regarding the safe, Tope, or Priscilla, he shed his clothes along the path to his bedroom and fell into bed. He didn't hear the phone ring late morning. He only learned that from his message light blinking on his voice mail when he awoke sometime later. He hit the button and heard Priscilla. Her voice sounded shaky as if she had been or was crying. She asked him to call her as soon as he received her message. He got up from his bed and wandered into the living room where he saw a piece of paper stuck under the front door. He picked it up and returned to the bedroom.

He sat on the side of the bed holding the note in Priscilla's handwriting and listened to the message again. "I'll be goddamn," he said. *One minute she'd run me over, the next she needs me to call. She is one crazy ass bitch.*

He showered, shaved, and found himself in a good mood. *The girl has come to her senses.* No rush to go to the office. Tope was gone, and anyone who'd call could wait.

He opened the fridge and was a bit stunned it was empty. *Damn, I was going to go shopping, but…* He went to a drawer in the kitchen and felt the bottom for some cash he would occasionally hide. He was rewarded with five one-dollar bills… enough for an egg and coffee.

By the time he reached the office it was near 3. He still hadn't called Priscilla. He had been empowered by her note and voice mail. Why ruin a good thing? The bitch could dangle a little while longer. He headed up the stairs to his office and was surprised the door wasn't locked. His imagination took off as he twisted the handle. Priscilla must be waiting for him. Was she sitting in a chair naked? Or, stretched out on a desk with a come-hither look? A jolt of energy went through him.

"Priscilla, you crazy woman," he said as he entered. "What the…? Priscilla?" The place was in shambles. Papers strewn all over, and chairs toppled. He took a deep breath. His heart thumped against his chest. He took a step or two toward Tope's office. He saw a black and white gym shoe sticking out the doorway. He drew closer. His gaze went from the foot to a leg to a body clothed in all black. His hands went to his face. He was about to puke. A woman he didn't recognize lay on the bloody floor. Her arm outstretched. A gun clutched in her hand.

Pappy didn't know how long he stood over the body. Maybe she was still alive despite all the blood on the floor. He was about to kneel and touch her, but her face was drained of all color. "She's… she's dead. No doubt about it." He looked around the office, then backed away. *Was this person after Tope? Did Tope sneak in and kill her? Did it have anything to do with Chicago?* He righted the receptionist's chair and sat. If he called police, they'd ask too many questions. If he didn't… He stood up and walked in a circle around the chair, then it came to him. He could call them later. The woman was still dead, but he wouldn't be here. The police answering his call of suspicious activity would find her. He stopped his pacing, his mind made up. He turned the chair over, then left the entrance door unlocked. The same condition he found it. He hurried down the stairs, hoping no one saw him entering or leaving. Maybe it wasn't the best plan, but it was all he could think of. He opened the lobby door a few inches enough to view part of the street. At 3:30 p.m. there weren't many people on the sidewalk. He wanted to run to his car, but having watched enough detective shows, he walked as normal as he could. Arriving at the parking lot, he stood at his driver's door for a second or two scanning the area, then quickly got in. His shirt was soaked with sweat. He sucked in a few breaths and started the car. His lips moved in prayer hoping no one had noticed.

Chapter Twenty-Nine

Brownsburg

Priscilla screamed. "You…you shot her. Just…like… oh my God. Is she…dead?"

"I hope so," Jenko said, "otherwise I am bad shot." He bent over the body and felt her pulse.

"But…but…"

"Why? She wanted to kill you   ." He straightened and took a step toward her. "So now, you talk, yes?" He saw her eyes go wide. "Where is this Pappy?"

Priscilla's mouth moved but no words came out.

"You want to join this woman?" he said, waving his gun.

"Please…no… I know… where he… lives. He… could be… at… home."

He glanced over her deciding what to do. "Hokay, you come with." He grabbed her arm and pulled her off the chair. "If behave you have no worries. You scream or make unpleasantness you wind up like her." He pointed to the corpse. "Look at me. You understand?"

She nodded.

One more thing. He made her stoop over the body. He grabbed her hand and placed it over the dead woman's gun.

She turned her head as he did it.

"Perfect, now we go."

They left the office, and he told her to sit in the front passenger seat. It wasn't a long drive to Pappy's house.

"This is where your Pappy live?"

"Yes, but he's not…" her voice shook. "I don't see his car."

"Phone him."

Her fingers shook as she punched in the numbers Jenko could hear the connection, then Pappy's voice mail announcement. "Tell him to call you," he instructed. She did.

They waited a minute or two before Jenko ripped a piece of paper from his notepad. "Write. Tell him to contact you immediately. It's important." He handed her a pen.

She obeyed.

"Go slip under door. If you think of running, I'm good shot from this distance."

She eyed his gun and got out. The sway of her backside enticed him. He knew she would do whatever he wanted. That is what happens when one was no longer bound by rules. He smiled, remembering that it wasn't that long ago when he was a nothing. This new life has given him everything he always wanted….

He already planned his explanation of Vera's demise. He was in the midst of mentally organizing the account when Priscilla came back to the car. He put his hand on her thigh. "You did good. We will wait at your place."

"My…ppl…house? Why? I…"

He saw her pale as she tried hard not to cry. "Woman. Where else can we go? Besides, it's logic that he'd come see you." He pressed on her flesh. "Yes?"

She gasped and slowly nodded.

"It's hokay. Everything is hokay." He held her thigh a second or two longer, then let go.

***

Paris

"Your things?" Felix said. "They're in the room. By the way I had a devil of a time finding that phone. It was like in a secret compartment."

Susan put a hand on her hip. She thought of saying something but decided not to.

"Besides that, what the hell you got in there…all your belongings… a weapon?"

Susan stepped into the room. "A Beretta," she called out as she dressed. A minute or two later, with her purse slung across her front, she met him in the hallway.

"Are you serious?" he asked. "A gun? Really?"

"Oh, Felix you are so naïve. It's late at night when we close. I'm single and live alone."

He grunted. "Do you know how to use it?"

"Don't piss me off and you'll never find out."

He moved closer. "Can I see it?"

Susan looked at him. "Why?"

"Well, …I… I don't know…curious."

"Forget it. It's not a plaything."

"You mean it's loaded?"

She laughed. "Felix, sometimes I… what do you think?"

He looked at her. "I don't know."

"You'd look silly in those boxers holding a gun."

"You'd look sexy."

"Are you luring me back to bed?"

"What do you think?" His eyes shone.

She took a breath and placed her hand over the purse strap and opening. A feeling came over her. It was Chicago all over again. Where a secret arms dealer, Hugo, tried to force her to fuck. She'd shot him.

"You okay?" Felix asked. "You seem not to be here and you're trembling."

"Yeah." She looked into his eyes. "I'm fine." She released her grip on the strap, then brushed some hair from her face and kissed him lightly. "*Demain* and *demain*. Tomorrow will see what it brings."

***

Susan's palm itched to grab the cell phone, but she waited until the cab let her off several blocks from her home. She didn't tell the driver the exact address. As Dumond advised many a time, "Don't give information away for free." It was early morning and there were few people on the street. Even the boulangeries hadn't opened their doors, but that didn't prevent the smell of fresh bread from wafting through the air. She took a deep breath. Paris at that hour was so restful, full of promise.

"Hey girlie, *tu veux couchez avec moi?*" someone shouted from a passing car going slowly down the street.

She gave him the finger and picked up her pace. "*Cochon,*" she shouted. "Pig!" She kept a watchful eye until the vehicle disappeared. She again was reminded of Dumond. Surprise was always hiding around the corner. She knew it was true.

Last night was her tour de force with Felix. He got what he wanted physically, but not completely. The sex was…*bon* for her but more importantly, it left him wanting more. She was the cat and he the mouse. The longing to have her again was a mighty weapon to wield. Finding her damn phone made her even more desirable. Her gun, mysterious with a touch of danger thrown in. It planted the seeds of jealousy. Poor Felix, like a child in a store full of his favorite things but told "not yet."

She reached her apartment. Felix was just a bit player

in what lay ahead. Once inside, she dug her phone from its so-called hiding place and scanned "recent calls." The rat had bit. She checked her watch. Act Three was about to begin.

Chapter Thirty

Chicago

"And where do you think you go'n?" Janine asked her husband.

"I thought you were sleeping?" Billy Dee stuffed a room key into his pants pocket.

"I was, but you made such a racket on that phone of yours. You talk'n with Shep?"

"Uh huh." He didn't look at her as he gathered his wallet, a pen, and notepad.

She sat up. "What is happen'n, Billy Dee? I know you go'n somewhere."

"You can have the car. Shep is picking me up."

"You ain't leav'n me behind for another one of your breakfasts. I won't stand for that."

Billy Dee faced her. "It ain't that. We're head'n to Indiana... Brownsburg."

"You what? Brownsburg? Where's that?"

"Indiana, like I told you."

Janine walked over and stood a few feet from her husband. "Don't play me for no fool, Billy Dee."

Billy Dee put both hands up as if he was shielding himself from a punch. "Remember that business card I found in Posen? It turns out that one of the fellows whose name is on the business is missing."

"Yeah, what's that got to do with anything?"

"Don't know, that's why we're go'n to take a look. It could be nothing," he shrugged, "or a connection to that blown-up garage in Posen and our house."

Janine took a few seconds. "So, what you tell'n me is you're on a wild goose chase."

Billy Dee sighed while giving her the eye. "Yeah, maybe, but if we don't look, we don't find. That's how investigations are."

"Okay, you win. Leave me some cash. I'm eating today with or without you. And Billy Dee, you come back now. Your pension is all we got."

Billy Dee picked up his jacket from a chair, then kissed his wife on the cheek. "I'll call when we get there. We'll be back later tonight. Pension, lord, lord, what a woman."

***

"I don't want to sound like a young'n but aren't we there yet?" Billy Dee asked. "I told you to get off at the Purdue exit for McDonald's. Lord my stomach been rumbling for the last seventy-five miles."

Shep took another puff of his cigarette. "That's all you do, Billy Dee, bitch and complain. It's not enough I'm driving to this godforsaken town. We made up a lot of time after getting out of Chicago and now we've got another twenty minutes or so. Your stomach can wait. As you said, there must be some better place to eat in town."

Billy Dee looked out the window. "You got me. I appreciate the wheels, but not that inferno thing hang'n from your mouth. But a fact is a fact, I'm hungry, and when I'm hungry I'm cranky."

"Here's gum."

Billy Dee swatted the package away. "That ain't noth'n." He opened the window a crack. "Damn your smoke."

"We're almost there. Give me the address again."

Billy Dee reached into his coat for the business card. "Need glasses." He found them in his shirt pocket. "All right now." He began to read the address, then stopped. "Didn't you put it into the GPS?" He heard the wind whistling through the window opening and the tires making a *wzzz* sound on the roadway before Shep finally answered.

"Yeah, I did. Just wanted to take your mind off your gut."

"Very funny."

They got off the highway and followed the directions. They found a parking space across from the building.

"This it?" Billy Dee asked.

"That's what the nice lady in the GPS box said. Look at the window. Isn't that the name of the company?"

Billy Dee glanced at the structure. "Yep. It'll be nice to stretch the legs."

They exited the car, crossed the street, and entered the building.

Billy Dee sniffed the air. The odor of staleness and look of the hallway and stairs was a throwback to some other time. "Smells like the fifties," he said.

"How would you know what the fifties looked or smelled like," Shep said. He wheezed as he climbed the stairs.

"Those cigarettes are talk'n."

"Shut up. You're turning into your wife and that's not a compliment to her."

They stood at the floor landing of the office. Billy Dee knocked, but there was no answer. "You suppose everyone went home?"

Shep looked at his watch. "It's only three-forty. I wouldn't think so."

Billy Dee tried the doorknob. "They're trustworthy here. It's not locked."

Shep shrugged. "The beauty of a small town. Let's go."

Billy Dee walked in. "Holy shit. What the…"

Shep moved in front and put his hand on the butt of his gun. "It was either a hell of a party or…"

Billy Dee went toward one of the offices. "Oh no… Shep."

Shep pulled his gun. They glanced at the body on the floor.

"Mercy," Billy Dee said, "we stepped into a murder. Who the hell was she?"

***

Jenko stretched out on Priscilla's couch. "Nice place you have. You live by yourself?"

She nodded.

"And all this is yours?"

"Yes," she said softly.

"Only in America. It is great country. Come, sit by me."

"I…I…"

He motioned with his gun. She got up from the chair across from him. "Why you way over at end of couch? Closer. We have time. Nothing to worry about. That woman back there was pain in ass. You not like her. Right?"

She shook her head and moved in a deliberative manner next to him.

"Put phone on table. When he calls, we'll see."

She hesitated for a second, then bent forward. Her hand shook as she let go of the cell. "How do you know he'll call?"

Jenko smiled. "He will. I have no doubt."

Her eyes widened.

"Despite what you said, I know there's something between you and this Pappy."

"No…there…"

He put his finger momentarily on her lips. "Shh… you lie. That makes me mad, and you don't want that."

She crisscrossed her arms across her front. "Okay, okay," then buried her head in her arms. "We did. We had a relationship," her voice muffled. She sat up. "But not anymore."

"See, truth is not so hard. Why were you at office?"

"I... I... wanted to...get..."

"What?"

She brushed her face with her hand and used the sleeve of her sweater to wipe her nose. "I was...upset...money."

He pulled her close to him. "I have better idea to make him pissed."

Chapter Thirty-One

Paris

Felix returned to bed after Danielle left. He lay on his back staring at the ceiling. *What just happened?* He thought he had taken control, but within minutes she dressed, kissed him on the cheek, and *au revoir*. He had spent a fortune on that dinner, and her reaction was the same as if the evening was a mere *le hamburger* from McDonald's. What did it get him? His hurt pride faded as a rush shot through him reliving the touch and movement of her body. She was not a shy one in bed. Whatever dreams he had she surpassed, and of course he knew he did well, too. That should have been worth something more than "*demain.*" Les femmes. They were all crazy. Not a sane one among them. The image of Denise, his former bedmate, popped into his mind. She was good, but not like… Besides, she talked too much and simply was too easy.

He shifted his weight and moved one of the pillows. Hah, if it wasn't for Danielle's damn cell, she'd be next to him instead of the empty space. He tucked his arm under a cushion. Always a mystery… What about that call? Another lover or wrong number? But, then why such a reaction? He wrestled with those questions but his brain soon tired of it. Instead, he lost himself in the images of making love.

He recalled the feel of Danielle's velvety soft skin and

the curves of her body. The dream was so vivid. He could hear her moan as he touched and licked her breasts. He saw himself slide down her stomach to her hips, planting small kisses along the way. His breathing was heavy as his fingers danced between her legs. He looked at her face and saw her closed eyes. Her lips taut as she moved to his rhythm. Little purrs escaped her throat. She guided his entrance, then gasped. The bed creaked along with her ooh's and ahh's. This was heaven and the Lord gave His blessings, but , then another sound intruded. Where was it coming from? Afterall he was in the midst of rapture. But it grew louder and more alarmingly, real. Recognition slowly dawned on him someone was at his door. The images of Danielle and their lovemaking vanished. *Merde.* He looked wildly around the room. "Danielle?" He was in his bed, alone. He smacked his forehead, what was he thinking? He grabbed a pair of running shorts.

Who the hell would be knocking this early in the morning? He got to the door. "*Oui*, who is it?" He didn't bother with the peep hole. He couldn't see anything through it, anyway.

"Please open," a male voice asked.

"Okay, okay." He undid the lock and pulled the door a crack.

"I'm Inspector   Alain Ricard of the Paris police." He flashed an identification card in front of Felix. "We have some questions."

***

Susan laid the phone on her table, then stretched her arms above her head. It had been a long evening, but all in all successful. She was sure Felix would do anything she asked. Her plan was to send him back to see Monte with another letter.

Dumont was a proponent of never letting up. Play on weakness. Monsieur Monte must be worried, or he wouldn't have called. Information was like food; without it one blundered or starved. How unfortunate for him if both occurred.

Susan went to the kitchen to boil water for tea. She wanted to concentrate on what to write, but tidbits of last evening filtered through her consciousness. There was, indeed, something about Felix that was desirable. He was a naive boy in certain matters but quite knowledgeable and appealing in physical attributes. She giggled and felt her face flush. *Arrêt! I am letting my imagination run.* The water boiled, just as her phone signaled an incoming message. She shut the stove, picked up her cell, and pulled a chair from the kitchen table. Would Monte dare put something in writing? She quickly realized it wasn't from him. She glanced over the words. The last two lines leapt out. Vera was dead. She stared. Was this a joke or real? She scrolled to the beginning and slowly reread the note. How could Vera have let this happen? She was sent to take care of the situation, not the other way around. Vera was not one who would lose in a struggle. Susan read the message again.

"Ve came to building. Vera went ahead. I parked. I was going up stairs when I heard screams. I hurried into office and Vera was on floor. There was voman who had gun in hand crying. She vas Pappy's girlfriend. I wrestled her and took gun. We wait for Pappy at girlfriend house. Vera is dead. Update later."

La connerie. It was bullshit. Did Jenko think he was dealing with a fool? The son-of-a-bitch shot the wrong man and now Vera was dead too. He was incompetent, but a cold, cold stone killer. She took a deep breath.

Poor Vera. Dumond had introduced them years ago in Paris. Vera was strikingly beautiful with long legs, high cheek bones, and fluid movements. To watch her was to admire a perfect painting that flowed. Vera's beauty overpowered her, and Susan was sure Vera's effect on Dumond was more than professional. He'd charmingly denied it and pointed out Vera was very good at what she did. His explanation left much to question, but that was Dumond. Nonetheless, Vera was proficient whether as a spy, a smuggler, or an assassin she did excellent work. Hard to believe Vera would let herself get killed by some *femme de ville*.

There were only two people remaining who knew what occurred in Chicago…this Pappy and Jenko. With luck, Pappy would be eliminated. As for Jenko, there will be a time and a place. "When mistakes happen, or plans deviate, take what's given and turn it to your advantage." Dumond would have a twinkle in his eye when he spoke those words.

Susan went to the stove and poured the hot water into a cup. The steam rose and the warmth felt good on her face. Dumond never considered failures. He viewed those as temporary setbacks. She wished she had his vision and nerves.

She stared at her phone and reread the message for a third time, then it hit her. The letter her new boyfriend Felix would deliver. It almost wrote itself. She envisioned Jack Monte's eyes grow wide. His body shaking, riddled with fear as the news of new corpses piled on his doorstep.

Chapter Thirty-Two

Brownsburg

Pappy's hand shook as he dialed 911. The time on his phone read 3:45. "Hello, hello, I think something's going on…"

"Brownsburg Police, what is your name?

"Name? Look there's something terrible happening at the real estate office of Topin and McDonald. I think I heard a gunshot. Send someone, please."

"Sir, calm down. Can I get your name and phone number?"

He clicked off. He was two blocks away. He drove down the street, made a left and, then another until he saw his building. In his rearview mirror, he saw lights, then heard sirens. He continued to drive down the street. He chewed on his fingernails as he drove. *Now what?* His head felt as if it was going to burst. He knew sooner than later the police would call him. If for nothing else than to tell him what he already knew. He had to be strong and keep it together. Hell, he didn't do anything, anyway. The bottom line whatever happened in Chicago was Tope's idea. He really had nothing to do with it. For the first time, he smiled. "Yep, that's the gosh darn truth," he said. His spirits lifted; Priscilla came to mind. He sure could use her loving. It would be just the thing to take all this goddamn stress away. Should he call or head over there and just take her? Hell, he'd be asserting his rights as her boyfriend as well as a man…a horny one at that. *Yes, sirree the bitch contacted me begging me to call her.* What else could it mean but that she wanted him as much as he wanted her. The only sane thing to do was to oblige her wish.

***

Shep knelt to examine the body that laid on the office floor. "Looks like one shot through the chest. Whoever did it meant business."

"Let's not mess up the crime scene. We better call it in. What time do you have?" Billy Dee said.

Shep stood and looked at his watch. "It's about three forty-seven. Who was the cop you talked to?"

"Ah, hmm, it's on the tip of my tongue."

"You've got a memory like an elephant." Shep said as he stood with his hands on his hips.

"Yeah? You don't remember, either. I told you the name."

"You think I listen to everything you say?"

Billy Dee looked up and snapped his fingers. "Wrap… Reynold's wrap."

"What?"

"The officer's name was Reynolds. I do have an elephant's memory. Don't forget a thing."

Shep glared and walked into the main area. "You know what doesn't make sense?"

Billy Dee followed. "What?"

"Why all this mess here and nothing where she's laying."

Billy Dee examined the scene. "The victim was searching for something, heard a noise, and went to that office, but before she could do anything, she was shot?"

Shep stroked his chin. "Possible," He looked toward the corpse. "But the way she's laying, the force of the blast would have her completely on her stomach."

"Wait a minute. You're bomb and arson, not homicide. What do you know about entry and exit wounds and trajectory?"

Shep straightened to his full height. "I've hung around those dicks enough to know what I'm talking about."

Billy Dee glanced at the body, then at Shep. "Uh huh. We better call this Reynolds." He

put on his glasses and ran through his recent calls. "Found it. These phones are a beautiful thing." He was about to press the number when he heard footsteps on the stairs. "Company?"

Shep went to the window. "Forget the call, they're here."

The door burst open before Billy Dee could react.

"Police. Get down on the floor."

Three police officers had their guns drawn. A short man with a Buzz Cut screamed further orders. "Put your hands behind your head." He pointed to Shep. "You, too. Get your ass on the floor."

"We're pol—" Billy Dee started to say.

"Shut up. The both of yous." He stepped over Billy Dee while his fellow officers trained their guns on them. "Holy shit. There's a woman in that office who's shot." He disappeared for a moment. "She's dead." He walked back toward Shep and Billy Dee.

"Motherfuckers. Did you rape her too? Sick." He took a breath. "What the hell is that humming noise?"

"It's my… my phone," Billy Dee said, "I'm getting a call, I think. Hey we're police…Chicago."

Buzz Cut bent down. "You're who?"

Shep perked up. "We're Chicago PD. We're looking for Officer Reynolds. We found the place turned upside down along with the dead woman."

Buzz Cut ordered the two other police to search them.

"My star is in my back pocket," Shep said.

"Mine too," Billy Dee joined in.

"Okay so you're Chicago cops," Buzz Cut said, studying the stars. "It don't explain what the hell you're doing in this office." He held onto the badges and while still examining them asked, "How did you get in here in the first place."

"Can we get up," Billy Dee asked. "It's difficult to talk from this position."

Buzz Cut hesitated, then said, "Go ahead, but we're not taking our guns off of you."

It took Billy Dee a few seconds. "The knees don't cooperate the way they used to," he said, struggling to stand. He took a breath. "Better. Here's the four-one-one. My partner and I are here because of a couple of bombings around Chicago. At the scene of one of them was a business card from this firm. I thought it was unusual. I talked to Officer Reynolds yesterday who told me one of the partners…Tope or Topin, was missing. We decided to come down to talk to someone about any connection to Chicago."

Shep, then continued. "We climbed the stairs, and the door was unlocked. We let ourselves in and found the office like this. The woman was stretched out where all of us found her."

Buzz Cut seemed to take it all down. He nodded and stuck several pieces of gum in his mouth. "You boys," he said finally, "are smooth and maybe what you're saying is all true, but we're going for a ride to the station." He cracked his gum. "The funny thing is we got a call of a break-in going on at this place. Sure enough, you boys are here along with the dead body. Coincidence? Or a dead-bang winner for us and a loser for you. Cuff'm." He walked to the entry door and examined it. "Don't seem to be any force used." He shook his head. "It's all weird. You comin' all the way down here just to talk to…" He looked at Billy Dee. "And you don't even know who you'd be talking to. Don't make much sense. No sirree."

Chapter Thirty-Three

Paris

Felix put his hand above his eyes to shield himself from the sunlight as he opened the door wider. "Who are you again?" He scratched his head.

"Inspector Alain Ricard, Paris police. May I come in?"

"Yes, of course." He stepped back and allowed the Inspector to enter. "Is this about the Café Deux Magots. Every euro is accounted for. I don't cook the books."

"Café Deux Magots? No. no, it is one of my favorite places, such history. You own it?"

"*Non*, I manage it."

"*Bon*. Is there a place we can sit?"

Felix looked across from the entryway. He pointed to the living room. "Sorry for the mess. I wasn't expecting… I should put on a shirt. Is that okay?"

The Inspector, who came up to Felix's shoulders, nodded.

"It won't take… a minute or two, I'll be right back." Felix hurried into his bedroom. *Why on earth are the police here? What did I do?* He racked his brain. Were there traffic tickets he didn't pay? Fines he may have missed? He took the first shirt he saw in his closet and put it on. As he went back to join the officer, he realized he'd misbuttoned. *Damn, so much for hiding my nerves.* "*Pardonnez moi*, I don't usually have police officers come to my home."

Inspector Ricard smiled. "I understand. I won't take much of your time. Please, sit."

Felix fell into one of the chairs.

The Inspector opened a manila file. "Do you know a Denise Jonpair?"

Felix moved to the edge of his seat. "Who?"

Ricard reached into his coat pocket and produced a pair of glasses. "Maybe I mispronounced the name. We are all getting older." He reread it.

"I know a Denise, but… the last name?" Felix shrugged.

Ricard took out a photo. "Perhaps this will help." He showed the picture.

"Yes, of course I know her. Why? What has she done?"

Ricard had a smile frozen on his face. "Did you ask her to deliver a letter to a Jack Monte?"

"A letter?" He sat back and focused on the Inspector. "*Oui,*" then he looked at the ceiling. "I did, I asked her to deliver a letter." His hands became clammy as he feared the direction of the next question.

"Do you know Jack Monte?"

"Jack Monte?" His gaze went passed the Inspector. "*Non,*" he shook his head. "I…I don't know him."

"Who asked you to deliver this letter?"

"Well…eh…" Felix shifted his weight, then he coughed to clear his throat. "Well, as I was saying…eh…"

"It's a simple question," Ricard said, "let me explain the need." He inched forward in his chair. "Jack Monte is a criminal and a violent one. He murdered one person that we know of, probably more. More importantly, he claims to be associated with a terrorist group. They call themselves the Serbian Liberation Army. This letter may lead us to other individuals associated either with him or the terrorists."

"Terrorists?" Felix shook his head. In his mind he dismissed the possibility. He laughed. "Terrorist? Impossible."

The image of Danielle's naked body flashed by. "Inspector, no… no way." He brought his hand up as if it was a stop sign. "Enough. I wish I could help … but…" He smiled as he shrugged.

"Surely you got the letter from someone?"

"*Oui,* of course, but you know I don't recall. It may have been a patron who asked a favor. Who remembers? All in a day's business. I took it and asked Denise to deliver it. I was being the good host."

"Wouldn't the request be somewhat unusual?" Ricard asked.

Felix felt himself perspire. "Well, yes and no. In my business…all sorts of people, I'm in hospitality. People ask all kinds of things. Mistresses, lovers, secrets kept and unkept. I'm a social worker, manager, provider. Somedays I don't know which hat I'm wearing."

Ricard sighed. "We are in similar occupations, monsieur. Dealing with the public forces us to wear many hats. Except in mine, I must learn the secrets before they become fatal." He drew a small leather case from his jacket. "This is my card. If you happen to remember who gave you the letter, please call." He stood. The look he gave went through Felix.

"I'll see you out," Felix said. His arms shuddered as he braced himself to get up from the chair. "*Au revoir,*" he said, opening the front door.

"Sorry to have disturbed your morning," Ricard replied, "have a good day."

***

Susan knew she shouldn't have made the phone call to Detective Jackson, but patience wore thin as she eyed the time. Hadn't she dangled enough bait? Perhaps she had asked too much? She scolded herself for falling into the-believing-her-own-invincibility trap. She was taught better. No immediate harm though, Monsieur Jackson never picked up, and the number was as false as she made herself out to be. She steeled herself for the inevitable wait.

To occupy the time, she plotted her next encounter with Felix. Should she arrive to work on schedule or provoke him? She gave a little laugh. After all, she was now more than just another employee. Hmm. How deeply had he fallen for her? She was aware that at work, Felix valued control and prided himself on punctuality.

She excelled in "poking the bear." Throughout her life, she tested limits. Dumond repeatedly reprimanded her concerning that trait. She laughed it off. As he said in resignation, "As long as you have that beautiful body and that head to match, you won't change."

She decided forty-five minutes late would be appropriate. She wouldn't call or answer his messages. *Non*, she'd walk in wearing her tight jeans and fitted blouse.

She envisioned the scene. A scowl would cross his face. He'd raise his voice in irritation and point to his watch, then the café and give a speech about responsibility and letting "the team down." If he was angry enough, he'd threaten to fire her. She'd respond demurely and speak softly. Her eyes playing havoc with him. Add her hand gently caressing him, along with a long and provocative kiss and *voila* all should be forgiven. But if not…, then maybe she was mistaken, and *au revoir* Felix. She'd find someone else.

***

Jack Monte slumped on his cot. Why did he disconnect so quickly? *Merde, merde.* He eyed his screen. Should he try again? He looked around the darkened prison tier. He was a fool to be so open with his phone. Someone might see or hear, but what if that was really the contact? Monte racked his brain, replaying the short conversation in his head. It was a male and he answered with an accent. Try as Monte might, the conversation was too short and quick to identify it.

Monte repeated in a whisper the question the man asked. "Who is this?" God only knows the location Monte called or the time of day or night. That may account for the person not knowing who Monte was, then again, if that was the contact, wouldn't Monte's number be the identifier?

Monte wiped his face with his hand as he kept vigil for any new sound that disturbed the snoring of the sleeping men. When he heard nothing unusual, he stood, gripped his phone, and began to pace. He lost track of time as he fell into a daze arguing with himself whether to try again. His mutterings must have been loud enough to disturb a sleeper who moaned a complaint. That stopped him. There must be little of the night left, and all this angst has made him tired. He laid down on his bunk and carefully returned his phone to its hiding place. *A demain*, he thought staring at the ceiling, and slowly drifted to sleep.

***

"Monte, get up," the guard known as Le Rouge said as he banged on the bars.

Monte first thought he was dreaming or in that state where reality and dreams intersected, but none of it made sense. The noise and the shout of his name pierced whatever was left of his sleep. "*T'as-toi, batard*, can't you see I'm sleeping." He opened his eyes and stared at Le Rouge. "What do you want? I have a right to sleep."

"You and your rights." He spat. "You are a prisoner. Get on your feet." Le Rouge paused and waited for movement. "Now."

Monte slowly slung his feet to the floor. "This is not right. It's still night. I haven't done anything."

Le Rouge signaled for the cell door to open. "You're all innocent, every last one of you, and none of your rot deserves to be here. Keep that garbage to yourself or your lawyer. Put your hands behind your back."

Monte knew arguing was useless. He obeyed. "Where are we going?" he asked as Le Rouge took him by his forearm and led him out of the cell.

"You've suddenly become important," Le Rouge said. "The warden wants to see you." He said it loud enough so that the prisoners on the tier heard.

"Why would you do that? You've just marked me," he hissed.

Le Rouge laughed. "It's because you are liked so much."

Monte heard his cell door bang shut. At least the guards weren't searching his quarters. A small victory as he wondered what the hell was about to happen.

Chapter Thirty-Four

Brownsburg

No one ever accused Priscilla of being book smart, but she had street sense. If her choice was sex with this monster or death, the decision was easy. She contemplated the mechanics of it and thought if during the act she maneuvered herself in such a way as to grab his gun, she knew how to use it. What were the chances, though? He acted like a professional hit man. But why would a hit man be after Pappy? Not that she should care. Was there something she didn't know about him? Impossible. He'd been a puppy ever since high school. There was nothing to him. But the question of why remained, then again, if this blue-eyed devil wasn't a hit man, , then he was crazy and more dangerous. Her mental wonderings ended when she felt the killer's arm pull her closer to him.

He said he had another way to make Pappy jealous. It didn't take a genius to figure what that was. She could satisfy him beyond his wildest dreams and maybe he'd allow her to live. Either way, she prayed and hoped for Lady Luck.

He kissed her cheek. She eyed him for a moment. He wasn't bad looking. Matter of fact he was sort of cute in an evil way. And those icy blue eyes… She could do worse. She *had* done worse. "We'd be more comfortable in the bedroom. Don't you think?"

A huge smile crossed his face. "You are smart girl." His hand brushed her breast. "But, if we go to bedroom, your friend, this Pappy, will not get whole picture. No, better he walks in and see. We do it here in living room on couch. This way watching you fuck will be last thing he sees. Sweet, no?"

A tremor went through her. She must have paled. He touched her face with the back of his hand. "Don't worry. It will all be okay."

His eyes seemed to penetrate her very being.

"Now, let's go to fun part. Undress for me …. slow."

"I…I… you mean like a striptease?"

He rubbed his chin with his free hand. "Yes, why not?"

***

Pappy pulled up to Priscilla's house and was about to turn into her driveway. Another car was parked there. He looked again and saw the vehicle had out-of-state license plates. Strange. He thought back to the day before. Not again. He gripped his steering wheel hard…the bitch. How could she? He grabbed his phone from the passenger seat and reread her message. This ain't right. Why would she want him to urgently call if she'd got someone there? Even for her that would be insane. She couldn't hate him that much. He backed out and drove a few doors down to park. He gently closed the driver's door and walked to the house. He stood in front deciding whether to repeat the other day's mistake. "Nah." This time he'd go around.

He went up the driveway but stopped to peer into the parked car. He was inches from the driver's window when he heard music. He swung from the vehicle and went toward the side of the house. It was definitely coming from there. The sounds were brassy with drums beating out a rhythm like he heard at a strip joint. *Jesus, the whore. Well, she's about to get the surprise of her life.* He resumed his walk up the driveway, his head bent, and shoulders scrounged forward. He reached the back door and tried the knob. It was locked, but he knew where she hid the key. He had told her thousands of times to find a better hiding place, but… He reached under the mat and there it was. He pushed it into the slit and twisted. He was in. Any noise he made was covered by the music. He went through the kitchen and, then the hallway that connected to the living room. He was halfway through it and saw Priscilla's silhouette on the wall gyrating to the beat. He went closer and was riveted by what he witnessed. Her hands clutched the sides of her panties. She pulled them up and, then ever so slowly down. Each movement revealing more and more of her well-shaped ass. Her panties were below her thighs when she turned. She must have seen him because she gasped, and her hands flew to her naked breasts.

"Get out!" she screamed.

He ran toward her. He was within a few feet or so of where she had been when he heard a boom and an instant later felt something hit him. He collapsed to the floor. He laid there a second or two and struggled for air. He tried to speak, but instead of words there was only a rattle sound, then two more bangs and all went black.

***

Da da dum. Even I know that sound. Wait. Da da dum. This makes no sense. She groped around and felt something underneath her. Her memory returned as to what happened. Was it a minute, an hour, a day ago? She had no idea. Pain shot through her arms and legs. She sucked in air and forced herself to open her eyes. Beneath her was a body. She jumped off and screamed, "Oh my God, oh my God." She stood frozen. "I can't believe… I…" She retched but managed to stop herself. *I need water…bathroom.* Before she took a step, she saw Pappy lying on the floor off to her side. "Pappy, Pappy, are you all right?" She went to him. His shirt was soaked with blood. She touched his wrist, then his neck, searching for a pulse. He was cold to the touch. She drew her hand away. It was smeared with blood. His? Hers? Had she been shot? She touched herself. She had blood on her chest and torso but felt no wound. "Jesus, the motherfucker missed. How?" She took another look at the body on the couch. "Fuck." She saw a gaping hole in the man's neck and upper chest area. *How the hell did I do that?* She eyed the gun and a cell phone on the floor next to the couch. The screen read Missed Call. *I have to wash. I have to…* She raced to the bathroom, stepping over Pappy's corpse. She flipped the toilet seat and dropped to her knees. She vomited, then grabbed hold of the bowl. Her whole body shook, her teeth chattered like she had a fever, then a surge of heat swept over with sweat pouring from her face. She struggled to breathe as another wave of nausea seized her. When she had no more to give, she felt for the handle and spent her strength to flush. She succeeded, but for the moment was too weak to move. She waited, making grunting noises until whatever energy she had left allowed her to crawl to the bath and turn on the faucet. She forced herself into the tub. She sat mesmerized by the steam as the water rose.

Chapter Thirty-Five

Brownsburg

"Hey, just wait a dang minute," Billy Dee said to Buzz Cut before his fellow Brownsburg officers prepared to cuff him and Shep. "Think about it. We each have guns that you didn't check. See if they'd been fired."

Buzz Cut eyed his officers. "You guys didn't… Shit." His face grew red. "Got to do everything myself. Get out of the way."

"It's on my right side," Billy Dee said.

Buzz Cut took Billy Dee's gun, , then went to Shep.

"Left side," Shep said.

Buzz Cut inspected each weapon. "They're clean as a whistle. I'm beginning to think I owe both you fellas an apology. We don't get many shootings like in the big city. Hell, I think this may be the second or third we had all year. This is a small town. Most folks know each other. Pappy, I mean Mr. McDonald, was a high school basketball star. Everyone knows him." He wiped his face with his hand. "Pappy kind of fell on hard times until this Topin fella showed up. It seemed his business got better. Now--he looked toward the dead body--"maybe everything's going to hell." He handed Billy Dee and Shep their police badges and weapons. He plopped some more gum in his mouth. "So, you fellas think Pappy or Topin had something to do

"

with some bombs that went off in Chicago?"

"Not exactly," Billy Dee said. "We weren't looking at them, but maybe a client. Someone had their card where an explosion occurred."

Buzz Cut popped a bubble. "I'm think'n." He turned to one of his fellow officers. "Call the sheriff and tell them to send an ET car down here, then dial the coroner's office to pick up the body. I'll let the captain know what's going on. If you boys stick around, I'll take you to Pappy's house or maybe I can get him on the phone. Someone will need to talk to him about what happened here, anyway."

Billy Dee gave Shep a look. "Thanks. You sure? Don't want to get in your way."

"Nah, you boys probably know more of what to do than me."

Billy Dee replaced his gun and placed his star in his back pocket. "If you don't mind me saying, I think we should seal off this office and step into the hallway until the ETs get here. Don't want to contaminate the scene any more than we had to."

Buzz Cut screwed up his face. "Huh?"

"Fingerprints, DNA, don't want to touch or step on any-thing until after…"

"Gotcha. Boys, let's go into the hallway." He motioned to the other officers.

They all moved outside the office door. One of the offi-cers went to his car and returned with yellow tape. He began to seal the entrance door. Buzz Cut went outside and met the sheriff's evidence technicians. Billy Dee and Shep followed. They stood several feet away and heard part of Buzz Cut retelling what occurred.

"Well, that's it for now," Buzz Cut said as the ET personnel went inside the building. "The captain will be here in a few minutes too. What a goddamn mess."

Billy Dee was about to remind Buzz Cut to reach out to Pappy when the officer's radio crackled. Billy Dee saw his face turn ashen as the dispatcher radioed "This is a ten-thirty-five all units, gunshots at ninety-five hundred Block E four hundred North."

"What's going on?" Billy Dee asked.

"Get in the car," Buzz Cut ordered, "all hell may be breaking out. The address, if my memory is correct, is the lady Pappy hung out with. What the hell did he do?"

***

Paris

Susan looked at the time, then her phone. So far, nothing had gone according to plan. Monsieur Detective Jackson didn't return her call and Jenko ignored her too. It was concerning, but not fatal. The true aim was Jack Monte. He needed to suffer for his attempt on her life and the murder of Dumond. Focus on what she could control. *Rien.* Time to dress and test Felix, her newfound lover. She chuckled at the connotation. Lover? She couldn't blame him for finding her attractive and alluring. She knew the ways around men. It was what she did, but for Dumond. Only he had captured her and held her spellbound. His was beyond just love. It was a combination of that, along with fear and admiration. He gave just enough of himself but never all. Maybe that's why she could never leave the web he spun. There was always more to uncover.

The Café Deux Magots was bursting with patrons waiting patiently for a table. Susan timed her arrival to be 45 minutes late to her shift. She hurried to the back to grab an apron and to learn the specials of the day. A few of her coworkers muttered *bonjour* as she passed them, then raised their eyes to a clock and shook their heads. Susan could guess what they were thinking. By now, it wasn't a secret she had slept with the boss. Another conquest for Felix. She had joined a not-so-exclusive club and her fate would most likely be the same as the others. She was the flavor of the day until someone fresh arrived. Susan knew better.

She went into the employees' bathroom to brush her hair and make final adjustments to her makeup. She worked quickly and the reflection in the mirror approved her work. "*Bon*, and now for the test." She walked into the restaurant and searched the room for Felix but didn't see him. She stopped a coworker on his way to the kitchen.

"Where's Felix?" She asked.

He stopped, scouted the dining area, then pointed. "He's waiting on one of your tables."

"*Merci*." She marched over and tapped Felix on the shoulder. "I'll be happy to take over from here." She said it naturally as if she'd been there all along and saw the need to help.

He wore his usual business smile, but his eyes flashed something else. "Very well." He addressed the table and introduced her as the new server. "When you have a moment, Danielle, see me," he said under his breath as he moved toward the front.

She half listened to the prattle of questions regarding what dish was better or fresher. Her answers were professional but lacked engagement. Most of her mind was elsewhere scrutinizing Felix's reaction and order. Did his tone mean something bad or a slap on the wrist? After taking her customers' dinner requests, she quickly scanned the café. She saw him hovering over a table. It was a party of four beautiful women. Had Felix already found a new flavor? She scolded herself for submitting to the jealousy game. Who cares if he did as long as she got him to do what she needed? Focus…all the rest was smoke.

Chapter Thirty-Six

Paris

Inspector Alain Ricard left Felix's home and returned to the station. He had been a cop for more than two decades and had developed a keen sense of observation. He learned to listen by watching. He could tell if one lied. In today's parlance, he'd put it another way: the individual was not forthcoming. He was sure Felix knew exactly who gave him the letter.

Why would he cover? It could be a myriad of reasons. The most typical…*cherchez la femme*…a woman. If not, perhaps his explanation held a grain of truth. Could there be a financial gain for Felix? Ricard sat back in his chair. He doubted it, but…

Was Felix involved with the SLA? He wrote that on a pad of paper and stared at it for a few seconds. *Non*, intriguing but… He reviewed the meeting with Felix. Not the type, too jittery, to be a part of a terrorist group. He drew a line through the phrase.

He reached into a drawer and pulled out a folder. He had done research on Felix before his visit. He opened the file and reviewed his notes. He knew Felix managed the Café Deux Magots for three years, and by all accounts, ran it well. Prior to Café Deux Magots, he worked at several different restaurants in Paris. He was also aware Felix had a reputation with the ladies. He imagined running the café helped in that department.

For the time being, he would keep an eye on him. Felix gave the impression he was uncomfortable with the situation regardless of how he got involved. As Ricard's countrymen would say, *laisse-les tremper dans son propre jus,* let them soak in their own juices. Ricard's profession had made him a very patient man.

The next order of business was to pay a visit to the prison and have a chat with Jack Monte. He reached for the desk phone and placed a call to the warden's office. After being transferred to several people and repeating his explanation for the need several times, an appointment was arraigned for 9:00 a.m. the next day.

***

Ricard arrived at the jail earlier than he expected. Traffic had been unusually light. He could remain in the car, but an hour was a long time, and it was cold. *What the hell?* It wasn't as if Monte had other engagements. He decided even if he had to wait, the warden's office was warmer than his automobile.

It took a good twenty minutes to pass through all the security checks before he was ushered into warden Rene Boucher's office.

Boucher didn't get up. He pointed to a seat and motioned for Ricard to sit. "You are early," he said. "Prisons run on a schedule and when that is upset" --he spread his arms wide--"chaos."

"Please accept my apologies, Warden Boucher. I miscalculated the traffic. However, my being here is to: one, warn you that Jack Monte is a dangerous man and two, he may be planning or has planned more crimes."

Boucher laughed. "Come Inspector, he is behind these prison walls. His cell is monitored and…"—he went closer to Ricard—"there's informants all over. We keep a tight ship." The warden hit an intercom button and instructed an underling to bring the prisoner. "It will be a few minutes."

Ricard partially listened as Boucher made small talk. He discretely took in the office and estimated it was last remodeled after the Second World War. The walls were painted pea green. The warden's desk was metal, and the chairs well worn. A crinkled pack of Marlboros was on top of a pile of papers. There was a picture of the president of France on one wall, and the Minister of Justice on another. In the far corner was a photo of the beach on St. Moritz along with bikini-clad women and half-dressed bronzed men. The warden himself was built like a fireplug, short, stocky, but muscular.

Boucher took a cigarette from the pack and lit it. "You don't mind, do you? In this place these are worth a fortune. The inmates would sell their mothers to get their hands on them. It's an effective tool. *N'est pas?*"

Ricard nodded with a knowing smile. "I'm sure cigarettes play an important role in the commerce of this place."

"You have no idea…gold." He plucked the packet from the desk and held it to the light. "I've been here over a decade." He turned to Ricard. "And this is the first time an Inspector from the Paris prefect has come in person. This Monte must be valuable?" He grinned.

"Valuable?"

"Come Inspector, you and I can level."

"I don't understand?"

"Inspector, we all dwell in the same milieu. Everything has a price. Cigarettes on the inside, euros perhaps on the outside. No one here works for nothing. Information is a commodity. Monte won't say anything unless you have something for him. I want to be prepared."

Ricard kept his silence.

Boucher leaned forward. "What I'm asking is, what are you giving in order to get?"

***

Susan found herself too busy to speak with Felix during the evening. The line into the café only stopped near closing. Around 1 a.m. the last patron shuffled out. The bartender washed and restacked the glasses, and the wait staff took over several tables to count their receipts, , then their tips. Felix sat by the computer near the back comparing the evening take with the slips the staff turned in. From the smile on his face, it had been a good night.

"Danielle," he said as she brought her receipts, "your evening went well?"

She patted her pocket. "*Oui*, very."

He looked from her to the computer, then said, "*Bon*."

She saw his attention return to the screen. He was all business. What happened the night before all but forgotten. She waited awkwardly for a second or two. *That's it?* She remembered the four women Felix catered to earlier in the evening. Were they the new flavor? At least there was no consequence for her tardiness. More importantly, it told her that he could no longer be part of her plans. She turned to leave.

"Danielle, we need to talk. Get yourself a drink and wait until I'm finished with the bookkeeping. It shouldn't be long." His expression was intense. "This needs to between only us."

She paused. "Business or pleasure?"

His facial expression didn't change. "Please do as I ask."

This was a change, then she thought, he was still in boss mode. He had to make it look good for the few employees who were tiding up. She shrugged. "Okay, I'll wait." Her tone was a bit tired and part bored. She walked to the front, subtly moving her hips. At the bar she studied the assorted bottles of cognac, then reached for Hennessy XO. If she was about to receive a lecture or reprimand, might as well drink the expensive stuff to soften the blow. She poured two fingers worth and took a chair near the front.

"*Bon soir*," a coworker said, winked at her, then left.

She didn't question what the co-worker meant. Was this how he did it? A pretense to reprimand? No more romance. Jesus, how disgusting. She took a sip and let the liquid slide down her throat, electrifying her taste buds and producing a warmth of comfort.

"Only between us," he said. Her hand encircled the snifter. Fucking would only be between them, she thought, unless… he invited those bimbos from earlier this evening.

She looked up and saw Felix bidding adieu to another worker, then he went to the back presumably to lock the door.

From her vantage point she looked around the café's dining area. What the hell did he have in mind? To do it on a table, the bar, oh God not the floor. But why do anything?

Her old friend Dumond appeared so real when he whispered, "Never give something away for nothing." She held the rim of the glass to her lips. No never. She knew that as well as breathing.

She heard Felix's footsteps. She took another long sip and watched him approach. Life was a chess match about to begin. What move will the queen make?

Chapter Thirty-Seven

Brownsburg

The sirens of several police cars had the neighbors out of their homes on the 9500 E 400 N block. Billy Dee could see them milling about in several groups. Buzz Cut, whose name tag read R. Callahan, pulled up to the house and left the car in the middle of the street.

"Let's go," he said.

They started up the walkway and saw another officer knock on the front door.

"Try opening it, maybe it's unlocked," Callahan shouted.

"No luck, Sarge."

"Can you see anything through the window?"

The officer moved to the side. "Nah, the shades and curtains are drawn. Can't see a fuck'n thing."

Billy Dee had stepped off the front porch and started for the driveway.

"Where are you going?" Callahan asked.

"The back. By the way did this woman…Pris…Priscilla own a car with out-of-state plates?

"Wha…?"

Billy Dee pointed.

"Hell, don't know." He directed another officer to run a check on the vehicle. "This is creeping me out. You hear anything from inside the house?" He waited as Billy Dee and Shep took a few steps toward the side bay window.

"No…" Billy Dee stepped closer. "Yeah, now I hear something. "Music. Wow…drums, horns, sounds like a honky-tonk party.

Callahan went toward them and cocked his head. "I hear it, too. You fellas should get out more." He laughed. "It's the shit played at a strip joint." He put his hand on his holstered gun. "Maybe you boys stay back. Ain't your jurisdiction and all."

Billy Dee glanced at Shep, who nodded. "Just write us out of the report if there's something. We've got your back."

Callahan hesitated. "Captain not going to like it, but what the hell. Our funeral, let's go."

They moved to the back door and Callahan was about to touch the doorknob.

"You got something for your hands?" Billy Dee asked.

"What?"

"Fingerprints. Don't want to mess it up."

Callahan took a breath. "Oh yeah, almost forgot." He dug into his pocket for a handkerchief. "This should do." He folded the hanky so that it only covered the outer rim of the knob and twisted. "I'll be damned. The door ain't locked." He looked at Billy Dee along with Shep and two other officers. He drew his gun. "Here goes nothing." He burst in shouting, "Police."

Billy Dee, Shep, and the others followed. Other than the bawdy music there was no other noise.

A minute or so later Callahan could be heard from the front room. "Shit, shit."

Billy Dee caught up. He saw a body on the floor near the couch and another one on the sofa. "God damn. I thought you said this is a quiet place, small town, and stuff. This looks more like Chicago. Do you know who they are?"

Callahan looked from one dead man to the other. "Crap,

the one lying on the ground is Pappy. This one here…no idea."

"Watch your step," Billy Dee warned, "it looks like the weapon is on the floor near the dead man's hand. Better wait 'til the evidence techs get here before picking it up."

Callahan grunted something inaudible and sighed. "Never seen anything like it. In all my years on the force, nope." He shook his head. "Like the last scene from the OK Corral. Jesus."

Shep tapped Billy Dee on the shoulder. "You smell water?"

"Water?" He sniffed. "Yeah… I do." He looked around while Callahan and the other officers busied themselves with the crime scene. "Didn't see anything unusual in the kitchen. What about the bathroom?" He pointed to a closed door on the other side of the living room. They walked over, and Billy Dee opened the door. There was water on the floor along with a soaked bloody towel. He stepped over it to observe the tub. It was full of pinkish water. "Well, we found the source of the smell. Where's the bather?"

****

Priscilla felt something by her lips that startled her out of her catatonic state. She slapped at it, then realized she was drowning in the bath. She jerked herself into a sitting position and looked wildly around the room. Her cough racked her body as she struggled to sit and breathe at the same time. It took several minutes to gain control. Water cascaded over the side of the tub until it dawned on her to turn off the faucet. She pushed herself through the bath water, grabbed the knobs and twisted them shut. The water stopped, and she burst into tears. The pain of everything plagued her. Pappy was dead. How? Why? She started to shake. "Have to get out," she told herself. "Can't sit in this shit any longer." She grabbed onto the sides of the tub and pushed herself up. She clung onto the shower door and forced her leg over the side. The other one caught the edge and she nearly fell. She swore, then wildly grabbed a hanging towel. After dabbing herself, she dropped it on the waterlogged floor and sloshed toward the door. What if someone else was out there? What if… She strained to listen over the bump and grind music for extraneous sounds. *I've got to get out.* That's all that mattered. She edged the door open staring at the exposed space, , then ran to her bedroom and grabbed whatever was hanging… a sweatshirt and jeans. She found shoes and put them on, then raced to the front of the house. Pappy's corpse stopped her. "Sorry Pappy, really, I am. I don't know why this happened, but… it did." She couldn't stay longer as tears formed. *I've got to get out.* , then she remembered her car was at Pappy's office. She stooped and snatched Pappy's car keys from his pocket. She took a step toward the front door when she heard a buzzing and looked toward the sofa. The phone on the floor next to it signaled an incoming call. "Fuck." She grabbed it and decided to run out the back. She'd go through the alley and hunt for Pappy's car. It had to be close by. After that, she didn't know.

Chapter Thirty-Eight

Paris

Jack Monte was led into the warden's office. His body and hair were thinner. He was unshaven and uncombed. He also looked ten years older.

"*Bonjour*, Monsieur Monte," the warden began, "you have a visitor, Inspector…eh…" He looked over at Ricard with a hint of a smile.

"Ricard," the inspector said.

"*Oui*, Ricard." Boucher narrowed his eyes. "He wants to ask you a few questions."

"*Baise-le*," Monte spat, "and fuck his mother too."

The warden glanced from the prisoner to Ricard. "See, my Inspector, it is as I said. In his base vocabulary Monsieur Monte asked the same question as I."

Ricard stood. "Monsieur Boucher, I must have missed his question." He looked from Monte to Boucher letting seconds of silence settle. He observed the desired effect of uncomfortableness, then interrupted it. "Is there a place where I can interview the prisoner with a bit more privacy?"

Boucher laughed. "This is a prison, not a hotel. I brought Monte as a courtesy to your enforcement agency, but…it's out of the question. You interview him here or nowhere." He stuck another cigarette in his mouth.

Ricard took a step toward the warden and spoke almost

in a whisper. "Do you know what I'm in charge of, Monsieur Warden?"

Boucher shook his head. "You are a detective from Paris. In my life I've seen dozens of your types. Paris"—the word came out guttural—"so what."

Ricard ignored the slight. "I'm in charge of monitoring terrorism. Potential, if we're lucky and investigating it if we're unlucky."

That didn't seem to faze Boucher. He continued to smoke, his cigarette perfuming the room with the smell of burnt paper and tobacco.

"I'll put it another way: if something happens in Paris or for that matter in France and the investigation leads to Monsieur Monte…" He stopped and waited to see if Boucher's expression changed. Noticing no difference, Ricard continued. "I'll spell it out for you, Monsieur Warden. You've been here, what, thirty years?"

Boucher didn't respond.

Ricard sighed. "If I don't receive your cooperation, you and all the Marlboros you have will find a new occupation or a new location….and that will be the least of your troubles. Do we understand each other?"

"Is that a threat, Monsieur Inspector?"

Ricard shrugged. "A statement of fact. Do with it as you wish."

Boucher began to cough. As he doubled over, he nodded. "Go ahead… I'll step out. *Allez*." He motioned his staff to leave.

Ricard asked Monte to sit after everyone had left. "You remember who I am?"

Monte rubbed his lips. "Of course, I do. You and the *cochons* from America put me here. That's not easy to forget."

"I suppose not." Ricard drew a chair near the prisoner. "Do you know why I've asked to speak with you?"

"Am I a fuck'n mind reader? Not a clue." His left eye blinked continuously.

"You had a visitor the other day." Ricard forced himself to ignore Monte's tick.

"Who says?"

Ricard stood and rested his hands on the back of the chair. "This could become very tiresome and the outcome not good for you. Dispense with the bullshit, Monsieur Monte…"

"Or what? You'll keep me here for another year? Who cares? Another 365 don't make a damn bit of difference." He glanced away for a second or two. His tongue licked his lips. "So, let's say I did have a visitor. Ain't against the rules. You know French prisons even allow fucking for spouses."

Ricard looked through him. "You don't have a wife."

A smile flew over Monte's face. "You got me there."

"Monsieur Monte, you may believe or want to believe that behind these walls you have disappeared. I assure you that is not the case. The woman who came to see you…"

"Woman?"

"Monte don't be stupid. She signed in." He opened a file and showed a prison document with her signature.

"I don't know her. Never saw her in my life."

"What did you talk about?"

Monte leaned back. "My mouth," he pointed, "is dry. Haven't even had what passes as coffee this morning." His attention shifted to the Marlboros on the warden's desk. "How about a cigarette to continue our talk?"

Ricard glanced at the desk, then went into his coat pocket. In his hand was a full pack of cigarettes… American also.

Monte tried to hide his excitement, but his eyes gave him away. He pointed to what Ricard held in his palm. "You don't play fair Inspector. Most of the fools in here would sell their souls for that. Me…"

"Really?" Ricard undid the plastic wrapping and opened

the pack. He hit the packet against his palm so that a cigarette popped up. "Have one, on me. No strings."

Monte let out a snort as he reached for it. "Inspector, there is no such thing."

Ricard lit the smoke for him. He let him take a few puffs before he began questioning again. "So, you never saw this woman before?"

Monte held his Chesterfield between his index and middle finger staring at the ash. "That's right. Never saw her before. But I'll tell you if there wasn't that glass between us, I'd take her. She was easy on the eyes."

"Monte, you'd take any woman."

The prisoner took another puff. "True, I would." He laughed.

"What about Felix? Do you know him? Heard of him?"

"Nah, the bitch blabbed on about him…boyfriend or something…I know nothing about him."

Ricard nodded and reached into his pocket again. "What about this note?" He held it up to Monte. Who is the 'we' and what does 'We Know' mean?"

The cigarette Monte held almost burnt to its end. His face turned pale. "I…I…don't… where did you get that? What's this about?"

"*Exactement,*" Ricard said, "that's what I want to know."

***

Felix stopped at the bar and poured himself a Scotch. With his tumbler in hand, he joined Danielle at the table. He had the same intense expression as when she turned in her receipts. He took a gulp of his drink. His gaze flited around the room until it settled somewhere below her face. He touched her hand.

"What's going on, Felix? You should be happy after a

night like this," she said. "The café did very well. Are you angry with me that I was late? It wasn't the worst thing in the world. I was tired after the night we had."

A smile crossed his face. "*Oui*. It was quite an evening. No, I'm not upset with you about that. Disappointed, but angry? *Non*." He suddenly stood. "I don't know even how to begin?"

"Just say it. I'm a big girl. Whatever it was, I'm sure I've heard it before."

He shook his head. "*Non*. I hope not. This was a new one." He took a few steps away from the table.

Danielle clutched her glass as she stared at him. "You're starting to scare me." She got up, went to the bar, and poured herself another finger of Hennessy XO. She took a sip, then held the snifter in front of her face. "Tell me."

"Okay." He sat down again, his focus on his glass. "Not long after you left my apartment an inspector of police came to my door."

"What? How come?"

"Please sit."

She joined him. He intertwined his hand with hers. "The inspector asked me questions about that letter you had me deliver to that prison."

"Letter?" She pulled her hand from his. "What did you tell him?" He had her rapt attention.

"Nothing…really."

"You must have said something."

He looked at her. "Well, yeah, I did. I told him I forgot who gave it to me. He kept pestering me. I finally told him it could have been a patron who asked a favor."

"Did he buy it?"

He shrugged. "For now."

"What do you mean?"

"That ended the conversation. He gave me his card and left."

"So, what's with the worry face?"

"The inspector told me that the prisoner Mo…, whatever his name, was a terrorist."

"A terrorist? I don't believe it. Oh my God. Terrible. The inspector really said that?"

Felix stared at her. "Yeah, he did. He mentioned some group… SUA or SLA, something like that."

Danielle gulped down the rest of her drink. "I'm so sorry I got you involved. Those relatives in Canada are distant. I didn't know. They asked if I could do them a favor. They said they had something personal to tell him. I had no idea."

"Is that the truth, Danielle? I must know."

She grabbed both his hands and locked her gaze on him. "Truth. Whoever this prisoner was this…Mo…Monte, I… Really, would I risk everything, my job, you…" She shook her head. "No way. Never. This is too crazy."

He looked from her to his drink. His finger twirled around the rim of his glass three times. , then he stopped and regarded her. His eyes set deep and serious. "That's all I wanted to know." He swallowed the rest of his Scotch. Like a fever that broke, his mood changed. A smile played on his lips. "If you want… I mean…" He chuckled. "You've spun my head around. I never had trouble asking a woman to bed."

"There's always a first." She stood. "I must go home. I want to change out of these clothes and give you something to remember. I'll be at your apartment before the sun rises."

"Interesting response. A little Hemingway?"

"Who?"

"Never mind. I'll be waiting."

She leaned down and kissed him hard. "Get some rest. You'll need it." She laughed as she went out the door into the night.

Chapter Thirty-Nine

Brownsburg

Billy Dee and Shep agreed something disturbing occurred in the bathroom. The pinkish water in the tub was up to the rim and there were one or two inches on the floor. "I don't think the two dead guys were the ones who took a bath before they were shot. So, who does that leave?" Billy Dee asked.

"Real good, Billy Dee, how did you come up with that obvious point?"

Billy Dee took a moment and gave him the look his wife gave when he said something stupid. "I just know."

They stepped from the bathroom into the living room. There were a lot more personnel than before. A chalk outline replaced Pappy's body. Photographs were taken of the corpse on the couch. Sgt. Callahan stood apart. He didn't yell orders like he did at Pappy's office. Instead, he watched wide-eyed as sheriff's evidence technicians and officers overran the scene.

"Pretty hectic," Billy Dee said, moving toward him. "Shep and I took a look at the bathroom." He pointed. "That's where the water smell was coming from."

"Smell? What smell?"

"You know like when you've taken a bath and water hangs in the air, sort of speak."

Callahan looked as if Billy Dee was a creature from

another planet. "What are you getting at?"

Shep spoke up. "There's a bloody towel on the floor and the bathwater was pink. Meaning whoever took a bath was bleeding."

It took Callahan several seconds. "Shit, you think Priscilla shot those two? I'll be damned."

"Let's not jump to conclusions," Billy Dee said. "It's a possibility, but why?" Billy Dee turned toward the couch and looked down. He stooped. "What's that under the sofa?

Callahan and Shep looked in that direction. "Hell, I don't know." Callahan moved an officer out of the way and went to the spot. He got on his knees and grabbed a bra, a pair of leggings, and a shirt that must have been pushed underneath. "That explains the music," he said as he got up.

"Yeah, I guess so," Billy Dee said, "but who was she performing for?"

The three of them looked from Pappy's silhouette outline to the couch and back again.

"My guess," Billy Dee said, "the girl was in front of the couch. Pappy came in, saw them, and…"

"Priscilla shot him, , then the guy on the couch?" Callahan asked. He shook his head. "Why? I get Pappy. It was common knowledge he was sweet on her, but she not so much. If anything, Pappy would have fired at her, but I don't think that happened."

Billy Dee stroked his chin. "You have a point. If Priscilla was the shooter, where did she keep the gun? The clothes in your hand paints a clear picture she was naked or pretty much so."

"Must have been a quite a scene. The gossip around town was Priscilla was a looker." He scratched his head. "Won't the gun tell us who handled it?"

"If the technician finds fingerprints. It's not like TV. They're not found all the time."

"Thanks for your optimism." Callahan stared at the couch. "How long you think before we get prints from the gun? It's been ages since I dealt with the Feds."

Billy Dee and Shep shrugged. "Could be within a day or who knows," Shep answered. "Depends how motivated they are."

"My God, what a shit show." Callahan took out another package of gum. "What about the dead woman at the real estate office? Is there a connection?"

Billy Dee held up the palm of his hand in a gesture to stop, then checked his watch. It was near 5 p.m. For a moment, the noise around him faded. His thoughts went elsewhere. He could almost hear his wife fret that she hadn't heard from him. Who knew how complicated this little jaunt would turn out to be?

In the old days he wouldn't have thought of Janine. The excitement of the investigation would be all-consuming. He missed that part. He took a quick glance around the room. Cops came and went along with more technicians. It really was getting much too crowded.

He thought of those days when he worked full time. Despite the horror of the crimes or maybe because of it, the adrenaline took hold. Everything at a crime scene became a possibility. Followed by the drudgery of countless leads that went nowhere. The untold cups of coffee, cigarettes, or in his case, cigars that with luck turned into the eureka moment. He long ago admitted that little of this was about crime and punishment. It was about ego and the ability to find clues that led to an arrest resulting in a file marked "solved."

He turned to Callahan. "Yeah, I think the woman at the office had something to do with these victims." He pointed to the side bay window. "That car may be a clue. Find out who it belongs to. Also have the evidence techs go through it."

Callahan mumbled something, then went to search for the officer he asked to contact the Secretary of State. After a few minutes he came back. "Too many people in here. Jesus. Can't find him. Maybe he's outside."

***

Priscilla put much effort into walking with a steady gait; not too fast or slow. If the neighbors heard anything they weren't in the street…at least not yet. Find Pappy's car and get the hell out, was her mantra. She reached the mouth of the alley and turned toward her street. Three cars in from the corner was the vehicle. *Thank God.* Pappy's old key slid into the lock and opened the door. She got in. She remembered Pappy had to jiggle the ignition slot to make it start. "Shit." Her hand shook and the key fell out. She flung the door open to find it, then tried again. "Come on." She half-closed her eyes and mouthed a small prayer. Luck was with her. The engine started. She quickly checked the mirrors. The street was still quiet. Escape was a turn of the wheel away. She took a deep breath and pulled out of the parking space. She drove toward the main avenue. Checking the rear-view mirror, she thought she saw flashing red lights blocks behind her. Was she imagining this? She lowered her window. Sirens? Someone had called the police. Her hands tightened on the steering wheel. Did anyone see her? She could taste the panic that rose within her. She fought to stay calm. She reasoned she was the victim, why run? Then the image of her shooting the man on the couch flashed. She swallowed hard. *Get away,* became her siren song.

She drove with no plan, then realized she was heading toward downtown and her parked car. She had to think this through. Cops would be all over there because of the shooting in Pappy's office. Bad idea. She pulled off the highway and idled without calling attention to herself. Police would be looking for her car, but not Pappy's. At least not this soon. Why not hide at Pappy's house for a few hours? The cops had their hands full with all the victims. They wouldn't get around to searching the place for a while. Besides, Pappy usually had money somewhere in the house. On occasion she even had left clothes there, or in his trunk.

An ease came over her. Warmth returned to her hands. The immediacy of where to go solved, her whole body relaxed as she drove toward Pappy's. By the time she reached his house, it was dark. The street appeared quiet, and she didn't see any cop cars. She parked a block down and got out. The chill in the air reminded her to check the trunk for clothes. She carefully eyed the area for passers-by, , then opened the trunk. "Jesus, what the fuck?" She stared at a safe, her mouth open. *What the hell?* Her mind raced as to whose it was. Pappy's? She ran through the possibility. As she stood trying to figure it out, she heard the distinct sound of a phone. She looked widely around and felt her pockets. She lowered the hood and opened the passenger door. The phone she took from the murder scene wailed. Impulsively she grabbed it and pressed "Accept."

"Hello, who is this?" she asked.

The call immediately went dead.

Chapter Forty

Paris

Susan rushed into her apartment. She had kept her composure during her Uber ride from the café but now…the myriad of reasons to be upset hit her. Cops nosing around, Felix, Monte, and that asshole, Jenko. Her designs for revenge were in jeopardy. She took a deep breath and went to her bedroom. She had to change and prepare herself for Felix to keep him happy. *Merde*, that wasn't what she had planned. She unzipped her jacket. Before she could even think of Felix, though, she had to try Jenko again. She went into her closet. Her safe was hidden behind the back wall. She batted a multitude of hanging dresses and coats away to get there. She , then hit a panel of the wall in its center. It lifted and opened. The safe had a tumbler which she twirled to the combination and voilà it opened. She grabbed the phone that rested on top of stacks of dollars and euros, dialed, and stepped back into her bedroom. A woman's voice answered, startling her. She quickly disconnected. "Who the hell was that? It wasn't Vera." She checked the number. It was correct. She sank into the side of her bed, gripping her cell. She was faced with a dilemma. Should she call back? Wait? She went to Messages and reread the last one from Jenko. He claimed Vera was dead and this Pappy's girlfriend was the shooter. Was that who answered? If it was, where was Jenko?

She closed her eyes and struggled for calmness. As Dumond advised, "Think it through." She played through the various scenarios regarding Jenko and concluded that if he was dead, it was a gain. All the ones who could talk about the bombed house and murders were themselves, forever silent. She let out a sigh of relief. But, then this Pappy. Was he alive? What did he know?

Dumond would often say, "Information is the coin of the realm." How does she find out without jeopardizing herself further? She looked around the room and her gaze fell on her lace corset hanging in the closet… Felix.

***

Monte shifted in his seat. "Monsieur l'Inspector, you must believe me when I tell you I don't know what that note means. I was minding my own business when Le Rouge took me out of my cell and informed me, I had a visitor. A visitor, who could it be? Who do I know that knows I'm in this place?"

"Go on," Ricard said.

Monte opened his eyes wide like a puppy dog pleading for a treat. "If you don't mind, Monsieur l'Inspector, another cigarette or two? My friends…"—he pointed to the cell block— "would…"

Ricard took several out. "Here's another. You'll get the rest after we're done. Depending…"

Monte grabbed the one. "*Merci, merci,*" and waited for the Inspector to light it. He inhaled deeply.

Ricard let him enjoy his puff and waited a few seconds, then moved a bit closer and directed his gaze. "Monsieur Monte, we have reason to believe you are somehow still in contact with the SLA."

A coughing fit wracked Monte. "Water," he struggled to say.

Ricard went to the water dispenser in the corner of the warden's office. Most likely the only improvement in the place. He filled a paper cup. "Maybe you should stop with the cigarettes. You'll be healthier." He handed the cup to Monte.

The prisoner gulped it down which brought on another round of hacking. He held up his hand asking Ricard to wait. The cigarette dangled in his hand. A few more throat clearings and he finally sat straight. "It's not good to do things fast. Something always goes wrong."

Ricard let that statement pass him. "Getting back to the SLA, Monsieur, are you still in contact?"

A smile crossed Monte's lips, then a hoarse laugh. "You don't really expect an answer, Inspector." His gaze roamed around the room. "There are ears where one doesn't see and eyes where one doesn't look. Particularly behind these walls." He shook his head. "Inspector, I would think you'd know." He took a long drag of his smoke. There was no coughing.

Ricard digested the response which confirmed his suspicion. It also made clear that somehow Monte was in communication with them. From the triangulation of the cellular towers surrounding the facility he believed he knew how. The prison was a haven for criminal activity even terrorism. For all he discerned, Monsieur Warden was part of it, but that was for another time. "Moving on." He dipped into his pocket and took out a small envelope. He pulled a photograph from it. "Do you recognize this person?"

Monte leaned forward, glanced at the picture, and turned his face to the inspector. His eyes blazed. "*Oui*, Monsieur l'Inspector, I know this *chien*. She…put me here. I never forget."

"What name did she use?"

Monte scratched his day-old stubble. "I believe… Susan."

"Did she use any other names?"

"We weren't that close, Inspector." His cigarette was near the end, and he took one last drag. After he exhaled, he stared at the picture again. "She was Dumond's whore, and I believe it's her life's work to destroy me."

"How so?"

He hesitated for a moment. "There are many ways, Inspector, especially in prison."

"Do you think she was behind that note?"

He licked his lips. "*Oui*, I do, *oui*. She is a devil, Monsieur l'Inspector and will stop at nothing to get me. My life is very much in danger."

"Do you believe she's in Paris?"

Monte shrugged. "I don't know, but…" He looked toward the warden's closed office door. "I may have said too much."

Ricard returned the photo to the envelope and placed it back in his pocket. He stood. " then, Monsieur Monte, we have an understanding."

"An…under… *oui,* we do. I will help you nail the bitch, and you will…"

"See that you're safe." He handed the rest of the cigarettes to the prisoner. "Make a lot of friends, Monte. You will need them."

The warden stopped Ricard on his way out.

"Monsieur l'Inspector, a word."

"*Oui*, what do you want?"

"I trust your report to your superiors will reflect my utmost cooperation." His arms crossed his chest.

"Of course, Warden Boucher, so long as you continue to do so. The prisoner and I have an understanding."

"You do?"

"*Oui*. You are to make sure nothing bad happens to him."

Boucher stared. "What do you mean?" He motioned Ricard to move away from the secretaries and re-entered the office.

"Simple," Ricard said once inside, "I'm holding you responsible for his well-being."

"This is a prison, Monsieur Inspector not a nursery."

"Let me be blunt. Your tenure here depends on it." He left Boucher gaping.

***

Ricard took a lungful of air as he got into his car. He treasured his good fortune that he could leave the dark gray buildings behind. It was a terrible thing to cage human beings like animals. On the other hand, what else was society to do when humans lose their humanity and act like wild dogs? His mind, then switched to other thoughts.

Monte believed Susan was in Paris. He had no definitive evidence of that; at best, it was a hunch. In reality, she could be anywhere… the United States even returning to Chicago. Under a different name, of course. She had so many. Ricard tapped his steering wheel trying to make sense of the received information. It was clear wherever she was, trouble followed. The note shown to Monte with the words WE KNOW could mean anything. However, it was directed to the prisoner. If Susan sent it, what was it that she knew? He had reviewed the chatter on the dark web a few days ago. It alarmed him to the extent that he had called Detective Billy Dee Jackson. Could the note and the chatter have had something to do with Detective Jackson's bombed house? He sighed. Perhaps, but such a long shot. He wiped his face. A more obvious question popped into his head. Monte. What was his role? His gut told him that Monte communicated with someone, someway. He would have to contact the techies in his department to decipher the cell phone communication. It wouldn't be beyond imagination that Monte had a hidden cell phone or the use of one.

The scenery flew by much too quickly as he entered the outskirts of Paris. He decided if nothing else, he'd give Jackson a call and relay the new developments. Monte was right about one thing; this Susan was a she-devil and a dangerous one at that.

Chapter Forty-One

Brownsburg

Priscilla's hand shook as she held onto the phone. The possibility of a wrong number was immediately replaced by her imagination running wild. She half jogged and half walked to Pappy's. Before opening the front door, she searched the street for anything out of the ordinary. Satisfied, she let herself into his house using his keys. Her first instinct was to turn on a light but realized that would attract attention. She used the phone's flashlight instead and nearly tripped over the clothes Pappy had left on the floor. "Idiot," she said under her breath. She knew the layout of the house well enough to find the kitchen and the less than secret drawer he kept money. Opening it, she found it was empty. The same with the fridge. "Shit, how did that man survive? Guess he didn't have to worry about that anymore. Poor Pappy."

He wanted so little from her. A blow job, an occasional fuck, and he was a happy man. She felt a pain in her chest for being such a bitch to him, but that was not the life she craved. She teared-up, as she went to his bedroom. His reputation as a small-town basketball star faded for her, but not him. In bed he would tell her afterward he still heard the roar of the crowd. She'd roll her eyes, none too pleased.

She had always wanted to get out of bumble-fuck U-S-A,

but now it was no longer on her terms. She sat on his unmade bed. The room was full of his basketball memorabilia. She glanced at his desk. There was a picture of her. She was in high school and the envy of all in those days. Pappy was her trophy, but each of them soon learned that was, then. Sleeping with a has-been didn't get one far.

She sighed and looked down at the phone taken from the murder scene. Five or ten minutes must have gone by and there had been no other calls. Maybe it was a wrong number. *That does happen*, she argued. She cut the phone's light, leaving it on the bed, and stepped over to Pappy's desk. She fumbled looking for the switch on the desk lamp. After two or three attempts, she succeeded in flicking it on. She studied the six-drawer desk, hesitated, then opened the top one and gingerly shuffled some of the objects. She became engrossed and began tossing things to the floor, old check books, pictures, birthday cards she had given him. He had kept them all. Without warning, she began to cry reading what she had written. God, did she play him. In another drawer, she found letters penned by him but not sent. She was taken aback by the feelings never expressed. The man loved her. She stared into the semidarkness, grasping the time-worn writings. She rubbed her eyes and searched for a Kleenex without success. She used her sleeve, , then sat motionless for a few seconds. A shiver went through her. She worked up her courage and reached for the bottom drawer. It was locked.

***

The moment they stepped outside of Priscilla's house, Shep reached for a cigarette. Callahan spit out his gum and asked if Shep could spare one.

"Help yourself, Sarge," and extended his pack.

Billy Dee glared at his partner. "I know Shep knows those are not only bad for you, but the smoke hurts the eyes. Come on, Callahan…"

"Yeah, yeah, you're preaching just like my momma. That's the reason I've been chewing gum, but" he shrugged, lit up, and inhaled deeply. "Chomping on that shit only goes so far," he said after exhaling. "After a day like today, I could smoke a pack."

"Yeah, it's been quite something." Billy Dee watched the cigarette smoke rise through the air. "You know all this smok'n, well…" He tapped his pockets.

"Oh crap, he's going for a cigar," Shep said. "Hell, there's always a price to pay."

"Damn right." Billy Dee unwrapped a Macanudo Maduro compliments of Shep from the other night. "Usually this goes after a good dinner, but improvisation is life's necessity." He cupped his hands around the open end and Shep dutifully lit it- "Boys if you're going to do the deed this …" He held the Mac away from his mouth and eyed the perfectly lit end, then took a puff. "Is what it's all about."

"Shit." Shep moved a few steps from his friend. "I'm not staying downwind from you, Billy Dee."

"Suit yourself."

An officer holding a clipboard approached Callahan.

"Where the hell you been, Davidson? I've been looking all over for you." Sarge edged his cigarette hand behind his back. "You find out anything about the car?"

"Yes sir, I did."

"Well?"

Davidson glanced at Shep and Billy Dee.

"It's all right, they're assisting. What's you got?"

The officer cleared his throat. "The car is registered in a place called Posen, Illinois, owned by a Calvin Thomas. This Mr. Thomas reported it stolen two weeks ago."

"Did you say Posen?" Billy Dee asked. "Jesus. Mind if I have a look at the paper you're holding?"

Davidson looked to Callahan who nodded his assent.

Billy Dee put on his glasses and leaned over the officer's shoulder to study the writing. He still couldn't see all the information. "Let me have that for a moment."

Davidson gave him the board.

Billy Dee planted the cigar in his mouth, holding the papers near his face.

"Any closer and you'll burn it with that damn thing in your mouth," Shep said.

Billy Dee glanced over to where his partner stood. "Just a moment," ignoring the comment, "if I'm right, this Mr. Thomas lived only a few blocks from the bombed-out garage. How's that for a coincidence?"

Shep craned his neck to peek. "You sure?"

"As sure as this cigar ain't go'n burn noth'n but the tobacco it's supposed to."

Chapter Forty-Two

Paris

Susan stood outside Felix's apartment building. She looked up to the third floor but couldn't determine if there was a light. Did he fall asleep and not believe she'd return before morning? Technically it was morning…very early…but the moon hadn't yet given way to the sun.

Her corset underneath her coat felt tighter and was beginning to chafe. Heaven forbid, she must have gained a little weight. That's what happens when working at a café. Not important, it would be a relief to have it off. How fortunate for Felix. She rang the outside intercom buzzard and waited. When no one answered, she counted to twenty in her head and pushed the bell again. She heard its shrill sound and hoped it didn't wake anyone. Another 20 count went by and still she remained outside in the dark of night half -undressed waiting for…

"Allo, who is…Danielle, is that you?"

She looked up toward Felix's apartment and noticed a light. "But of course, I told you I'd return."

"*Oui*, you did."

His voice sounded tired as if he was either just waking or annoyed. The door lock clicked, and Susan let herself in. She decided to use the stairs as the clang of the elevator could disturb those asleep.

She arrived at his floor a little out of breath and found his door closed. *Qu'est qu c'est?* She gently knocked. "Felix?"

She heard shuffling of feet, then whispers. A snap of a lock and Felix stood in the doorway with a towel around his waist.

"Danielle, you surprised me." He had an embarrassed smile on his face.

"You should know by now that's what I'm all about." She stepped forward, but he didn't move out of the way. She was a foot or two from him. "Don't you want to see what's underneath this coat?" Her hand toyed with the zipper.

His eyes went to the vacated space. It had an immediate effect, but he remained where he was.

She looked from his bulge to the pained look on his face. "Don't you…you have company?"

His face contorted turning red. He, then shrugged. "*Oui.* After I locked the café a…eh…friend…I bumped into… well, you know…"

"One of the guests who sat at the table earlier in the evening."

He hung his head and held up two fingers.

"A *ménage* à *trois*. *Très bien*, Felix. You do have stamina. I don't want to spoil your party."

She zipped her coat and stepped back.

"*Merci* and forgive me. I really didn't…"

"No problem. This is Paris and these things happen." She waited a second or two. A smile returned to his face. "A favor, Felix. Can I use your phone? Mine died. I won't be long."

***

Le Rouge waited in the corner of Boucher's office. The warden had some words with Monte, then motioned for the guard.

"Take this shit back."

"Yes sir."

"You are a good man, Le Rouge, take care of that one." The warden dismissed them.

***

"Walk faster," Le Rouge commanded.

Monte did what he could to keep up. It was difficult to retain his balance while walking with his ankles chained. "You are doing this on purpose. What's the rush? My cell isn't moving nor am I."

"Shut-up." Le Rouge placed his large hand under Monte's armpit and almost lifted him. "I'm making you look good; you fool. Bad treatment from me means your little visit with the warden didn't go well."

"Nice of you to consider my welfare. What's the cost?"

Le Rouge removed his assistance and Monte stumbled to the floor. "Get-up."

He made two attempts but tripped on the chain. "How about a hand? Or is that extra?"

"I should make you crawl back to your miserable hole, but I'm a humanitarian." He stood over Monte. "That means…"

"I know the meaning and your display to me certainly fits the definition."

Le Rouge wrinkled his face. "Huh?" A second or two went by. "*Oui.* I show it every day by not shooting the lot of you. I'd be doing society a favor, plus our taxes would be so much less, but I'm not that kind of man." He slid his arms underneath Monte's shoulders and pulled him. "You're back on your feet." He remained behind his prisoner, then whispered, "The price for my kindness is cigarettes and part of the contraband I know your grubby hands have access to. It will be on a weekly basis."

"But…"

"I'll let you know if your contributions are sufficient. *Tu comprends, mon ami?*

Monte tried turning in his direction but was pushed forward. "*Oui*, I understand."

"Live and let live," Le Rouge said and pushed Monte along until they arrived at his cell. Le Rouge motioned to other officers in the control room to open the door. "Have a pleasant day, Monsieur Monte. Get next to the bars while I remove these charming ankle bracelets from the other side."

***

Monte lay motionless on the poor excuse for a bed. The inferno tier lights were dimmed but never off. He wondered what was worse, night or day. True, during daytime one could move around, but that came with a price.

In prison, information about others, guards, even the warden, was the grease that oiled all relationships. The key was to learn more about them than they knew about you.

Night was supposed to bring quiet and safety from the noise and chatter of the day. But everyone knew the darkness was for other things. Deals through information acquired in the light of day came to fruition in the night. Scores were evened and arguments and jealousies settled.

Monte listened to the nighttime sounds of men snoring or laughing like hyenas. He considered jail disgusting and an imposition. A man like him who schemed his way out of many difficulties, shouldn't be kept in a cage. He was too valuable an asset to be held in storage. If he'd only done away with that bitch when he'd had the chance.

Night afforded him the time to review as he glumly recognized there was not much else to do. Susan or whatever name she was calling herself caused his downfall and for what? Back, then in Chicago, he realized now it was his dick that did the thinking. He could have taken the bitch and done whatever he wanted, but he believed he had time. Given the luxury of perspective, she wasn't worth the risk. In truth no woman was, then again, as he stared at his cell's ceiling, that conclusion was easy.

The truth, though, if it hadn't been for her, those Keystone Kops in Chicago would never have found him. She was the one, like the dog she is, who pointed those Chicago dicks toward him and forced him to confess to Dumond's murder.

His hand felt clammy as he touched his face. Now, he was sure Susan was out to finish him. Who else could it be? The SLA had no reason. He was important. He was one of their idea men. They owed him. But her… He would use his phone again…later when he was sure everyone was asleep. Someone answered his call last night. This time he would message. He knew full well that left a trace, but he was running out of options. With the likes of Le Rouge, Boucher, and Ricard, an enemy could indeed turn out to be a friend.

Chapter Forty-Three

Brownsburg

Priscilla didn't understand why Pappy locked a drawer. Was there something she didn't know about him? That was *People Magazine* stuff. The quiet ones who passed through lives never giving them a second thought. Turns out they hid away millions.

She licked her lips. Everything else had gone to hell today; perhaps this could be the reward. She pulled on the handle, but the lock didn't give. She looked at the pile on the floor; maybe a key was mixed in with the papers and the various objects she'd tossed. She got down on her hands and knees and sifted through the heap. God this was for shit. What was she doing? She caught her breath while sitting cross-legged her hand rested on the handle. She never thought of herself as a bad person. A little crazy, out-for-a-good time girl, but evil, not her, then why didn't she feel more remorse or sadness? Pappy was dead, and all she thought of was to learn his secrets. She glanced at the photos of him hanging on the wall in his basketball glory. Same god-damn pictures she'd stare at while he did his thing. Damn. She gripped the handle and after a wobbly start, stood. She grabbed the phone from the bed and took a step or two. What if there really was money in that drawer? If she was to get out of this mess, she needed cash. Her gaze fell on the locked fortress.

The key had to be somewhere. She dropped the cell on the bed and attacked the desk again. But her luck didn't change. Cleverness was not one of Pappy's attributes. The key was probably in plain sight. She checked the night table and his chest of drawers. "Jesus, Pappy where's the damn key?" she said, and at the same moment knew how stupid she acted. She surrendered to defeat and sat on his bed. She put her hand in her coat pocket. His keys, of course. She whipped them out and stared at four of them. One for the car, the house, the office, and wouldn't you know it. The small one fit like a glove and popped the lock.

She eyed her prize. "Pappy you've been holding out on me all this time. Here I thought you were just making it by the skin of your teeth. You little devil. You squirreled away all that green and it was right there every time we fucked. I was a fool to let you go." Her fingers entwined the handle. She felt the metal against her palm. "Okay now, here it goes." Her grip tightened.

Music suddenly erupted from the stolen phone. She could tell it was different than the one heard at her house, but Russian sounding all the same. She froze, then gasped.

***

Paris

Felix still didn't move after Susan asked to use his phone. "Felix? Your—"

"Phone?... Oh yes, of course. I'll get... Do you mind waiting out here?"

She shrugged. "I have no intention to be part of a *ménage à quatre*. Someone would be left out." She allowed a thin smile to grace her lips.

He opened his mouth, but no words came. He motioned

with his index finger to wait, and then disappeared into the apartment. She heard whispers, which became loud apologies and, then his plea for his guests to stay. He returned, tossing his cell to her. "Leave it inside the door when you're done. I've opened the phone." With that he left to attend, Susan guessed, the pleasures awaiting in his bedroom.

***

This was working better than she first thought. She quickly downloaded the app that hid the identity of the true number from which the call was made. It took a few minutes. Once the app was operative, she dialed Jenko and walked down a flight of stairs to make sure Felix didn't hear. She heard the buzz of the line waiting to connect. She hoped it would be the woman who answered before. If it wasn't, if she was wrong about Jenko, then… oh my God…

The phone indicated a connection was made by notating the passing seconds. "Hello…hello…" She heard breathing on the other end. "Jenko?"

"Who?" The female voice sounded tremulous.

"Where is Jenko? Where is Pappy?" Susan asked, her voice disguised through the app's technology.

"Who are you? What do you want?"

"Just answer the questions and you'll be safe."

"I want to know who's talking."

Susan paused and moved the phone from her ear. This was taking too long. She cleared her throat. "If you don't want any more problems, answer. Are Jenko and Pappy dead or alive?" Susan stared at a spot on the wall. The bitch better not hang-up. *Merde.* Don't hang up.

"I want…to know…who…"

"I'm not the police. I know you shot Vera…"

"What? How… do…you…? Oh my God."

Susan could hear sniffling.

"Leave …me… alone. Jenko … Vera… leave me be."

"Listen carefully. Your life hangs in the balance. Just tell me about Jenko and Pappy and you'll never hear from me again."

The words tumbled through a crescendo of crying and heavy breathing. "I… don't…know… please…please… leave …. me… Pappy… dead."

A wail erupted through Susan's receiver.

"Dead? Pappy is dead?" Susan could barely make out the answer of "yes." But she was sure that's what she heard. She ended the call and breathed a sigh of relief.

***

Brownsburg

Priscilla couldn't control her sobbing. What did they want from her? She couldn't decipher whether it was a man or a woman on the other end of the call. Who was Jenko? Was that what that shit called himself…Jenko? Jenko the hitman? She dropped the phone on the bed and rubbed her eyes with the sleeve of her jacket. This was too much. Why did anyone care…? She took several deep breaths to stop her trembling and tears. She stumbled to the bathroom and hunched over the sink. She twisted open the faucet handle and stared. The water poured out. She stood immobilized… watching. After several seconds or maybe minutes she dipped her hands under the nozzle and splashed her face. The coldness felt good as she washed herself. When done, she shut off the faucet and stood upright. No need to look at the mirror above the sink; she knew how unflattering the image would be. She returned to Pappy's bedroom and sat on his bed. There would be no end to this dilemma until she figured out the puzzle of calls and crazy persons.

Jenko and Pappy were obviously connected. Jenko was sent by someone to murder him. Why him and not Tope? Then it struck her. Tope had vanished a day or two ago. Pappy was surprised by his partner's disappearance. She was sure Pappy wasn't acting. The poor man couldn't keep a straight face when telling a lie. Besides, Tope left his car in the parking lot. How far could Tope go without his Land Rover? Then there was the matter of the safe in Pappy's trunk. Whose was it? Where did Pappy get it? For as long as she knew him, he never mentioned he had one. She glanced at the phone on the bed. Her hand shook as she retrieved it and studied the recent received number. The area code was unfamiliar as well as the number itself. Should she call back? What if she told the person that Jenko was alive but ran away? What if… She cast a glance at the unlocked bottom desk drawer.

***

Billy Dee took the cigar out of his mouth. "Now that we have a clue about the car in the driveway, anyone find Pappy's or Priscilla's vehicle? It's, what, five miles from the office to here. I doubt he walked."

Callahan nodded. "Good point. I know Pappy's. It's an old jalopy." He stepped toward the street. "Don't see it." Callahan looked at his watch. "You boys ain't going to believe it, but my shift is over in five minutes. I'm not allowed overtime unless the captain says okay."

"Are you going to call him?" Shep asked.

Callahan cleared his throat. "The amount of paperwork ain't worth it. To tell you the truth, I've had it." He dropped his cigarette and rubbed it out with the heel of his shoe.

"I've seen more blood and bodies in the last few hours than in all my years on the force. I'm turning things over to my replacement, Sgt. Brody. He should be here in a few minutes. I'll give you a lift to your car if you'd like."

Billy Dee glanced at his partner. "I guess we'll take the ride."

They stayed at the scene for another ten minutes. They were introduced to Sgt. Brody and Callahan briefed him as to the developments. That done, Callahan motioned Billy Dee and Shep to get in his squad. It didn't take long to drive back to Pappy's real estate office. The building was surrounded by yellow police tape and cops were still at the site.

Callahan rolled down a window as he pulled next to one of the officers in front. "Anything new, Sam?"

He sidled up to the driver's window. "That you, Callahan?"

"Yeah, it's me."

"Who are…"

"They're cops from Chicago," he said in an irritated tone.

"Chicago? That's a long way from here."

"It's a long story. What about…?"

"You mean what's going on in there?" Sam pointed to the building.

"Yeah, in there."

"We're waiting for the prints on the victim. One shot did her. Ballistics thinks the bullet came from the same gun found at Priscilla's."

"Well, that's progress."

Sam smiled. "Guess so. You going off duty, Sarge?"

Callahan sighed. "Yeah, need a whole lot of somethin' after today. I'm letting these two Chicago guys off. Their car is nearby. Give them a hand if they need anything."

"No problem, Sarge."

Billy Dee and Shep got out of Callahan's squad.

"We'll keep in touch," Billy Dee said.

"Sure thing. Goodnight boys. Have a safe trip." Callahan drove off.

"I've been thinking," Billy Dee said as they reached their vehicle.

Shep stopped. "That's a bad sign."

"Listen, Callahan never mentioned if anyone went to this Pappy's house. We know Priscilla left. Where did she go and how? I've got a feeling…"

"Shit, you and your feelings. Do you know the time? If we leave now, we won't be home by midnight."

"True, but… I'll call Janine. She'll understand."

Shep eyed him. "Your wife has become more understanding? You're old and you've lost your mind." He pointed to the cigar. "Must be all that smoke from that damn thing in your hand." He shifted his weight. "Forget about it, I'm pretty sure my bosses won't like it."

Billy Dee waited a minute or two. "Hell, what's the difference if we're home at midnight or three a.m.? We're going to feel like shit in the morning. What if we get something to eat, then go to that house? I'm sure you'll feel better."

"I don't know… I am sort-of hungry. Okay, let's get something to eat, then decide."

"You got it. Just in case, I'll ask Sam for the address and directions. Shep, you'll do better on a full stomach."

Chapter Forty-Four

Paris

Ricard parked in front of the headquarters of the Prefecture de Police at 1 rue de Lutrec. He should have been home with his new wife, Giselle, enjoying the bliss of recent marriage. Instead, he was at headquarters for an appointment with Monsieur Robert Suvé, tech wiz with cell phone transmissions.

Giselle being an ex-officer herself would certainly understand. He smiled, then winced as the memories soared through his head.

He lost his first wife about a year before Giselle came into his life as his assistant. He was working on the Dumond murder case, and Susan, the very same Susan, Monte believed was out to get him, had surfaced as a person of interest due to her relationship with Dumond. Giselle superficially looked similar to Susan. A disgruntled and violent investor in one of Dumond's schemes kidnapped Giselle, believing he had taken Dumond's mistress. He wanted to even the score. Luck showed its hand, thank God, and he rescued Giselle before any more harm came. Susan disappeared…until now. As for Giselle, the rest as they say, was magic.

Ricard sent his wife a brief message with regrets that he would be late. He sighed as he got out of the car. He was feeling his age. A man in his late fifties having served more than two decades was more than enough. Perhaps he should retire, then again, what would he do all day? He knew himself better. There was something to be said for working through a case. Despite the many defeats and blind alleys, reaching that singular moment when the pieces came together was what drove him and those like him. It was the satisfaction in making a small difference but a difference just the same.

He marched up the sweeping staircase and entered the building. He showed his I.D. to the sergeant at the desk and waited for him to call Suvé. After a nod and instructions to take the "D" bank elevators he went on his way.

Ricard was familiar with the building and had no problem finding the correct elevator. He had been to Suvé's cramped office space in the basement a few times. It was easy to miss, though. The powers that be were only beginning to appreciate the intricacies of the modern world that included the internet and cellular activities.

Suvé met Ricard as he stepped out.

"*Bonjour* Robert," Ricard said as they shook hands.

"*Bonjour,* what brings you to my desert island?"

Ricard explained his meeting with the prisoner Monte and his belief that he was using a hidden cell phone. They reached Suvé's office. His desk as well as the area around him had all sorts of equipment strewn about.

"Just move the stuff and find a seat. As you can see, space is at a premium. "Tell me again what you'd like me to do."

Ricard went over the information he had.

"What you are asking is not impossible, but it will take time." Suvé took out his cell phone as well as a blank sheet of paper. "All cell phones have identifying numbers. One is called IMEI which is tied to the SIM card and is used to identify the subscriber and services." He looked at Ricard.

"You understand so far?"

"*Oui*, of course."

"I'll write all this down."

"*Merci*."

"Where was I?"

"Something about IMEI."

"*Bon*. The other is IMSI, which is a number unique to the SIM card. Once the phone connects to an IMSI catcher, the identity of the caller is revealed. The IMEI acts like a fingerprint. The fifteen-digit number assigned to it is unique to each device." He handed Ricard the paper.

"*Merci*." Ricard stuffed the note in his pocket and leaned forward. "So it sounds like Monte's phone would not be difficult to find."

Suvé sat back. A smile crossed his face. "*Oui* and *non*. We will need an Inquiry to get the records from the tower near the prison. Then, we would have to find a way to eliminate the calls used by personnel."

"I see." Ricard felt a pit in his stomach. "How long would it take?"

Suvé shrugged. "Depends upon the volume of calls and the period you request on the Inquiry. The shorter the time the less to review."

Ricard drummed his hand on the desk, then got up. "I'll have the application for Inquiry on your desk by tomorrow, then you'll get started."

Suvé stood. "As you can see, your matter is not the first."

"I'll owe you one if you squeeze me in. It's important."

"It's always important. I'll see what I can do. *A demain*."

***

Prison taught Monte patience. When he got on the outside, that attribute would be his difference. Another long night lay ahead, but this time there would be success. He was sure of it. There was obviously someone attached to the number he called yesterday. It must be the same contact that set-in motion his idea to inflict pain on the Chicago *flic* by blowing up his house. What a surprise that must have been. As far as Ricard and the other bullshit, they needed time to catch up. He was still ahead. The idiots and that included Bucher and Le Rouge haven't found his phone, and he was pretty sure, they wouldn't. He had to strike while he still had the chance. He had to find the bitch and put an end to her, then on to the next chapter.

***

Susan deleted the app on Felix's phone, then walked up the stairs to his apartment. She stood by the door for a minute or two. A smile crossed her lips at hearing erotic sounds escaping from the bedroom. Whether it was her pride or libido she considered changing her mind and joining in. Why wear the revealing corset for nothing? Her looks, body, and knowhow would add spice to the party. She imagined the effect on Felix. He'd be drooling all over himself. Then she heard a woman's voice scream his name. That changed everything. It was not worth coming in at the end. She placed his closed cell inside the door and left. She had other things to do.

It was still dark outside as Susan began to walk. She kept an eye for a cab, but at this hour, she'd be fortunate to hail one.

Paris in the twilight between night and dawn was not asleep. Lovers walked slowly down a boulevard. On another street, women appearing to be in their 30s or 40s made their way home. Some would have stories they kept warm in their hearts; others seem to plod, each step displaying the heaviness of an affair gone wrong.

Susan noticed it all. She knew Paris well. She walked along, her mind turning to the information learned from her recent call. Whoever she had talked with confirmed that anyone who knew of the mayhem she caused wasn't around to tell the tale. Now she had to maneuver those deaths to Monte's doorstep. The letter option with Felix acting as the delivery boy was no longer viable. She'd have to use her other phone to, as it was said in America, "drop a dime" and let the consequence enfold.

Chapter Forty-Five

Brownsburg

Priscilla looked from the stolen phone to the unlocked bottom desk drawer. It was now or never. She clutched the cell in one hand, knelt, grabbed the drawer's handle, and pulled. The rollers on the bottom screeched as if they hadn't been opened in a while. She put the phone on the floor and used both hands. She overcame the resistance and stared at a row of thick manilla file envelopes. *What the hell?* She yanked one out. There was a name on the front and an address. The file was packed with papers. She grabbed a few and flipped through them, not understanding what they meant. She groped her way through the file, letting the papers fall at her feet. As the file thinned, she gripped something that hugged the bottom of the folder. She held the envelope between her legs and peeked inside. *Holy shit…cash…* "Ernest money" was written on a yellow sticky note that clung to the first of a wad of bills. The money had a large rubber band wrapped around it. A tremor went through her. It couldn't be. Quiet, unassuming Pappy kept, stole? client's money? No wonder someone wanted to kill him. She turned to the drawer and tried to quickly count the number of files. She got to 10 when she heard noise. A car door slammed, then voices. *Maybe they aren't coming here.* She tried to calm the pounding of her heart. Cops? Friends of what's his name… Jenko. She grabbed the phone and the money. She glanced at the cell's blank screen. Her breathing reverberated around the bedroom. She heard footsteps trudging up the front stoop. *Oh my God, it has to be cops. I got to get out…hide…do something.* She jumped up and grabbed her coat from the bed. Wildly looking around the room, she almost tripped on the papers. *Shit.* She looked at the desk…the light… The doorbell rang, then came pounding on the front door.

***

"Billy Dee give me one good reason why we didn't stop to eat first. You said yourself I do better on a full stomach. Damn it, I'm hungry. But…nooo… you drag me to this godforsaken town, with bullet-laden bodies falling all over the place, and somehow, I listen to you and wind up driving to this Pappy's house. Why am I such a fool?"

"Shep, you carryin' on worse than my wife. We're just go'n to take a look-see, then sit down to a fine dinner." He paused to let Shep soak up the full effect. "My treat."

"Damn right you're pay'n, and we're not going to some drive-in McDonald's or something."

Billy Dee turned away and glanced out the passenger window. "I think we're close. Hard to tell which house." Billy Dee strained to catch an address number as they drove down the street onto the next block. "Stop. Didn't Callahan say Pappy drove a beater?"

Shep pulled alongside an older model vehicle. "Yeah, he did, but he didn't say anything else."

"You see any other jalopies in the vicinity?"

"Not at the moment. I'll drive to the end of the street, then come back and find a parking space." Shep checked the mirrors, then made an illegal 3-point turn at the corner. It took driving two blocks until they found an empty space.

"Well, I'll be, I think Pappy's is across the street. Looks pretty dark."

"Why wouldn't it?" Shep said getting out of the car, "isn't he dead?"

Billy Dee nodded. "Uh-huh, then what's his car doing here." He raised the palm of his hand to quiet his partner. "I know what you think'n. The beater may not be his, but what if it is."

Shep sighed. "We could be halfway home by now."

"Come on, Shep. What's another few minutes? This could be the break in the case."

"Jesus, you are one…okay, we'll check it out."

They crossed the street and climbed the three steps of the stoop.

"You do the knocking," Billy Dee said.

"Why me?"

"You're the one with the real badge."

"It don't make a difference. We're not in our jurisdiction."

"Right. Do it anyway. I'm behind you."

"Damn it, I'm listening to you again."

Shep rang the bell, then pounded on the door. No one answered.

"Try the knob. Maybe it's unlocked," Billy Dee suggested.

"Wait now, even if it's open, we don't have a right to go in without someone from this town with us."

"Shep, we've been with Callahan and his boys all day. They aren't a crackerjack force. If there's something to see, we'll call them."

Shep put his hand on the doorknob. "We're talk'n a big juicy steak, now. Don't even think of getting away with anything less."

"Gotcha. Open the eff'n door."

Chapter Forty-Six

Paris

Susan let herself into her apartment. The sun was peeking over the horizon. For most a new day, for her, it was nearing the end of a very long one. She slipped off her coat, then stepped into her bedroom and took off the damn corset. She caught her naked reflection in the floor-length mirror hanging from the closet door. Felix certainly missed out. She grabbed an old flannel shirt off a hanger and put it on. The length went below her thigh. *Much better*, then she retrieved her other phone from the concealed safe at the back of the closet. She went to the kitchen, filled a tea kettle, and turned on the stove. Coffee might not be the right drink before sleeping, but there were things yet to do. She filled her French press with ground espresso beans taken from her job at the Café Deux Magots. While waiting for the water to boil, she popped a croissant into the microwave. That never would have happened had she not lived in Chicago. The very thought of microwaving pastry was so un-French. *C'est la vie.* There was no time to visit a patisserie. Besides, they wouldn't open for another hour or so.

The microwave and kettle finished within seconds of each other. She placed the warm pastry on a plate and set it on the small kitchen table. The steam from the kettle felt good on her face as she poured the water into the press and worked the plunger. The coffee dripped dark into her cup. She took a sip before sitting. The strong bitter taste jolted her. The bitterness dissipated after biting into the croissant. They made for a wonderful combination. She eyed her phone as the flavors melded in her mouth.

Bon, she had dallied enough. Another sip, then she opened the cell. Her eyes widened as an uncoded message was displayed.

"Contact me. There is a traitor among us."

Qu'est que c'est? She instantly recognized the number. Her hand slammed the table. The bastard. How stupid leaving a plainly worded text message, then again, Jack Monte thought he was smarter than most. She stared at the text, then realized the little shit believed he'd reached the SLA. The thought went down better than the espresso and croissant. Time was ticking, Jack Monte, but not in a good way.

She saw the message was sent an hour ago. He must be anxious. The pressure had gotten to him. Poor boy. It must be hard to wait in a prison cell. She wondered what he did to pass the time. She smiled. All those men and nothing to relieve the tension. A pity.

She finished her espresso and croissant and brushed away the crumbs. More than 20 minutes had gone by. It must be unbearable for him. Would he send another message? She decided to wait another 10 minutes. She washed the plate and cup, then returned to the kitchen table. She reopened the phone. There were no other posts. She pressed the app that concealed the true telephone number as well as voice. She heard the clicks, then the buzz.

"Allo?" a male voice tensely whispered after the second ring.

"You broke the first rule of communications," her voice disguised, "you know better. You have put all of us in jeopardy and you will pay for this stupidity."

"I'm sorry," he pleaded, "but..." The whine of air passed

through the connection. "I … don't … much…longer…" His words poured out, "Find Susan Dumond. She was the traitor."

She swallowed hard when Monte said her name and squeezed her hands. "I will break a rule too." She paused. "Monte," her voice crackling, "it was your idea to bomb that cop's house in Chicago. There are now five dead bodies because of your idiotic plan. Five. This Susan Dumond had nothing to do with that. But you, you, Jack Monte, did." She clicked off.

***

"Allo, allo," Monte repeated into the phone. He took the cell from his ear and stared at the blank screen. His hand shook. Five deaths. Impossible. How? He fell into his cot, his phone concealed in his hand. He was done for. They would come for him whether in the dark of night or the brightness of day. Would it be a guard or a prisoner? He wiped his face with his free hand. Did it matter? His hope was that it would be quick… a knife to the heart. He slowly stretched out and returned the mobile to its hiding place. Perhaps he should get rid of it. He had no more use for it. He played with that notion as he stared at the ceiling.

The sound of a man screaming interrupted his thoughts. Another inmate having a bad night. Someone yelled "shut up" and the noise stopped. He eyed the small crack near the corner of his cell. How could he have been so stupid as to send an uncoded message? He argued his defense. Time and fear played a part. The walls were closing in, and he had panicked. His mind reviewed the entire conversation. Did the voice at the other end change when he spat out the name, Susan Dumond? Did he imagine it? He lay still waiting for an answer, then something struck him. He turned and grabbed the phone from its hiding place and examined the number to which he sent the message to the number attached to the call. "*Merde*." They were different. He sat up. Was the she-devil behind all of this? Was that Susan herself? It was preposterous, he argued. The fantasy of a crazy and desperate mind. How was that possible? He got off his cot and began to pace. The voice he heard was…hard to tell…male, female? The language was French, but the accent blunted, as if a machine… A machine. He looked at his cell again. Technology could make anything possible. If that was the she-devil… then he… he must save himself if only to have the tables turn on her. There was not much left of his life. It would be worth the price. He would have to wait until later in the morning, then he'd contact Inspector Ricard. He glanced at his cot and decided why not. His body crumbled into the mattress. He fought off sleep to re-hide the phone. After that, he stared at the same spot in the ceiling. His breathing became shallow, he could feel a smile cross his lips. That old saying of something about the enemy of my enemy… he chuckled and closed his eyes. Morning.

***

For Felix, daylight came as a surprise. It seemed only 5 to 10 minutes had passed since his delightful guests left and he fell asleep. The clock on his nightstand told a different story. Still, he figured at most he had three hours of sleep, not enough to get through the day, much less a night of work. He stayed in bed and marveled at how fortunate…*non*, that was the wrong thought. It wasn't luck that attracted those women. It was his magnetism, and his persuasive abilities. He was sure they each had a good time. Hell, he certainly did. Their names already forgotten but not their bodies. *Il fait bon vivre á Paris.* Life was good in Paris.

He fought nature's call for as long as he could, but finally got up. He lumbered his way to the bathroom and relieved himself. Should he return to bed or make coffee? He rubbed his arms to loosen the ache in his muscles. It had been some kind of night. The two women were quite physical. He congratulated himself on his stamina and endurance even though 40 was not in the too distant future. He decided he could recount the triumphs over a morning brew just as well as lying in bed. He trudged his way to the kitchen, then remembered he didn't have his phone. He returned to the bedroom and searched. After a minute or two he stopped, scratched his head. A gnawing feeling began to well in the pit of his stomach. Did one of those bitches steal his phone? What about his wallet? He quickly found his pants. His wallet was securely in its back pocket, then it dawned on him. Danielle. She came by. For a second or two, he wondered if she too participated, then remembered. He hurried to his front door and spotted the cell. *Thank God.* He picked it up and opened it. There was a message thanking him for using an app and, then informed him of the many ways the app can hide messages and phone calls. *What the hell?* Was this a joke? He looked further and saw a phone number and a time. What was this? He retreated into the kitchen. Coffee would be just the thing to have. After that, he would sort this out.

Chapter Forty-Seven

Brownsburg

"Before I open this eff'n door, you better have your piece out," Shep instructed Billy Dee. "We're not going to shoot up the place."

"No, but if that car parked on the street was Pappy's and he's dead, then someone drove it here, and that's got to be Priscilla."

"You make a fine detective. I'll go first and you cover me. You've got the badge and the right to that weapon."

"So do you. Don't you?"

Billy Dee shrugged. "Yeah, I guess, but you're official and I'm not."

"Jesus. I'm telling you again we should call Callahan, then our behinds are protected."

"Given that he's already signed out, he won't be happy if we don't find something."

Shep took a deep breath. "Arguing with you is exhausting. Okay, go first. I'll cover."

Billy Dee and Shep changed places. He waited a second or two, then turned the doorknob. "Damn, where the hell is the light?" he said stepping over the threshold.

"Use your phone."

Billy Dee stopped and patted his coat pockets. "Never can find the damn thing when you need it." He, then tapped his pants. "Got it." He stared at it. "Where the hell is the flashlight on this thing."

"Move out of the way. Jesus, you are a pain. You cover, okay?"

Billy Dee stepped aside and drew his gun. "I got your back."

Shep glanced at his partner. "I have all the confidence in the world. You see a switch?"

Billy Dee followed the beam. "It's on the wall to your left."

Shep went in that direction and flipped it. Light revealed the living room.

Billy Dee let out a low whistle after holstering his weapon. "Lord have mercy. Either someone went through the place, or…"—he shook his head—"a poor excuse for a bachelor pad. Janine wouldn't stand for something like this. Hell, she'd kick me out of my own place…clothes on the floor, dishes on the couch."

"You're lucky she doesn't throw you out now."

"Thanks, you're a real friend."

"I try to be. You see anything of interest; blood, something more out of place?"

Billy Dee inspected the couch. A dish with some sort of red sauce crusted on it sat near a faded pillow. Across from it was a chair with newspapers on its seat and arms. He bent down and examined the clothes on the floor. "Nothing other than he was a slob."

"What's the date on those papers?"

"Got to get my glasses." Billy Dee retrieved them from his shirt pocket. "Looks like…two days ago. Wait. There's one from yesterday."

Shep took a step toward his partner. "I say we've done enough. There's nothing here."

Billy Dee's jaw dropped. "What's wrong with you? There's the rest of the house."

"Yeah, I know, but…" He moved closer. "I got a funny feeling," his tone almost a whisper. He pointed to an object on the floor next to the chair.

Billy Dee looked, then retrieved it. He held it between his forefinger and thumb. "What's an earring doing there?" He caught Shep's gaze that led to the hallway, and he assumed the bedrooms. He and Shep redrew their weapons and took defensive positions behind furniture.

"Priscilla," Billy Dee called, "this is the police. Come out with your hands in the air. We know you're there. No one is going to hurt you."

The two looked at each other after waiting several seconds. "Try again," Shep said.

"Priscilla, Sgt Callahan sent us to find you. We want to know what happened. You know Pappy's dead as well as the other man. What went on at your house?"

Seconds ticked by, then they heard rustling as if someone walked on paper. "Don't shoot, please, don't…"

A shadowy figure emerged. Her arms were raised above her head as she came into focus.

"I have…a…phone… It's in my hand. Don't shoot." Her voice was a mixture of a plea and hysteria.

Billy Dee moved toward her. "Everything will be all right, miss. Bring your arms down slowly. Anyone else with you or in the room back there?"

"No, just me." She lowered her hands.

He saw the phone. "Have a seat," Billy Dee brushed the newspapers from the living room chair and holstered his gun. "You are Priscilla?" Billy Dee stepped closer.

She nodded. She seemed lost in the chair. Her face tearstained. Her hair unkempt. Callahan was right about her figure even though she was disheveled.

"That's Detective Sheppard and I'm Detective Jackson. You're not under arrest. We'd like to know what happened.

I'm sure it's been a terrible day for you."

Her eyes widened. "You have no idea. It's…" She trembled and her jaw quivered. "I…was…Pa..Pappy's…girl…" The dam broke and she began to wail.

Billy Dee stood motionless for several seconds, taking it all in. "Sorry about Pappy. This must be very hard. What happened?"

Priscilla wiped her eyes with her hand and used her sleeve for her nose. She fought to catch her breath and after two or three attempts quieted down. "Can you get me a Kleenex? There's some in the bathroom."

Billy Dee asked Shep to get it.

He returned a minute or two later. "Bathroom is clear, here's a box." He pulled Billy Dee aside and used his index finger to point to the hallway. "I'll check it out."

Priscilla blew her nose and held on to the tissue.

"How did all this happen?" Billy Dee asked, brushing chips off the couch.

She glanced at Billy Dee. "I went to Pappy's office. Pappy wasn't there, then the guy you found at my house, I think his name was Jenko, busted in along with a woman."

"How do you know his name?"

"What? Oh, his name. This is his phone. There was a message sent to him…"

"Hold on, lady. How did you get it?"

"I took it. After the shooting at my house, I took it. I don't know why, but I did, then someone called and…and…"

Billy Dee put his palm up. "Slow down. Tell me exactly what happened. Start again from the beginning."

Priscilla took a deep breath. "Okay," nodding, "I'll try again."

As Priscilla began, she stopped every few seconds and not so subtly looked toward the bedroom area. Her eyes widened and her face turned paler. Her recounting of events rambled even more. Billy Dee's focus strayed toward where Shep had gone. "What'cha doing back there?"

His partner returned a few minutes later with two files in hand. "There's more, but this is all I could carry. Explain these?"

"I…I…don't know. I had no idea Pappy…"

"I'll tell you what it looks like," Shep said, putting the files on the floor. He reached into one of them and clutched a fistful of hundreds. "Pappy seemed to have been playing with other people's money."

Priscilla hung her head. "Yeah, I…never knew."

Shep turned to Billy Dee and said under his breath, "I'm calling Callahan. He better get his ass down here."

Billy Dee nodded, then turned to Priscilla. "What did you know?"

Before she could say anything, the phone she'd been holding went off. She gasped.

"Aren't you going to answer?"

"No…no… it must…be… Here!" She threw the cell to him.

He put the phone to his ear. "Hello, this is Detective Jackson. Who's this?"

Chapter Forty-Eight

Paris

Felix sat at his kitchen table with a cup of espresso in
hand. The warmth of the liquid and caffeine made the
morning bearable. God, he was sore. He smiled into his
cup. Who needs a gym when one can get a great workout
by other means? He laughed and ran his hand through
his thick hair. *Oui*, it was quite a workout. He looked
across the table, knowing there was no one else there.
A small inconvenience, not to share the morning with…
It'd be a headache. She'd complain, the coffee wasn't…
She wanted a baguette, and he served pastry. No, it was
better this way. Have fun with them at night, and then
resume your life. He was the boss. He took another sip.
But… He waved away the thought. It came back. Danielle.
He caught his breath. Would she be sitting across from
him this morning?

Their lovemaking of the other night had intensity if not
all the physical razzle dazzle, but even while doing it, she
was there, physically hell yes, but… mysterious, like holding
onto the tail of a tigress for a second or two, but the energy
forced you to let go. *What the hell did I do?* Why did he
need those others?

Trust. He didn't believe she would come back to his apartment. Those other women fell in his lap, so why not? A sure

thing versus a strong wind. Nothing to be guilty about. It was a great night.

He ran a finger around the rim of his cup. He would once again use his charm on Danielle. Hell, she seemed to understand. She'd forgive him. All women wanted to have a chance to tame him. They saw it as a challenge. Danielle… was no different.

He held the cup to his lips and realized there was no more. He put it down, then saw the phone. What was all that about an app and…? He grabbed and opened it. He stared at the number. He was sure the prefix was USA. What the hell? He pressed on the digits. He heard connections being made, then a voice.

"This is Detective Jackson. Who is this?

"Allo, *bonjour. Qui es tu?*"

"What? Are you speaking French?"

Felix stared at the phone. Detective? Jackson? He was aware of his heavy French accent. "I must have the wrong number," he said in English, and quickly disconnected. He slid the phone away from him as if it were poisonous. "What the fuck did Danielle do?"

***

The soft purring of an alarm clock intruded on Inspector Ricard's sleep. He opened his eyes. His wife, Giselle, was blissfully curled next to him. He gazed at the rhythm of her breathing, amazed at his good fortune. As quietly as he could, he leaned over to the night table and hit the Off button.

"Who's calling this early? Is it morning?" Giselle asked.

"Ssh, go back to sleep. It's only the alarm." He sat up and had one foot on the floor.

"You're not leaving, already?"

"*Non*, it'll be a minute. I'll go to the other room."

She sat up and wrapped the bed sheet around her. "Alain, is this about…?"

"Not to worry. I'll explain later. You're safe." He kissed her on her forehead, , then left the bedroom. Other men would think him crazy to leave a warm bed with such a woman. He must be and sighed. *Always the work, it never ends.* He took his cell phone off the charger in his small office and closed the door. He checked the time again and loosely calculated that it was around 10 p.m. in Chicago. He opened his phone contacts, then dialed.

"Allo, Billy Dee Jackson?"

"Who's this?"

"This is Inspector Ricard… Alain. How are you?" He heard breathing into the phone.

"Inspector… Alain? Paris? Lord, this is a surprise. You're not going to believe…"

"Anything is possible."

"Ain't that the truth. You were right about that Internet chatter you heard a while ago. My house was blown up."

"*No! Je suis désolée.* I'm so sorry. I had a terrible feeling when I read all that talk. I wish somehow, I could have prevented it. Were you or your wife… eh, Janine, hurt?

"No, it happened while we were in the air returning from Paris. The bastards' welcome home gift, I guess."

"*Mon Dieu.* Terrible news." He grasped the phone tighter. "Listen, Billy Dee, I may have information that's a little more helpful. I paid a visit to Jack Monte in prison."

"That little shit."

"The same. He told me an interesting story with a familiar character, *la femme* Susan Dumond."

"Susan Dumond. I'll be a dog looking for its tail. The woman gets around. What did she do now?"

"We don't know exactly, but…" He searched for the

proper English words. "I think Monte has a cell phone that he used to contact the SLA. This Susan may also be communicating with him. It is only a guess, but…my gut tells me somehow your house and these two were involved."

"Holy crap. Those two again." He cleared his throat. "What's this about a cell phone?

"*Oui*. I'll be looking into it later this morning.

"Jesus, Lord. I'm in the middle of an investigation right now and not just ten minutes ago, someone called. He spoke French. When I asked his name, he said in English he had the wrong number."

"Do you remember Monte's voice? Did it sound like him?"

"Hmm. Monte…no…no I don't think so. I'd recall it. This guy's French and accent sounded real unlike Monte's. The call came in on the phone that belonged to a foreign guy who we believe was a hit man."

"A what?"

"Hit man, a guy who kills for money."

"Clever. You have a name of this 'hit man'?"

"Let me see, I wrote it on my pad…Jenko, J..e..n..k..o. Don't know whether that's his first or last name. Funny thing when I tried calling back, the call failed."

"That was strange. Billy Dee, you know there are, how you say, ah, apps that decoy telephone numbers. I'm not sure how it works, though. What was the number you dialed?"

Ricard heard Billy Dee ask someone how to find that information, followed by several voices.

"Okay got it."

Ricard wrote it down. "One more thing, do you have Jenko's number?"

"It'll take me a bit. I'll text it to you."

"Very well. *Merci. Mon meilleur a* Janine. I'm sorry about your house."

"Thank you, Alain. Best to yours."

Ricard returned his cell to the charger, then sat at his desk. He envisioned a very busy morning. There was an Inquiry to prepare, and these telephone numbers to track down. What stuck in his mind, though, was the call Billy Dee received. Was it from a Frenchman? Did the call come from Paris? He stared at the number. He knew the prefix for Paris and France was "331," and the incoming call Billy Dee received had those numbers. Although, given technology, it wasn't a certainty that indeed the call came from France. Why not start there? He went to his phone and dialed. The mechanical voice claimed it was a nonexistent number or misdialed. How strange. He was back to square one. He walked around his desk to the window. It was still dark outside, much too early. He shut the light and returned to bed. He wrapped an arm around his wife.

"Everything all right?" she asked in a sleepy voice.

"I guess, for now."

She opened her eyes, and a smile crossed her lips. "Alain, let's have a cozy dinner at one of our favorite places…Café Deux Magots."

"Dinner? It's not even… Deux Magots… Giselle, you are a genius". He sat up. "Felix."

Chapter Forty-Nine

Paris

Susan stood by her breakfast table. Dumond had warned her about the danger of seeking revenge.

They were in Dumond's kitchen. As he waited for the water to boil, he gave Susan one of his looks. His eyes grew wide. The eyebrow over it endowed with the ability to question. Were they at breakfast, after dinner, or after…? Did they argue? Did she threaten to get back at him for some slight. She didn't remember.

The scene though, stayed with her. He leaned over the table, using his arms for support, his face near hers, and stared at her for a moment, then he went to the sink and picked up a knife. He held it gingerly, then ran his hand over the top. He held out his palm. "Not a scratch or a nick, but revenge, unlike this, has a razor edge on both sides. The chances of getting cut are quite good, no matter how careful you may be."

Was her scheme to finish Monte backfiring? He's probably figured out that she was behind the note, the calls, the bombing, and murders. How does he blame it on her without admitting his role? She glanced around the room, then answered her question. He couldn't. They would both go down if he had the balls. She drummed her hand on the table. He may have decided, what the hell, he was already in prison, more years added was of little consequence, and worth the chance to destroy her. What connected him to her? Easy, the goddamn phone lying on the table. Get rid of the cell, and if the police can't find her... She lifted her empty coffee cup from the table, gazed at it for a moment. *Voila'*. She didn't need to drop a dime on him. He'd do it himself.

***

Monte stood in the breakfast line, shifting his weight, scanning his surroundings like he had some sort of radar antenna. Get the food, find a place to sit, then subtly leave and get to the warden's office to contact Ricard. No wasting time on the riffraff and gossip. Eat and disappear. In the real world a simple plan, but in prison…*merde*. There was always a hiccup or two. A nosy son-of-a-bitch who out of the blue makes conversation. If he's ignored, then he's insulted, and that could lead… It was exhausting running down all the possibilities. Patience, Monte counselled. Smile at the bastard. "Pardon, I didn't hear. What was it you said? *Excusez-moi*, no disrespect. Please take my seat. You can have the rest of my pastry as well as the coffee. I must go. See you around."

The usual guards were posted at various stations. They were there to protect inmates from fights, or worse, stabbings. In truth, not a one could be trusted. A couple of euros or cigarettes or whatever the coin and their eyes glazed, looking elsewhere until the deed was done.

Monte was a few steps from the doorway that led to the corridor. He slipped a 10-euro note into the palm of one of the guards who suddenly moved away. He no sooner crossed over the threshold when Le Rouge, the guard, came out of nowhere and stopped him. His smile was of a giant ready to pounce.

"Did you already forget our conversation from yesterday, Monsieur Monte?" He spit out the last two words. "There is a cost for my benevolence and watchful eye over you."

Monte lowered his gaze and stared at the floor.

"Do you have a pass? If not, you broke a rule and that, *mon ami*, costs."

Monte shuddered; the pressure from everything built within. He fought to steady his emotions although a part of him envisioned tearing the arms off Le Rouge. He couldn't do it. His frustration took over and he looked his tormentor squarely in the face. His voice unnaturally steady, "I'm going to the warden's office to contact Inspector Ricard. I have information." He paused, never taking his eyes off Le Rouge. "Lay a hand on me and you'll answer to higher powers. *Comprendez vous?*"

Le Rouge continued to hover over Monte, but his facial expression, especially his eyes that were seconds ago fierce and alert, showed a tinge of fear like the dread prisoners felt upon his approach, then like a snake whetting its appetite he changed and said, "*Excusez moi*, please Monsieur Monte, let me escort you to the warden's office. I'm sure he'd be most pleased."

Monte grasped his mistake as they began their walk. *Think!* The fatigue from little sleep attacked. Through the haze, he realized the warden would never let him call. Each step brought his demise closer. *Think.* He stopped and did something he shouldn't. He grabbed Le Rouge's jacket. "Listen, you are a pragmatic man. Let me use your phone to reach Ricard. I will tell him how you helped. I'm sure you'll be rewarded."

Le Rouge stared at Monte's fingers clasping his uniform. He slowly placed his huge hand over the prisoner's. "Don't you ever…" and applied pressure as Monte's face paled. Tears glistened at the corner of his eyes

"Please, please, I'm sorry, please," the words spoken in gasps as the pain grew.

A smile decorated the guard's face. "So, you are not so smart after all, Monsieur Monte." He loosened his grip. "You do not want to see the warden? You lied? Were you thinking of escaping?"

Monte shook his head wildly. "*Non, non*, please." He caught his breath. "I… have… Ricard…" He looked up at Le Rouge. "… stand… next… to me. Believe me, I have… nothing to gain… by lying. I swear. Ricard… will advance… your career." He rubbed his hands slowly, trying to recover.

Le Rouge grabbed the front of Monte's shirt and half dragged him to an empty room off the corridor. "You expect me to take the word of a worm like you? A disgrace of a man? A cockroach I caught sneaking out of the mess hall with a bullshit excuse of wanting to see the warden. How stupid do you think—"

Monte's knees crumbled. He would have sunk to the floor had Le Rouge let go. "Call Ricard," he said in a whimper. "I'm begging."

The guard held him for a second or two longer, then watched Monte stumble as he removed his grip. "Stand like a man."

Monte tried to obey. His hands went to his sides, head straight and chest out as best he could. His eyes, though, blinked as he waited for either a punch, a kick, or…

"What is the information you say you have?"

Monte licked his lips. "It's about… about…" He took a deep breath. "Chicago. I know something of what happened there a few days ago. Please." Sweat dripped down his face, but he didn't move.

"Chicago? What does that have to do with…"

"It's complicated. A terrorist group was involved. I know."

"Are you a terrorist?"

Monte's shirt was soaked. "No… no…I'm not, but I have knowledge of…"

Le Rouge stared at him as if time stopped. The sound of their breathing amplified a thousand times. Finally, Le Rouge stepped back. "I like playing cards. Do you, Monsieur Monte?"

"I…I…" and shrugged.

"When the cards are dealt, that's when the betting starts. I'll call your bluff." He took his phone from his pocket. "What's Ricard's number?"

Chapter Fifty

Brownsburg

Billy Dee motioned for Shep to come closer. "You ain't go'n… my God…"

"What the hell was going on? You look like you've seen a ghost." Shep swept the room with his gaze. "I ain't see'n any ghosts."

"If there were any you wouldn't see them. They're ghosts." Billy Dee grabbed Shep's jacket. "Priscilla, sit tight. I need a word with my partner."

"Did I…? Am I under arrest? What the fuck…?"

Billy Dee scowled at her. "Just do as I ask, okay? I need a minute. Callahan is on his way." He looked at Shep for confirmation which was given by his nod.

He led his partner partially down the hallway toward the bedroom and out of earshot. He pointed to his phone. "Ricard just called," he said, his whisper rising.

"Who?"

Billy Dee held the phone to Shep's face. "Ricard, the guy from Paris…Inspector Ricard."

Recognition formed on Shep's face. "Yeah. What did he want out of the blue?"

"This is what's so nuts. Remember Jack Monte, the shithead we caught at the storage place?"

"Sure. Who could forget? He had something to do with

a broad he almost killed. Didn't we ship him to France for the murder of…"

"You got it. Dumond."

"Okay, what about Monte?"

"You ready for this? Ricard has a hunch that Monte and that broad, Susan, was somehow involved with my house blowing up."

"Holy shit. Really? How?"

"I don't know exactly, but the connection may have to do with a cell phone."

Shep looked toward the front room. "This is like a bad dream that won't quit."

"Hey, I can hear what you're saying," Priscilla stood watching the two officers in the hallway. "I'm not deaf. Maybe there's a connection between the dead guy Jenko, and everything that's happened, including your house."

Billy Dee and Shep approached Priscilla. "What does that…? What else do you know?" Billy Dee asked.

"Well, nothing really, but" she shrugged, "a whole lot of coincidences. Pappy had a partner in the real estate business. I knew him as Tope. He blew into town about a year or two ago. Out of the blue, he offered to help Pappy's failing business. Pappy never told me the how or when stuff, just business got better, then…" She took a breath and her face reddened. "Two or was it three days ago," she pressed her hand to her mouth for an instant. "So many things have happened, I've lost track of days or time. Pappy came over and well… I… had company. Anyway, he was pissed. He told me I'd be sorry 'cause any day now, he'd be a very rich man. After that Tope disappeared, then like the next day this Jenko along with a woman busted into the office, pointed their guns at me, and demanded Pappy." She started to sway.

"Why don't you sit down," Billy Dee offered.

It took a second or two before she reached for the chair

and plunked herself down. She blinked at the officers. "Okay, where was I?"

She was interrupted by a loud bang coming from the front door.

"Must be Callahan," Billy Dee said.

Shep put his hand on the butt of his weapon. "Don't be so sure. The way things have gone… It could be another hit man."

"Take Priscilla toward the rear of the house. I'll answer." Billy Dee unbuckled his holster and drew his revolver. He approached the alcove adjacent to the door. "That you, Callahan?"

***

Paris

Ricard had difficulty returning to sleep. He lay on his back with ideas and faces swirling. Could Felix be a terrorist? Was he the one who called Billy Dee? The "why" nagged him. It was as screwed up as his jumbled thoughts. What reason would Felix have? The research on Felix indicated the man had no connections with Serbs or their Liberation Front. He was French, through and through. He didn't seem to need money and had a successful position. Ach, so what? Many times, it was those who appeared innocent but were devils behind the unseen curtain.

Ricard flipped his pillow and turned on his side, then there was Monte. Could he be trusted? He claimed Susan was involved, but… He also wanted his sentence shortened. He'd sell his mother if… His reflections were disturbed by the sound of ringing. At first, he stared at the alarm clock, then realized it was his phone. He threw the covers and stepped quickly to his study. His head pounded with guilt for oversleeping. If his wife said anything he didn't hear. He was too intent on grabbing the phone.

"*Bon*, Inspector Ricard."

"Inspector Ricard, this is Sergeant Georges Clemont, I am a guard at the prison outside of Paris. I have someone here who claims he knows you. He says he has information."

"Who would that be?"

"He is prisoner four one five seven, Monte, Jack."

Ricard wiped his face with his hand. He glanced at the number that appeared on his cell's screen but didn't recognize it as being from the prison. "Who is this again?"

"I am Sergeant Georges Clemont. I am known in the prison as Le Rouge. I've worked here for ten years. I'm calling on my personal cell."

"Because…?"

"Inspector, how well do you know the warden?"

Ricard cleared his throat. "*Oui, je comprends.*" He moved to his desk and sat. "Can I speak to Monte, please." He heard Clemont say, "Here, he wants to talk to you."

"'Allo, Inspector Ricard?"

"*Oui*, what do you want to tell me?"

"I have…I…eh…"

"Monte? What is it?"

"Okay, okay, before I…promise me you'll get that bitch. I don't care what happens to me, but she…"

"Monte, I want to catch all terrorists. If your information points in that direction, *oui*, we will pursue her until we get her. Now what do you have."

"Come to the prison. I'll give it to you, then."

Ricard's fist struck his desk. "You are playing games, Monte. I don't have the time… What will you be giving?"

"A package. I promise… I'm risking everything."

Ricard stood and walked around the room. *Merde*, was he going in circles? He stopped at the window. The sun had risen. "Okay, Monte, this is what I'll do. My assistant, Lemont, will pick it up. Give me Clemont to make the arrangements."

***

Brownsburg

"Who else were you expecting? Of course, it's me," Callahan yelled.

Billy Dee faced Shep, who was with Priscilla about 30 feet away in the hallway. "It sure sounds like him, don't you think?"

Priscilla came forward. "It's him. I know the voice."

Billy Dee lowered his gun, then opened the door.

Callahan stepped through and stood in the small vestibule. He was out of uniform and didn't look happy. "Your partner said…" His gaze went past Billy Dee. "Priscilla, honey, are you all right? What the hell happened at your place? Jesus, your house was a war zone."

She began to cry again. "I…I…poor… Pappy."

Callahan curled his arm around her and led her to the couch in the living room. He motioned Billy Dee or Shep to clear some space.

"I can catch you up on what she already told us." Billy Dee tossed a beer can from the furniture onto the floor. "She was about to tell us about this Jenko and the woman he was with over at the real estate office."

"That's right." She wiped her face. "I was." She sat next to Callahan and placed her hand on his knee. "This Jenko character had an accent. It could have been Russian or something Slavic. I have an ear for those kinds of things. They argued… I couldn't understand their language. All the while the woman had her gun pointed at me. I think she would have shot me if hadn't been for Jenko. He wanted to fuck me instead, and, then shoot Pappy. That was why after he killed that bitch, he forced me to take him to my house. He somehow knew Pappy would show up." Her face reddened.

"That explains the dead woman at the office." Callahan now had a small smile on his face, and his hand was over hers.

Billy Dee had taken the chair across from her and Shep found space at the other end of the couch. "How does that have anything to do with my house being blown up or the money found in the files?" Billy Dee asked.

"Money?" Callahan asked.

Priscilla shrugged. "I don't know. It's a mystery. Oh, I forgot to tell you. There's a safe."

"A safe? Where?" Billy Dee and Callahan asked at about the same time.

"In the trunk of Pappy's car."

Chapter Fifty-One

Paris

Ricard ended his conversation with Clemont and punched in his assistant Lemont's number.

"Lemont, this is Inspector Ricard."

"Good morning."

"Yes, morning to you. I want you to go to the Paris prison and pick up a package from a prisoner, Jack Monte."

"You want…"

"It's all arranged. You are to see Sergeant Georges Clemont. He's also known as Le Rouge. Whatever you do, stay away from the warden. And Lemont, take some petty cash in case…"

"*Oui*, I'm on my way."

"*Bon*, call me when you're done… and…" His concentration was so intense he didn't notice his wife, Giselle, leaning on the doorpost of his bedroom office until he felt the air change. He looked up and saw her sheer thigh-length robe that reminded him he was indeed newly married. He quickly finished his conversation.

"*Bonjour*," he said, "did I wake you?"

She yawned. Her hand partially covered her mouth. "Non. Why are you up so early? What is going on?"

What to tell her? His first impulse was to say nothing but get out of his chair and take her to bed. He was a man

239

of a certain age, though, with the supposed ability to tame those impulses. Was his maturity the shining attribute that attracted her to him? He sighed, what he'd like to do, well… He met her gaze and cleared his throat. "Giselle, you remember Jack Monte and Susan Dumond?"

Giselle stepped toward his desk. "Of course." She shuddered. "How could I forget? They almost got me killed. What happened now?"

He explained his meeting with Monte and his conversation with Billy Dee Jackson. He told her his belief those two were somehow involved in the bombing of Jackson's house. He finished with the mystery of the phone call Jackson received and his hunch that Felix of Café Deux Magots was involved. "But you see, darling, I can't figure why."

Gisselle went over and kissed his cheek. "You will, and you won't give up until you do." She stretched her arms and touched his shoulders. "You are a bulldog, and your persistence will pay off."

He grabbed her around the waist and kissed her with passion. For a moment all the mayhem in his world flew away. Her intoxicating presence argued for abandoning the unseemly things of life and give in to its pleasures. Had he been younger, no doubt he would have.

He broke away from their mutual embrace. "Gisselle," he caught his breath, his arm still wrapped around her, "I'm late. I need to shower and be on my way."

If she was disappointed, she didn't show it. "I'll make you coffee." She straightened, then added, "Be careful, Alain."

***

Felix was woken by the persistent knocking on his door. Unable and too tired to figure out what Danielle had done to his phone; he had retreated to his bedroom to catch a few hours' sleep. He felt as though his head had just hit the pillow. He glanced at the clock and was surprised at how much time had passed. "*Attendez une minute.*" His feet searched for his slippers. "*A venir,*" he shouted as he shuffled his way to the front door. It had to be Danielle with some bullshit explanation about the phone. Or, and his imagination soared, the ladies from last night wanting more? Insatiable. That was a delightful thought. "Okay…" he would have used their names if he only remembered, "Give me a second." He unlocked the chain and opened the door. To his dismay it wasn't the two from last night, nor was it Danielle or any woman; instead, it was a man, the same Inspector from a day ago. How damn disappointing. He tried to cover his surprise, but he was sure his face revealed his true feelings. "Inspector, I can't say it's nice to see you."

"Not many people are happy when I appear. May I come in?"

Felix held fast to the door. "What's this about?"

"It's easier to explain inside."

The Inspector's gaze met his. "I…I…" Felix looked at watch. "Jesus, I'm late. Another time, Inspector, I have a meeting and my God, I am way behind."

"Very well, perhaps we can meet tonight at the café. My wife wants to have dinner there. Can you make the reservation?"

"Tonight? I…what time?" Felix fiddled with the latch "About seven, for two."

"Two?" Felix held up the appropriate number of fingers. "At seven."

Ricard smiled. "*Oui,* that's right. We can talk, then. *Au revoir.*"

Felix watched him leave, then he shut the door. Danielle and that goddamn phone. What else could it be about? He went straight to his bedroom, picked up his cell, and searched for the number he used earlier this morning. It was gone.

Chapter Fifty-Two

Brownsburg

Billy Dee, Shep, Callahan, and Priscilla stood by the trunk of Pappy's car as Priscilla inserted the key and lifted the lid.

"Damn, it's a safe all right," Callahan said. "Do you have the combination, Priscilla?"

"Me?" She shook her head. "No way. I found the damn thing in there. I didn't know Pappy even had a safe."

"Let's bring it into the house," Billy Dee grabbed one side and shifted it. "Not too bad, Shep, give me a hand."

The two lifted it out of the trunk and cautiously made their way. "Careful with those steps," Billy Dee warned as he took the first one.

"You don't have to remind me. My back already knows."

They got it through the door and dropped it where the living room met the foyer.

"Good job, boys," Callahan said staring at the tumbler. "Know any safe crackers?"

Priscilla piped up. "Why don't you start with birthdays. Here's mine."

The suggestion hung in the air until Billy Dee tried. "Nope, that didn't work. You have another?"

"Pappy's."

"Okay, give it to me." Billy Dee spun the dial to those

numbers but that failed too.

"Maybe you did it wrong," Callahan stepped forward and gave the dial a whirl but had the same result.

"Anyone in your department or tech guys know how to open a safe?" Shep asked.

"Not us, maybe the sheriff's department, but not at this hour. We're not a big city like you fellows."

Priscilla took Callahan's place and stared at it. She spun the dial to the left, then the right.

"What are you doing?" Callahan asked.

"Ssh, I'm concentrating." She then twisted it left. The door clicked open.

"What the hell?"

Callahan helped her up. "How…?"

"I used Tope's birthday."

"Tope?"

She shrugged. "Maybe this isn't Pappy's?"

***

Paris

Felix couldn't believe it. How the hell did all the information disappear? He scrolled through his recent calls, then apps on his screen, emails, messages, gone…no trace of the number he used. It had been such a wild morning, could he have imagined talking to a detective in the States? He had to sit down. He stared at the screen. It didn't make sense. Why else would that Inspector show up? It had to be that call. Should he warn Danielle? He became restless and got up. He'd shower and shave, then think of a plan. Even though it was mid-morning, he was sure Danielle would still be at home. Her bedtime couldn't have been much earlier than his.

He followed through and felt much better. His plan filled in. He would apologize to her about last night, then convince her to invite him over. Hopefully, he'd get some answers.

He put on his blue crew neck sweater, then straightened his hair. The thought occurred, if he played his cards well, there would be the possibility he'd bed her. She did come to his apartment and was almost persuaded to participate. He put his comb down and scolded himself, as that was not the purpose. He had to get to the bottom of whatever Danielle's scheme was. He wanted to avoid a scene at the café, bad for him, bad for business. He strode into his living room and picked up his cell. There were no messages. He'd phone her. He began to dial, then stopped. If the Inspector asked for his phone, he would see the call was made soon after he left. *Good thinking*. The only option was to go to her apartment. He'd even buy flowers on the way.

***

Ricard weighed whether to place an undercover car outside Felix's apartment. He didn't believe for a minute that he had a business meeting. He lied either to protect himself or someone else or both. *Felix what have you gotten yourself into?* Ricard parked in his designated spot and went into his office. He asked his secretary, Stephanie, what form to use to request an inquiry from a magistrate. She brought it at the same moment he got comfortable in his chair and was about take a sip of coffee.

"Here's the form you requested. It's several pages and must be filled out in triplicate."

The amount of work before him must have been reflected in his face.

"Not so bad," she said.

"Who's the magistrate?"

She glanced at her clipboard, "it says Magistrate Jacques Ghosav. Ever hear of him?"

He shook his head. "Must be one of the new ones the Government appointed. Crime is up as well as terrorism. Don't disturb me unless Lemont calls or something very important."

"*Oui*. Will that be all?"

He picked up his glasses and glanced at the form…. always paper and more paper. This will take most of the morning, if not the day. When he looked up, she had left.

He decided to fortify himself with the coffee Giselle had given him. The irony of that didn't elude him. It was because of that drink Giselle and he… why go down memory lane? He had work to do. He looked across the room. He couldn't focus or help himself. The aroma reminded him of the bistro they went to.

She had been working on lists of new arrivals in Paris and happened on Susan Dumond, although that was not the passport name Susan used. It was Simone Dubois. He picked up a pen and twirled it between his forefinger and thumb. He made it wiggle, like this Susan who managed to evade him in Paris and Detective Jackson in Chicago. No one can be that smart. Somewhere she had made a mistake. All he had to do was find it.

His call line lit. He was about to berate Stephanie, then realized it had to be either Lemont or something important. He lifted the receiver. "Allo, Inspector Ricard."

"Inspector, I picked up the package from the prison."

"Any trouble?"

"If you mean the warden, *non*, but the guard, that Le Rouge, had a big palm that had to be greased. The prisoner, Monte, acted like a dog in freezing water. He hemmed, stuttered, stalled, then Le Rouge got into it and settled the situation."

"Thank God. What did he give you?"

"I'm in my car. I'll open the envelope."

"Okay, careful when you do that. Write your initials and date." He heard tearing. "Well…?"

"Inspector, all I see is…a cell phone."

Ricard slapped his desk with his hand and jumped out of his seat. "Did you say a mobile phone? *Mon Dieu, mon Dieu.* I'll meet you at headquarters at Suvé's office in the basement. Don't stop for anything."

Chapter Fifty-Three

Paris

Screw the flowers, Felix vented as he sat in traffic. Danielle was a goddamn nuisance. He was the one being inconvenienced. There were better things to do with his time than sit in the middle of Paris trapped in a line of cars that wasn't moving. What was her game? Revenge of a sort because he met up with those women? Was it all a sick prank? He tapped his steering wheel with his hand. His eyes closed for a second. It almost made sense. He would be pissed if it happened to him.

Traffic opened a bit, allowing him to travel three blocks before it slowed again. The lights were out at the corner. A policewoman attempted to direct traffic. Horns blared, brakes squealed, as she flailed her arms this way and that, blowing her whistle…utter confusion. He had a few choice words for her as he passed. The trip should have taken 20 minutes at the most, turned into an hour. To his amazement his clock in the car informed him the morning had melded into early afternoon. Would she still be home? He found a parking spot a block away.

He walked to her apartment. He felt stupid showing up empty-handed, but why would she leave a number to the police in the USA? The more frightening question was… Jesus…she wasn't worth all this. He should fire her ass and be done with it. He climbed the steps of her building. Maybe she made a mistake. The dinner they had together. That night they spent. There was real emotion and sensuality, wasn't there? She didn't do that with just anyone. He entered the foyer and searched for her name in the apartment listing. As his hand hovered over her buzzard, an older woman fumbled with the security door while handling several pieces of luggage.

"Let me help you," he said, catching the door. "Going on a long vacation?"

She nodded and continued pushing her belongings.

He noticed her pock-marked face as she walked by. She wore a hat that partially covered gray streaked hair. From the back, her rear hugged her pants and her coat clung to her figure.

"I hope it's someplace sunny."

She struggled with the suitcases approaching the front door.

"I'll get that for you, too."

She half-smiled. "*Merci*."

A cab pulled up as she stepped outside. The driver shouted, then got out of the car and helped her with the luggage. Felix watched her enter the taxi, then stepped back into the vestibule and rang Danielle. While waiting, another building dweller walked by and opened the security entry. Before it closed, he walked through and caught the elevator to her floor. He knocked several times on her door with no success. Could she still be sleeping? He checked the time. *Non*, possible but not probable. She was out somewhere having a *petite dejeuner*, which reminded him he was hungry. It wasn't until he got back into his car that the woman with the luggage came to mind. There was something about her... her eyes...the way she said "*Merci*" ... He started the motor. Couldn't... no, her face was nothing like Danielle's.

His head was playing tricks. It was afternoon already, what did he expect? Why would she be waiting for him, especially after what he pulled last night? It all made sense. He shouldn't have driven over. She pranked him. That's all. He'd apologize to her at work, and she'd laugh at the joke she pulled. The inspector was barking up the wrong tree. He patted his stomach. All this would straighten out after getting something to eat.

***

Brownsburg

Billy Dee looked to Shep, then Callahan. "Who's this guy, Tope? He gestured to Priscilla. She told us somethings, but what do you know about him?"

Callahan stooped like a catcher and reached into the open safe. "I don't know what Priscilla told you, but as far as law enforcement and the town, he was an okay kind of fellow. Hell, he saved Pappy's business. What he got to do with all this, I don't know." He grabbed several envelopes and loose papers and stood. "The fact he's missing, and his car was involved in a fatal accident, is all the information we have. Priscilla, honey, do any of these papers and envelopes make sense to you?" He handed her loose maps of Brownsburg and Indianapolis.

Billy Dee glanced over her shoulder as she viewed several areas circled with scribbles next to them. "I don't know. He and Pappy were in the real estate business. Maybe these were properties they were interested in."

Callahan bobbed his head. "Yeah, I can buy that. You're a levelheaded girl." He handed her another loose paper. "This looks like a map of Chicago."

Billy Dee grabbed it from her. He looked at it for a

moment, but it was blurry. "It's getting so, I can't do nothing without these." He put his glasses on. "I don't believe it. I… Shep, look."

Shep moved to his partner's side. "What am I seeing?"

Billy Dee pointed.

"Holy mother of god, it's your street, your house."

"Give me those other papers and envelopes," Billy Dee told Callahan. He took them to the couch and laid them on his lap. He pulled two sheets of paper from a packet. "Shep, there's Cyrillic writing on this." He flipped the envelope and read the address. "It's to Anton Topeski in Brownsburg. Is that Tope's home address?" He pointed and showed it to Callahan and Priscilla who were hovering by him.

"I've never been to his house," Priscilla said, "but Pappy mentioned it was in a rich neighborhood and that address is a highfalutin' one."

Callahan examined the writing and agreed.

"This is getting more and more baffling. This Tope or Topeski wasn't at all who he claimed to be. No sir." Billy Dee tapped his hand on the envelopes on his lap. This guy…I can't believe I'm saying it, was part of some foreign organization. Terrorist? SLA? Damn…"

"Bingo, look what I found."

Billy Dee looked over to the safe where Shep now stood holding something in his hand. His partner grinned like a Cheshire cat.

***

Paris

Ricard grabbed his coat and raced out of his office.

"Where are you going?" Stephanie asked as he sprinted by.

He waved her off. "Out. Headquarters." He got to the

front door and tapped his pocket. "Keys." He patted himself down. *Must have left them on the desk.* He walked back to his office, muttering.

Stephanie looked at him with concern as he passed her again. "Are you all right?"

"*Oui*, can't drive without keys." He held up his hand and an embarrassed smile crossed his face. *Merde*, he'd also left the file.

He was so close to tying Monte, Susan, and maybe Felix to the bombing of Detective Jackson's house. His head pounded with the thought that this could be Susan's "gotcha moment." Her mistake finally revealed.

He took a breath and loosened his tie…*Settle down.* He wasn't a kid anymore or a bright-eyed rookie who believed with the snap of a finger *voila* the case was done. He knew better. His years taught him there was no sure thing. Matters could go awry. He picked up his keys and the manila folder. He stopped at Stephanie's desk and explained what had occurred and where he was going.

"*Au revoir.*"

"*Bon chance*," she said.

There was no rush. The answers to the puzzle were either there or not.

***

Suvé had his sleeves rolled to his elbows, and a cigarette dangled from his mouth. He either hadn't shaved or had a heavy beard.

"So, what do you think?" Ricard struggled to keep his voice even. He had dismissed Lamont with thanks after receiving the package. Too many eyes led to too many wagging tongues.

"Well," Suvé opened, then closed the phone.

Ricard felt as if he were at his doctor's office waiting for the results of his tests…cancer…benign…? What the hell was Suvé doing?

Suvé began again. "Your Monsieur Monte was nice enough to give his code, so opening the phone will not be a problem. We should be able to obtain his messages, emails, and calls within a few hours, even the ones Monte believed were deleted. Let this be a lesson, Inspector, nothing is ever erased."

"Thank God."

"… then the real work begins."

"What do you mean?"

"The tracing of the numbers. Whose were they? Isn't that the point of all this? Who did Monte call, email, and text?"

"*Oui*, of course. That's exactly why I'm here. How long will that take?"

Suvé rubbed his chin. "I don't know. A few days if I'm lucky, and if I'm not… weeks." He shrugged. "I can see you are disappointed, Inspector. Look around this shithole of an office. There are files from Interpol, theft, sex, and murder cases. All wanting the secrets of these mobile devices unlocked. You're not my only case."

Ricard placed his hand on the desk. "This matter is one of national security, Monsieur Suvé. I believe what you are holding, Monte's phone, is evidence of a plot that led to a bombing in the USA." He pointed to the piles that filled the room. "This case is your priority. If I must, I'll notify the Minister of Justice. Am I understood?"

"You know the Minister?"

Ricard took out his phone and began to punch in a number. "We went to the University together." He was about to hit Call.

Suvé took a deep drag on his cigarette, then let the smoke curl to the ceiling. He looked past Ricard, sighed, then settled on him. "You don't have to do that, Inspector. I will do as you ordered."

***

Brownsburg

"A Goddamn phone, also with Cyrillic lettering. Obviously not American," Shep said while examining it. "Can your people open it?"

"This is above my pay grade." Callahan went toward Shep. "This is a quiet little place. Murders, foreign crap, spies, this isn't that kind of town. We'd have to get the FBI boys from Indie down here. And at this time of night?" He shook his head.

"I've got a better idea. The Chicago crime lab handles these things all the time."

"Shep, I can't let you waltz out of this jurisdiction with evidence. The captain would have my head."

Billy Dee joined the discussion. "That phone Shep is holding is also part of the investigation of the bombing of my house. Think about it, Callahan, everything that happened here, the murders of all these people, leads right to Chicago. It was a conspiracy." He got up leaving the envelopes and maps on the couch. "Where's that other phone Priscilla took from what's his name…Jenko?"

"It's on the table." Priscilla pointed to it.

Billy Dee stepped over and grabbed it. "Now, my gut tells me the proof of what I said will be on those two mobiles. Come to think of it that call I received a few minutes ago, it… Lord have mercy… leads to Paris…"

Shep came toward Billy Dee. "And Paris leads to Jack Monte and Susan Dumond."

"Who? Paris as in France?" Callahan slapped his thigh.

"No shit. Who would have thunk we've got an international conspiracy in this town few ever heard of?"

"You're a genius, Callahan, that's precisely why Brownsburg was chosen. Call your captain. This can't wait." Billy Dee winked at Shep. "Time to move."

"What about that dinner you promised?"

"Later. McDonalds has a deal on Big Macs."

Chapter Fifty-Four

Chicago

"Janine, baby, it's me, Billy Dee."

There was a pause. Billy Dee heard breathing.

"Billy…Dee…?" Sleep wore off her voice. "Why, you still remembered your little woman alone in this motel. Good of you to finally call. What time is it?

"Now Janine—" That's as far as he got. Billy Dee moved the phone from his ear.

Shep had to turn away to keep from laughing. "You're cooked, now," he said, "lucky for you I'm driving so that you can give your wife all the attention she needs."

Billy Dee glanced upward. "Thanks for your support."

"What was that?" Janine asked. "Shep in the car with you? I should have known. I've been worried sick, and you didn't have the decency to…" Her voice faltered.

"Janine, I'm sorry, but things down here in Brownsburg have gone from zero to one hundred."

"Uh-huh."

"I didn't want to worry you, but…"

"You what? Worry me? Billy Dee, you must have shut down your think'n."

"No, I mean, with what has happened down here. Several people have been killed…shot. Hard to believe but it all leads back to Paris."

"Now you're talk'n crazy. Paris…ha."

"No, it's real. I'm getting ahold of Ricard. We had talked earlier this evening. Those same characters, Jack Monte and Susan Dumond, had a hand in our house getting blown up."

"No, no, no I don't want to hear such foolishness. How's that possible? Get your bootie home. You're tired, overworked."

"Janine, Shep and I are not nuts. Neither were the captain and sergeant in Brownsburg. It was one giant conspiracy."

"Jesus give me strength."

"We're heading to Chicago, but we've got to stop at the crime lab before I get home. Go back to sleep. I'll see you sometime tomorrow."

"All right, all right. I don't understand, Billy Dee. Why? What do those people want from you…from us? I can't stand this. It's too much."

"It'll all work out. I promise." He sighed and gripped the phone a little tighter.

"You say that… I hope for all our sakes. Be safe, Billy Dee, and Shep as well."

"Will do. Love you."

Shep flashed his attention toward his partner. "Nice touch."

***

Paris

Susan got into the cab satisfied her disguise worked. Felix was such a simple man. He concerned himself with tits and ass; faces and persons meant little.

"*Ou allez?*" the cabbie asked.

"*Le Hotel des Arts, cinq rue Tholoze.*"

The driver's eyes reflected in the rear-view mirror. "I'm familiar with the address, Madam."

"*Bon*, it should take about three minutes, *n'est pas?*"

"Thereabouts, depending on traffic."

"No matter. I have a meeting. The luggage, *s'il vous plait*, should be dropped off at Air France, De Gaulle airport. Henri will meet you in front of area five, terminal two. Here's his number." She handed him a slip of paper.

The cabbie reached behind and grabbed it. "Ah, Mademoiselle, I had no idea I was going to the airport. It is out of my zone."

Susan opened her purse. "Will one hundred euros suffice?"

"One hundred… *oui*, it will suffice very well."

As understood, her ride was short. The taxi pulled in front of the hotel's entry 5 minutes later. The driver got out and opened the passenger door.

"One more thing, I need one of the suitcases from the trunk."

"No problem." He hit a button on his fob and the trunk lid popped opened.

Susan went to the rear and bent over the space. She pointed. "That one, if you'd be so kind."

"*Oui*." He moved several suitcases out of the way, then lifted the one she wanted.

"*Merci*. I wrote down your name and cab identification, and here's my number in case there's a problem." She handed him another piece of paper.

"*Très bien*. I'll call you after this Henri takes your luggage." He closed the trunk, then got into his car and drove off.

She waited until the cab was out of sight before walking away from the Hotel des Arts. One can never be too careful exiting a situation. Dumond had drilled that lesson into her. She followed rue Tholoze to 57 rue des Abesses, a 1-minute walk. There she entered the Hotel Basss. Once registered using her Lebanese passport with the name Francoise Bélut, she was given a magnetic key card to room 1406.

"Enjoy your stay," the male receptionist said, "if there is anything you need, please do not hesitate to call on us." He rang for the bellhop.

"That won't be necessary. *Merci*."

She took the elevator to her floor. She had watched the receptionist enter information into his computer. By way of positioning, she read the screen indicating another room near hers was empty. It wasn't difficult using a portable RFID writer to change the magnetic information on her card to the one for 1410. She eyed the hallways. Seeing no one, she stuck her transformed card into the slot of the new room. The click sounded and with a twist of the doorknob, the door opened. The room was sparse. A single bed by the wall, a small bathroom with the usual necessities. At least it had a nice view of the street. No matter, she wasn't going to stay long. She double locked the door, then heaved her luggage onto the bed. She unlocked the suitcase, unzipped the secret compartment, and took her phone. She held it in her gloved hand and walked to the small chair near the window. She sat and glanced at the street scene. It was so Parisian. People strolled, some sat at the outdoor cafés despite the weather sipping their espressos or lattes.

She studied the device. This was the only thing that tied her to everything…Chicago, Brownsburg, and…Jack Monte. She tried to think of a way to learn whether Monte had, as the expression went, "given up the ghost." Did that miserable bastard spill his guts to the *flics*? Should she chance it by calling? The virtual sim card in her cell distorted her voice but could the call be traced, despite a fictitious number? What to do? She checked the time, then gazed out the window. *Bon*, it was, in her final analysis, the only way.

***

Suvé counted to twenty after Ricard left. Everything was an emergency. He was tired of Inspectors telling him what cases to pursue and when. They all seemed to think their rank and clout moved him. It didn't. He would do what he wanted and when… Minister of Justice be damned and Ricard too. Murders, bombings, sexual misconduct occur all day, every day. He was the magician with the ability to unlock secrets. Yet, his office was in the bowels of a building few could find. It will be on his own time.

He stared at a wall where a window should have been. Luckily, few understood the intricacies of cellular systems. Thus, the magic he plied provided ready excuses. Ignorance was his shield. He gazed at Monte's phone and chuckled… then spat out, "Minister of Justice." He found a 9x10 yellow envelope, wrote Monte's name across the front, and dropped the cell into it, then he flipped the packet into a banker's box and slid it to the opposite wall. "I'll get to you when I get to you." He lit another cigarette and decided to step away and visit a café for a cup of espresso. There would be time to deal with all this later.

He enjoyed sitting at the Café Othèque of Paris. It was a cozy coffeeshop whose baristas knew the art of coffee, particularly Beth. She always had a smile for him along with his espresso and chocolate biscotti. He'd sit at his regular table, sip the bitter liquid, and chase it with a bite of his pastry. He didn't think of work or inspectors, or all the horrible things found on people's mobile phones, they never believed would be seen. No, the time passed with thoughts of Beth and what it would be like… if only. Besides *bonjour* and *merci,* no other words were spoken between them…less was indeed more. A whole world the way he envisioned…perfect.

45 minutes later he went back to his little office in the basement, sighing for the vision he left. Before resuming

his seat, he inadvertently glanced at the space where he had slid the box with Monte's phone. It was gone.

***

"What do you mean… gone?" Ricard was at his desk in his police station.

"How else can I explain it to you? It's not where I left it. It's not in the office. I've searched every nook and cranny. This has never happened. I… don't …." Suvé tapping on some surface could be heard.

"   "The phone can't walk. Find the damn thing. It must be somewhere in that mess of yours."

"Inspector… I… calling…" he gulped, then took a huge breath, his voice barely audible. "I think… someone… took…" he struggled with the last word, "it."

"Be careful, Suvé. That could be an even bigger problem."

"I'm aware. I'm not stupid."

Silence greeted the next few seconds. What more could Ricard say? He needed to regroup, think this out. Why out of all Suvé's files would Monte's be missing? Was it sinister or happenchance? Multiple scenarios began their march through his head. He gripped the phone tighter. "Listen, Suvé," he broke the quiet, "call me when… call me in an hour whether you found it or not." He hung up and stared at a blank spot on the wall. Who would have…no…who had knowledge Suvé had the phone? A few people came to mind: Monte and Le Rouge. But they only knew that he, Ricard, would receive the phone. There was only one person who knew the mobile would be given to Suvé… Lamont.

Chapter Fifty-Five

Chicago

Inspector Ricard, good morning, it's Billy Dee."

Ricard held his cell as if it had a plague. This was not what he wanted to do at this minute, having little or no interval to digest Suvé's news. "Good morning, although it is afternoon in Paris. What's on your mind at your time of day?"

"You sound a little… Did I catch you at a bad moment?"

Ricard glanced at the ceiling. Couldn't have been a worse time. Monte's goddamn cell phone was still missing. His whole case collapsing. For a moment earlier in the day, he was the striding hero, now an old fool seeking cover. "No, no, Billy Dee, always a pleasure." He hoped his voice didn't betray his true feelings. "What can I do for you?"

"Nothing for me, but what we can do for you. Shep and I are at the Chicago crime lab with two cell phones. One taken from that hit man, Jenko, the other from someone named Topeski or as he was known in Brownsburg, Tope."

Ricard sat a little straighter. "Interesting, go on."

After telling Ricard the connection Tope played, he continued, "The lab guys found this ghost number using a machine called Stingray. You ain't go'n to believe what it can do."

An image of Suvé flashed by and he wondered if Suvé

had similar equipment. If he did, why the bullshit? Ricard groaned.

"What was that?" Billy Dee asked.

"Nothing, *excusez-moi*. My mind wandered to our own technician and if he had that machine. Anyway, please go on."

"This Stingray catches the IMSI data. You follow?"

"I've heard of it."

"Okay, bottom line, despite using apps and ghost numbers we're able to trace the calls to the user of the mobile phone."

"*Mon Dieu*…fantastic… And…"

"We also recovered text messages and emails that, you ain't going to believe, has our two, what did you call them, a-m-i-s, friends in the thick of it. Jack Monte suggested the bombing to who he thought was someone in the SLA. Tope or Topeski did the recon work. He went to my house, surveyed the surroundings, provided maps, and reported it to who he also believed was an SLA member. But it was Susan Dumond who was behind the whole thing. She hired the crew for the bombing then used Jenko to kill his accomplice; including Dijana, she was the one who helped Jenko with the explosives, Vera, Topeski, and Pappy McDonald."

"Who? Pappy Mc…"

"Yeah, he was collateral damage. His partner was that guy Tope or Topeski. Pappy was at the wrong place at the wrong time although he probably had an inkling about the bombing in Chicago"

"I see. Those emails and texts, can you send copies?"

"I…I got to clear that with the higher ups. Red tape and bureaucracy."

"I know it very well. Did you come across someone named Felix?"

"Felix?" Ricard, then heard Billy Dee ask someone.

"No, the boys found nothing like that."

Ricard felt heady as Billy Dee continued to relay other information. He could feel justice's breath closing in not only on Jack Monte but finally on Susan Dumond. He made his hand into a fist. There was one more thing needed.

"Billy Dee, did that mobile phone have an address?"

***

Paris

Susan stood by the corner of the window in room 1410 and dialed Monte's number. She stared at the street scene below while anticipating the connection. By the fourth buzz, her finger hovered over the End button. She was not going to leave a voice message. On the fifth try, there was a click, then rustling…someone finally grabbed the ringing cell. She waited until she heard, hello or something.

"'*Allo, qui est ce?*

The voice was male and French, but it wasn't Monte. She was sure of that. A second or two passed after the voice asked who it was. She hesitated to respond. Dumond would not approve but she had gone this far. "I noticed a recent call," she explained, "so I'm calling back."

"I'm so sorry, I must have phoned you by mistake."

Susan noticed a car brake at the corner. The driver got out and had his hand by his ear like he was holding a phone. He seemed to be searching. A second man raced from the passenger side to the first man and pointed to an area near her window. *Merde*, they're *flics*. She threw the phone into the suitcase and zipped it closed, then cracked opened the front door. The corridor was still empty. She waited to catch her breath as her heart pounded. She left the room and went a few doors down to the one originally assigned to her. She took out her magnetic keycard. The elevator down the hall rung. There wasn't time to use her portable RFID machine. She searched for the stair exit and found it seconds before hearing the elevator open. She took the stairs and cursed as her suitcase clattered from step to step. She had to get rid of the phone. She made it to the next landing, and with one eye peeled to the exit door above she reached into the suitcase. The phone was still on. She gasped, , then sucked in a deep breath and punched "End" several times until the mechanism turned off. She looked around for a place to dump the beast. There was nothing but concrete stairs. She hoisted the suitcase and went slowly down to the next level, praying her luck wouldn't give out.

***

Lamont ran into Ricard's office as Ricard ended the call with Billy Dee. Before Ricard said a word, his assistant spoke rapidly. "I know I shouldn't have, Inspector Ricard, but that oaf Suvé strolled from his office to a café down the street after you left. His office was unlocked, leaving all that evidence open for anyone to steal. Here's Monte's phone." He placed the yellow envelope on Ricard's desk.

Ricard stared at the packet. Relieved but disturbed, what should he do? "*Merci*," escaped from his mouth. He sat back in his chair.

"Inspector," Lamont interrupted, "I have something else. My background was in computer technology before I changed career paths. I also took from Suvé's office a portable machine known as a gossamer. It's a device that gathers data on mobile phones in targeted areas. Monte's phone was kind enough to have left the number used to communicate with—"

Ricard leaned forward. "Wait, Lamont, I have…" He looked at the notes he jotted from Billy Dee's call. "Here it is. The location. We need to go to Montmartre somewhere on the rue Novins." Ricard grabbed the envelope and with Lamont a step behind, left.

***

Monte's phone rang in their car as they neared 57 rue des Abesses. It was difficult to tell whether the caller was male or female. The gossamer indicated the call came from the Hotel Basss. Ricard stopped near the corner and jumped out. He stared at the hotel, holding Monte's phone. Lamont came over and pointed to an upper floor. Both ran in. Ricard flicked his badge and ID to a startled receptionist. "Elevators."

The employee pointed to the right.

"*Merci*," Ricard said as they rushed in that direction. "Whoever called hung up," Ricard informed his assistant while they waited.

Lamont shook his head. "The gossamer is indicating the fourteenth floor. The phone wasn't turned off."

The light above the elevator car announced its arrival. They got in along with another couple who punched 5. An uncomfortable silence ensued. Ricard and Lamont stared at the numerals as the car made its slow upward climb. Their eyes cursing the couple. Too much time was passing before reaching the 14th. They stepped out and within a second or two heard a door close. They looked down the hall. It was empty. The gossamer was still reading a location. "Was it a door to a room?" Ricard wondered aloud, then he saw the exit door at the end of the corridor and motioned Lamont to follow.

Reaching the exit, Lamont tapped Ricard on the shoulder. He pointed to the gossamer. "Look. It's no longer reading." Ricard pulled the door open and heard somewhere below him a door closing. He glanced down the stairwell, but it was empty. "Come."

Chapter Fifty-Six

Paris

Felix found a small café a mile or so from his apartment. The maître d' handed him a menu that he casually reviewed. He settled for a ham and cheese sandwich and an espresso. He had his choice of outside tables and despite the chill informed the wait staff where he wanted to sit. He liked to view the passing scenery. He fidgeted with his silverware while sipping the coffee. He was restless to get to Café Deux Magots for his shift. Excited on the one hand to see Danielle, but a little anxious if he was wrong about her prank.

Inspector Ricard reminded him of Javert from *Les Misérables*, popping up when least expected. He was certain when Ricard appeared for his reservation at 7:00, all the intrigue would be put to rest. How else could it be? Danielle was no mastermind criminal or spy. Foolish to even imagine. He'll send Champagne to Ricard's table on the house. "No hard feelings, Inspector, *n'est pas.*" They would have a good laugh. Felix rubbed his hands together. *Oui,* it would all be fine. After work, he'd ask Danielle to help him close. He'd be his most charming. His boyish smile put to good use. Irresistible. He would dim the lights and share a few cognacs. She'd forgive him and he'd persuade her to spend the night. In the morning, he would brew espresso and lay out an array of croissants.

The waiter interrupted his thoughts, serving him his order. He looked up from his musings. "*Merci*, "and pulled the plate closer. There was one other couple braving the cold as he. No matter, he looked at his food, then realized how ridiculous and juvenile his previous reflections were. His affair with Danielle, if he could call it that, was one night, and he'd had many one-nighters… big deal. But her image, the way she… ach.

He took a bite of his sandwich. The bread wasn't crisp and the mustard barely noticeable. He thought of sending it back, but what the hell. A new one probably wouldn't be better. He took another sip of his espresso, then tried the coleslaw. The taste missed the mark. He checked on the other couple. They seemed oblivious to the cold or to him. It was apparent they were lovers; most likely illicit. He leaned back and closed his eyes for a second or two. Danielle. That smile of hers, welcoming but…with an allure of intrigue. That was what was so…mysterious and desirable. He held his cup midway between his mouth and the saucer and gazed again at the couple. Danielle, one moment sweet and sexy, the next she's holding a gun. Jesus, he almost forgot, she had a pistol in her purse. Damn. He raised his hand for the waiter.

"Check."

"*Oui*, monsieur. Was everything all right? You hardly ate."

Felix shrugged and swallowed a bitter taste. "Have to go," and patted his stomach. He paid with a credit card and hurried to his car. The clock on the dashboard indicated he had a few hours before work.

***

Susan had had a lifetime of running from flics, despondent lovers, duped or misguided investors. She and Dumond had left many a hotel or restaurant through side doors, fire escapes, even jumped from rooftops. The predicament she found herself in now joined a long line of such episodes.

The 12th floor of the Hotel Basss looked the same as the 14th but for the flower arrangement on the table opposite the elevator bank. If fortune held, she had a little over a minute before those two men would figure where she was. Would they come by the emergency stairs as she had, or elevator? The wrong guess and… She put the compromised phone in her coat pocket and moved toward the elevator bank. She pressed the Up button and took a deep breath. The door slid open to an empty car. She got in pressed 14 and as the door closed heard the bell of the other elevator. She said a silent prayer to a Deity she rarely believed in. As the elevator climbed, she touched her hair and straightened her clothes. The car stopped at her floor and the door opened. She put her hand by the rubber edge, bent forward and looked both ways. Seeing no one, she stepped out and began to walk toward her original room, 1406, pulling her suitcase behind. A calmness settled over her. She anticipated using her RFID machine…

"Mademoiselle Susan Dumond?" A male voice asked.

Startled, she did what Dumond had instructed her never to do: she stopped.

A man moved away from behind a column near the elevators. "I am officer Lamont, Paris police. Inspector Ricard will be here in a few minutes. He's in the stairwell searching for you. I believe we have much to discuss."

Susan regained her composure. "I'm afraid you've mistaken me for someone else."

Lamont moved toward her. "Madam, this is no mistake."

Susan thought quickly. "Officer Lamont, you really do have the wrong person.

"You stopped when I called your name."

"I stopped because you frightened me. My name is Francoise Bélut. My passport is in my pocket." She fished it out and handed him the document.

Lamont checked the name, then turned the pages and examined the stamps. "*Oui,* it appears to be legitimate," and returned the booklet to her, "but we must wait for the Inspector."

Susan made a show of looking at her watch. "Really, Officer, I'm going to be late. I am not this Susan… whatever her name. You have no right to keep me here." She tapped her toe as she waited.

Lamont eyed her carefully. According to Inspector Ricard, Susan Dumond was young, had long brown hair, and attractive. The woman in front of him appeared middle-aged with a pock-marked face. She was nothing like the description given. He looked around again, but the Inspector was nowhere in sight.

"Really, Officer, I must leave. It's a very important meeting with…"

"Okay," he sighed, "you may go."

"*Merci.* It's too late to use my room." She pressed the elevator button. The car came quickly, and she vanished.

Inspector Ricard arrived from the stairway a minute later. "Any luck?"

Lamont thought a moment. "*Non.*"

***

Monte sat on his cot. Sweat soaked his shirt. That morning he'd given his phone to Le Rouge along with the codes he used. He knew the consequences of his act. His solace was that it would lead to Susan Dumond's downfall, causing misery to her life. No more parties, fine dining, or freedom to do what she wanted. No, she would face the drabness of everyday prison mixed with the anxiety of staying alive. He chuckled and opened his hand as if he let a bird fly from his palm. Sweet revenge. It would stoke the warmth of his future winter years.

***

A month later he received news from a laughing Le Rouge. "Congratulations, Monsieur Monte, the government has decided to charge you with new crimes." He took out a pair of glasses and read. "Conspiracy to commit murder, conspiracy to commit arson, conspiracy to commit a terrorist act. Oh, Monsieur, the list goes on." Le Rouge gave Monte the stack of papers. "One more thing, I heard after you've been tried here, you may be going on a little trip."

"Trip? Where?"

"You should know."

Monte grabbed hold of the bars. "I…I…don't."

"*Qui vivra verra*. Time will tell. *Au revoir*."

Chapter Fifty-Seven

Paris

Café Deux Magots was busy. At a table where nearly a century ago the likes of Hemingway, Picasso, and Sartre, dined, Inspector Ricard celebrated with his wife, Giselle, Billy Dee, and Janine.

Jack Monte's trial where Billy Dee testified had ended a few hours before. Justice prevailed with a finding of guilty. The Court ordered Monte to be continuously held in custody while awaiting his sentence in another month.

"I can't thank you enough," Ricard began, "without your assistance…" He gazed at the ceiling and shrugged.

"No, it's you we have to thank." Billy Dee smiled. "You helped us and because of that, here we are again. My wife's eyes almost popped out of her head when I told her we were returning to Paris."

Janine used a napkin to dab her mouth. "Now, Billy Dee, don't go on and on." She glanced at Ricard and his wife. "We are mighty happy to be here. I'm sure Billy Dee's friend, Shep, would have liked to come, but…flying isn't his thing."

Ricard nodded and was about to launch into a new subject.

"*Excuse-moi*, Inspector." Felix held a bottle of Champagne. "It is the least I can do. If it weren't for you, who knows what would have happened. Danielle, or as you informed me, Susan Dumond….a terrorist. *Mon Dieu.* I almost stepped in a lot of…" He glanced at the bottle, then showed the label to the Inspector. "Nicolas Feuillatte, 2020, *très bon*. Did I tell you she once pulled a gun on me?"

Ricard turned to Felix. "*Non*, you didn't, but given how smitten you were, forgivable."

Felix twisted the cork and poured a glass for all at the table, then he reached behind and took a goblet from the next table. "To Inspector Ricard and his American counterpart."

They raised their glass and clinked.

"Excellent." Ricard took another sip.

Billy Dee smacked his lips. "Ses la vee. Great stuff."

Felix went on to attend to other guests after many *mercis*.

Billy Dee reached for the bottle, attempted to read the French label, , then refilled everyone's glasses. "And about Susan Dumond?" He looked at no one in particular.

Ricard held his flute aloft. "Tomorrow, we will see. *A demain*."

***

Susan had made her way out of the hotel. She didn't run but kept a normal pace. As the distance grew between her and the Hotel Basss, she waved down a taxi. Her time in Paris was finished. She was well trained by Dumond in the art of disappearing. There was money in her suitcase and before she left the city, she tossed her compromised phone into the Seine. She would travel to Provence and use several of Dumond's past hideaways.

Another name, a new passport, the pockmarks gone, her long, red, dyed hair blew gently in the soft wind. The sun, good wine, pleasant meals, and occasional companionship made for a wonderful way to pass the time.

She kept abreast of Monte's trial as reported in the newspapers. She sat on her terrace and caught a glimpse of the setting sun. The paper sat folded next to a half-filled glass of golden Chardonnay. It was a moment to reflect. Revenge was truly sweet.